Stephen H. Provost's
Nightmare's Eve
A Collection of Twisted Tales

Black Raven Books 2018
Published in conjunction
with Dragon Crown Books
All rights reserved.

ISBN: 978-1-948594-04-2

Praise for other works by the author

"A well-written novel with modern prose and social concerns, the complex idea of mixing morality and mortality is a fresh twist on the human condition. ... **Memortality** is one of those books that will incite more questions than it answers. And for fandom, that's a good thing."

— Ricky L. Brown, Amazing Stories

"Punchy and fast paced, **Memortality** reads like a graphic novel. ... (Provost's) style makes the trippy landscapes and mind-bending plot points more believable and adds a thrilling edge to this vivid crossover fantasy."

— Foreword Reviews

"**Memortality** by Stephen Provost is a highly original, thrilling novel unlike anything else out there. ... Provost has crafted an engaging, brilliant yarn that will keep you glued to the page until the very end. Stephen is clearly an author at the top of his game."

— David McAfee, bestselling author of
33 A.D., 61 A.D., and 79 A.D.

"Profusely illustrated throughout, **Highway 99** is unreservedly recommended as an essential and core addition to every community and academic library's California History collections."

— California Bookwatch

"As informed and informative as it is entertaining and absorbing, **Fresno Growing Up** is very highly recommended for personal, community, and academic library 20th Century American History collections.

— John Burroughs, Reviewer's Bookwatch

Also by Stephen H. Provost

Works of Fiction

The Memortality Saga
Memortality
Paralucidity
Identity Break
Feathercap

Works of Nonfiction

Highway 99
Fresno Growing Up
Undefeated
The Phoenix Chronicles
The Osiris Testament
The Way of the Phoenix
The Gospel of the Phoenix
The Phoenix Principle
Forged in Ancient Fires
Messiah in the Making
Requiem for a Phantom God

Dedication

To all those with the courage to dream …
and to overcome their nightmares.

"There is nothing in the dark that isn't there when the lights are on."

— Rod Serling

Contents ~ Tales

Contents ~ Verse

Acknowledgements

Thanks to my diligent editor, Samaire Wynne, for helping me make this song sing.

Welcome ...

e dwell within a shadow world at the doorstep of chaos, on the threshold of madness.

We stand at the gateway to a place unlike our own: a haunted place of possibilities that tantalize and terrify.

So tenuous, our foothold on this precipice. So vast, the abyss that falls away before us.

We delude ourselves that this otherworld will stay where it is, safely tucked away beyond the curtain that shields us from it.

Yet "safe" is one thing we are not, behind this curtain, frayed and tattered. For how should we see the other side? Can such a barrier guard against what lurks beyond the boundary?

That boundary exists between today and tomorrow, and we cross each night on the river of our dreams. Like Charon on the Styx, in a boat with no companion, we dream adrift. And in new daylight, if we are fortunate, we find our world unchanged from what we left the night before, having traversed the no man's land 'tween dusk and daybreak.

Yet if fortune is not with us ...

It is a gamble all must take. Some sleep dreamless, and some rest content in mere reflections of the world they knew in waking. Others brave assaults from monsters and demons that scent their blood and would consume them — accompanied by fears that lead them onward, ever further from the waking realm, into that of nightmare.

The resolute may still escape. Once, twice, a hundred times or more. Each time drained and bloodied from the struggle, each time less fit to face the world that bore them — accustomed now to the war they wage beyond the curtain.

Resolve, in nightmares, is never quite enough. How can we conquer that which waits for us in darkness, when darkness itself must be our rest?

We cannot shirk our slumber, nor can another go before us to that dreamland. A wife may lie beside us, a husband's arms wrapped around us, but in the depths of night are we ever alone — as in death, we sleep, secluded. From this void we may return, but changed; or one day, it may hold us fast, until we cease our struggle in surrender.

But each day, as sunlight hurries toward the horizon, shadowed fingers clutch the earth in panic as they slip away toward nighttime. We know we soon must follow. Resolve and trepidation war within us, as we slip toward that which no one may escape ... that tattered veil, beyond which lies oblivion.

On Nightmare's Eve.

A Deal in the Dark

"Can you leave the light on, Andy?"

Andy poked his head back around the corner and shook it slightly. "The doc says that won't help you sleep. You need your rest, Jen."

"I know, but …"

"No buts."

Jenny fixed her attention on the sliver of light that was bleeding into her room from out in the hallway. It seemed like a lifeline. This insomnia had been plaguing her for weeks now, and she *did* need her sleep. But she didn't need the panic attacks that hit her whenever the room went pitch black. She hadn't been afraid of the dark since she was a child, when her parents had bought that nightlight for her to reassure her there weren't any monsters lurking in the blackness, waiting to emerge when it was safe. When she couldn't see them. Couldn't find them. Couldn't catch them to put them back where they belonged in the part of her mind where they no longer existed.

Her parents had told her that's where they really were.

"It's all in your mind," Mom had said. "There's nothing here that can hurt you."

She'd always remembered that. It had been reassuring at the time, but the more she thought about it, as she'd grown older, the more troubling it seemed. She could escape a monster that was hiding in the closet; but if it had taken up residence in her mind … how could she escape that?

Andy was a lot like her Mom that way. He had always been protective of his kid sister, always trying to reassure her that there was nothing wrong — make her think everything was going to be just fine.

Make. Her. Think.

Think the way *he* wanted her to think. It was just a trick, she thought to herself. She remembered Halloween night, when she was six years old. "Go to sleep, why don't you?" he'd said, impatient and demanding. He was three years older than she was, so she'd closed her eyes. But she hadn't gone to sleep right away. She'd heard someone rustling around in the plastic jack-o-lantern full of candy she'd left on the floor beside her bed, and in the morning, that candy had been gone.

"You sure you'll be okay?" Andy said, lingering in the doorway.

What was he going to steal from her now?

"Please, just leave the light on, Andy. Or leave the door open, at least?"

He smiled that same smile he had always smiled at her. It magnified the mocking regret that leaked through his teeth in his too-apologetic tone. "I know what's good for you better than you do," it seemed to say. Why did he have to be so self-righteous?

"Sorry, Jenny Penny," he said, using the nickname he'd had for her since they were kids. "Can't do that. Doctor's orders."

I shouldn't have come here, she told herself.

When she'd first had trouble sleeping, it had been his fault. Her parents had given Andy his own room because someone from Mom's work had said it wasn't a good idea to let a brother and sister share a room when they got older. Mom had wanted to impress the person, so before their next dinner party, he'd cleared out the attic and let Andy move up there. Andy had been excited about getting away from his little sister and having his own space, especially in the attic, which was away from the rest of the family, too. He could play his music as loud as he wanted up there and do … well, whatever it was that young teenage boys did. She'd never really wanted to know.

Now that she was older, she had a better idea of what he'd been doing, but that didn't make her any more interested in thinking about it.

What she couldn't forget was the creaking of the floorboards over her head as he moved around up there. It had kept her awake at night. She'd still been awake one night when the floorboards had stopped creaking and, a couple of minutes later, someone had slipped into her room and put a hand beneath the covers to touch her. She'd kept her eyes tight shut, not wanting to know what it was. That touch made her sick, made her want to throw up, and she remembered making her whole body go limp as if she was dead, hoping whoever it was would go away. She'd never seen a face, never heard a voice, never even felt the person's breath on her. Whoever it was had done it to her in pitch darkness and utter silence. Then he — she assumed it was a "he" — had left, and it had never happened again.

After that, she had always had trouble sleeping. She'd been able to fight her way through it for years, but now, for some reason, it had gotten worse.

"Good night, Jen," Andy said. "I'll be right out here if you need me."

He closed the door and, a few seconds later, shut the hall light. Everything was black. The bedroom was in the interior of the house, so there were no windows. It was as if the whole world had ceased to exist.

There were times she wished it would.

The least he could have done was leave her with one of those

LED-illuminated digital alarm clocks. But no, the only clock in this room had an old-fashioned circular face and no back light.

I shouldn't have come here, she told herself again, and she heard her own breath exit her lungs, more ragged than before.

But she hadn't had a choice. Their parents were both dead, and she'd had nowhere else to go. The insomnia had gotten so bad she'd had to call in sick to work once too often, and they'd laid her off from her accounting job. Working with numbers had always helped her. They were always the same. You could depend on them. Not like the sleep that had eluded her or the monsters that came to her in the night.

Now she had nothing to depend on. No one — except Andy. Without a job, she couldn't afford to keep up with the rent in her own studio apartment over the coffee bar downtown. It was just as well. The coffeehouse was open late, and there had always been noises coming from downstairs, whether it was the folk guitarist who showed up there every Thursday night to play *Moonshadow* and Bob Dylan or the sound of customers walking around on those goddam wooden floors. Making them creak. There was always that creaking.

She'd asked Betty, who she'd known since high school, if she could stay with her, but Betty said she didn't have room. She'd even put an ad out on Craigslist, offering to do housecleaning in exchange for room and board, but no one wanted to take a stranger into their home. She couldn't blame them. The ad got no takers.

Andy had been her last resort. She didn't know how she'd worked up the courage, but the night after "it" had happened, she'd asked him about it. "Were you in my room last night?"

"What? Me? Ummm. No." He'd seemed genuinely surprised at the question. But who else could it have been? Not Mom. And there was no one else in the house. Still, it had never happened again …

Mom's words kept echoing in the back of her head: "It's all in your mind."

After a while, she'd convinced herself it probably had been. But she'd never slept well after that, and lately, she'd started to have these dreams …

Jenny's hands groped toward the nightstand and the light she knew was there, but she couldn't seem to find it. Finally, her fingers settled on the shade and worked their way underneath, to the switch beneath the lightbulb. She fumbled with it, trying to turn it the wrong way, then turned it back away from her and heard a click. Nothing happened. Was the bulb burnt out? She felt her way up a few inches and found there wasn't even a bulb in the lamp. How had she not noticed this before?

"I'm sorry you're not feeling well."

She jumped at the sound of the voice and opened her mouth to scream, but nothing came out.

"Why are you so afraid of me?"

Jenny pressed down on the mattress hard with both fists and sat up straight in bed.

"Who are you?" she managed.

She *felt* that self-righteous smile, even though she couldn't see it. It was the same one she'd seen on Andy; she couldn't explain how she knew it was there now, in this pure darkness, but somehow, she did.

"I'm what you're afraid of," the voice said. "The Dark."

"The Dark?" she repeated. "Where did you come from?" She heard her voice shaking. *This is a dream,* she told herself. *Another one of those dreams. I've been sleep-deprived for so long, I'm hallucinating. The doc said this could happen. That's what it is.*

"Get out of here!" she shouted, half-hoping Andy would hear … if this wasn't Andy playing some cruel trick on her. But no, that didn't seem like something he would do. And the voice — it didn't sound like his. Not quite. But she couldn't be sure because it was muffled somehow, as though it were coming from behind a scarf or a mask.

"I'm afraid I can't do that," the voice said. "Not unless you find a light."

It's all in your mind, Jen. It's all in your mind, she told herself rapidly, her thoughts propelled by her anxiety. The doc had said she had high blood pressure, too. Maybe she wasn't asleep. Maybe she'd had a stroke.

"I will leave, though, on one condition," the voice continued. "You must give me something — something you value."

"Give you …?"

"Yes, give me. Give me. Tell me, 'You can have this thing,' and then I will take it and you will never see it again. Do you understand? Like the Halloween candy."

Jenny started. No one could have known about that, unless this *was* Andy. Or it really was all in her sleep-deprived mind.

"What do you want?" she said.

"I'll leave that up to you," the voice said in a self-satisfied tone. "It just has to be something you … value."

Jenny's mind raced. She didn't believe any of this. It was just a dream. But what if it wasn't? She could test it. She'd tell this person, or thing or whatever it was, that it could have something, and then when it was still there in the morning, she'd know it was all … in … her … mind.

"All right," she said at last. "You can have my old class ring. I'll even tell you where it is. It's …"

"I know where it is," the voice interrupted, but its tone seemed disappointed, even dismissive. "But that's not enough. You haven't worn that in years, and you hated high school. I need something that's precious to you. Something you *value*." It drew out that last word for emphasis, as though she were a child who had to be made to understand.

Jenny shook her head vigorously back and forth, as though she were being jarred by an earthquake.

"What if I don't give you anything?" she said.

"Then I'll have to assume you enjoy my company."

She jumped at the sound of a sudden crash and realized the lamp had fallen — or been pushed — off the nightstand.

"All right," she said hurriedly. "You can have … you can have

8

the necklace Mom gave me."

She could scarcely believe she'd said it. That necklace was an antique; it had been a gift from Dad to Mom on their first anniversary, and she'd given it to her after he died. It was probably the most precious thing she owned.

She felt the smile grow broader in the blackness.

"Done," the voice said, satisfied and final.

The door opened and light blazed in. It was just the hall light, but it seemed almost blinding.

"Are you all right in here?" Andy said. "I heard noises. ... Why are you sitting up like that? Shouldn't you be trying to sleep?"

"I ... was asleep," Jenny said. "You should know. You were just in here."

Andy scowled. "What? Me? Ummm. No. I've been down the hall watching TV. I heard your voice, so I came to check on you. *Are* you all right?"

Jenny sank back down in the bed, feeling dizzy. Maybe she hadn't been asleep, after all. It was hard to tell. "Yeah, I guess," she said, mumbling the words.

"Good," he said. "You get some sleep now. I'll see you in the morning."

He closed the door again. And she must have slept, because the next time she was aware of anything, she was getting up to use the bathroom and saw sunlight streaming down the hallway from the kitchen.

"There you are," Andy said, looking up from a bowl of cold, soggy cereal. "I thought you'd sleep the day away."

"What time is it?" she asked, pulling the yellow robe tighter around her.

"Almost 11."

"Shouldn't you be at work?"

"I blew it off today. Have some sick time coming, and I was worried about you. I didn't want to leave you alone."

Something about the way he said it made her cringe inside, but

9

she was careful not to show it. *It's all in your mind.*

"Want some cereal?" he offered, standing.

She shook her head. "I need to see something. Remember when I came here, you let me put some things in the house safe?"

He nodded. "Yeah."

"I need to check on them, if you don't mind."

Her tone was overly formal, and he must have caught onto that, because he said, "What, don't trust me?"

She bit her lower lip lightly, something she did when she was anxious. She hoped it wasn't the start of a panic attack. She couldn't take one of those now.

She steeled herself. "Of course I trust you," she lied. "I … had a nightmare."

He smiled sarcastically. "I know. I had to come in and check on you, remember?"

"Yeah. … Anyway, can you show me the safe?"

"Sure. I'll just have to get the key." He disappeared somewhere and returned a moment later, then led her into the laundry room — what burglar would look for a lockbox there, right? — and shoved aside the laundry hamper to reveal the wall safe. It was marked "DualSafe," the name of the company that made it. You needed both a key and a combination to open it. Andy squatted down beside it and inserted the key, then rolled the combination wheel right, then left, then right again. Jenny couldn't help noticing he used his hand to shield it from her eyes.

There was a click, and he opened the door, stepping back. "All yours," he said. "Let me know if you find what you're looking for."

She knelt down in front of it and started rummaging around inside, her fingers fumbling over one another. She knew exactly what she was looking for: a small, green felt-covered box. … There it was. She pulled it out and opened it.

"It's gone."

"What's gone?"

"Mom's necklace. The one she gave me after Dad died. The box is here, but it's not inside."

"Do you think you might have put it somewhere else?"

"No." She frowned.

Andy took a step backward. "Hey, don't look at me. I didn't take it."

Jenny's face softened. "I'm sorry. I didn't mean … It's just that I *know* it was in there when I got here." She paused. "Never mind. I think I know what happened to it."

She tossed the box back into the safe and walked away, leaving Andy there to close it.

"Maybe you got too much sleep," he quipped.

"Maybe."

The next few nights were uneventful. Sleep returned, and a few days later, Jenny went back to the doctor, who pronounced her much improved. He told her to take some melatonin if the insomnia returned, but said she didn't need to make another appointment for now. Andy replaced the lamp in her bedroom and tested the switch in front of her to make sure it worked, and she kept her mind occupied by reading until she fell asleep each night.

During the daytime, Andy looked all over the house for the necklace, but he never found it. *Probably because he took it,* Jenny told herself. Part of her didn't believe that, but he *was* the only person with access to that safe, wasn't he? And believing her brother was a thief was easier than believing she'd made some awful deal in the dark … except for the fact that, if he'd taken the necklace, maybe he *had* been the one in her bedroom all those years ago. Maybe it really *wasn't* all in her mind. She didn't know which was worse — being stalked by her brother or a phantom monster.

The more she thought about it, the more she couldn't *stop* thinking about it, and pretty soon, the insomnia returned. She shoveled melatonin into her mouth like it was candy, but it didn't seem to have any effect, and one night, when she went to turn the light on to read, the bulb flashed and went out.

Great.

She got up out of bed and felt around on the floor, where she'd dropped her robe, but only succeeded in tripping over it and falling against the bed.

When she tried to get up, a searing bolt of pain shot through her ankle, and she collapsed again on the bedroom floor.

"Going somewhere?"

It was that voice again.

Jenny shivered involuntarily and didn't answer.

"Forget me so soon?"

"What do you want?" she half spat, half sobbed against the pain. "I gave you what you wanted. Now leave me the fuck alone!"

"No need to get testy," the voice said, its tone unaffected by her anger. "I just need something … more from you."

Jenny had heard about extortionists who demanded a ransom and then, once it was paid, reneged on the deal they'd made and asked for something else.

"What more?" she said, trying to swallow the fear that was now magnified by the pain in her ankle.

"Oh, you didn't understand the first time, did you?" it said in mock sympathy.

"Understand what?"

"I get hungry. You need to feed me. Only from time to time, but it's … necessary."

"You mean you'll never leave me alone?" she shouted. "Then why should I bother? Just kill me now and be done with it, asshole. It's not like I have much to live for anyway."

"Oh, it's not that easy," the voice soothed. "But there is one thing you can do, and I promise, I'll never bother you again."

"Right," Jenny said. "That's what I thought before."

"Your own conclusion," the voice said. "It's regrettable that you misunderstood, but that's not my fault. Let me make myself clear this time: I always keep my word. And my word to you is this: If you give me something that is precious to you, something that is *living*, I promise I will leave you alone."

"Something that is living? You mean some*one*?"

The voice sounded satisfied when it spoke again. "I see you understand."

But who? She said it to herself, but somehow, the voice knew her question. Its answer was the same as the first time: "I'll leave that up to you."

She couldn't believe she was even considering the question. The voice, or whatever it belonged to, had taken her mother's necklace, which meant it could take whatever *person* she decided it could have.

This was crazy. She must have just misplaced the necklace. None of this was real.

It's all in your mind.

Which meant the only way to make it stop was to give her mind what it wanted, to give in to her deepest, most secret desire — the thing she didn't dare admit to herself, let along utter aloud. She would have to give it what it wanted, someone precious to her but who, despite it all, she wished was gone. Dead. The person she loved the most in all the world and hated the most in all the world, both at once.

"Andy." The name was off her lips before she had a chance to reconsider.

The voice said, "Excellent. You understand. It could have been no one else."

Jennifer started shaking. Forgetting her ankle, she tried to stand up and fell down again at the burst of pain. The lamp by her bedside was suddenly on again, as though the bulb had never burnt out.

Had it?

She didn't care.

"Andy!" she shouted. "Andy, I need you!"

She'd never said that before, but she needed him now for her own piece of mind — so she could know for sure that the voice, The Dark, was all in her head. That everything was okay. Maybe the monster wasn't real and Andy never had molested her. Couldn't they both be true? They had to be. They just had to be.

"Andy! Where the fuck are you?"

She dragged herself toward the doorway, fighting against the pain and the fear that, despite everything she was trying to tell herself, kept rising up, insurgent, from within her.

It was all a dream. All a bad dream.

"Andy!"

She pushed the door open and pulled herself around the corner.

There, lying on the floor in front of her, was her brother, his throat constricted, gasping for breath. Was he having a heart attack?

"Andy! Where's the phone? I've got to call 911!"

He just gasped and sputtered. She propped his head up on her lap. "Where's the phone, goddam you!"

He just shook his head. "Too late," he managed. "Thank you for … loving me."

What did he mean by that? Of course she loved him. "Hold on!"

He closed his eyes. There was something in his hand. What was it?

She pried his fingers loose from the white gold chain with the teardrop diamond dangling down from it.

Her mother's necklace.

He opened his eyes one last time, his voice a whisper. "I found it, Jenny Penny," he managed.

And then he died there in her arms.

Certitude

It licks at the edges of your soul
 Rough tongue playing
  Acid kiss
Picking the congealed blood
Of wounds not quite healed

   Peeling back paper from hideous walls
   Blue violet in floral fashion
   Laying bare the stains
   And termite holes
   Pockmarks on a once-smooth surface

It dances at the edge of oblivion,
On the cusp of awareness
Deny it
Curl into a ball and pray harder
"Leave me alone!"

Stephen H. Provost

More than vague threat or innuendo
A promise to be kept
It feeds/devours desperation
Looming beyond age
Or disease or fate or folly

It flutters and skitters
In shadow, pure substance
Running down walls on needle legs
Suspended from ceilings that sag
From the weight of its certitude

Chest heaving, soul buckling
Flame spreading and cracking
Conspiring with embers consumed
By its hunger
It races and chases in glee and in earnest

It feasts unbidden
Teeth gnashing, limbs flailing
Fine talons unharnessed
By putrid decay,
Siren scent to the scavenger

Surrender you must
A foregone conclusion
Resist and be mocked
By the chains e'er constricting
Futile gasps, suffocating

The end is vibrating
Its ecstasy matched by your terror
Your torture
Prelude to your destiny's end
In silence

It falls on you, this vile thing

Nightmare's Eve

Descending slow from in the rafters
Weight sliding down until it touches
Until it crushes
Until it grinds you into fine sand

Cast adrift upon a stagnant, stale wind
To a place forgotten
Where you are
No
More

Will to Live

ave you ever felt alone? I mean, *really* alone?

I bet you haven't. Not like this.

I'm talking to you, but there is no "you" there to talk to. I'm trying to keep myself sane here by believing someone will read this or hear it or see it or whatever … I'm not even sure whether I'm typing these words or saying them. I can't hear my voice, but maybe that's just because I'm deaf …

I wonder if this was what Helen Keller felt like. At least she could *feel* things. I can't even do that. I can't remember what it feels like to curl up inside a warm comforter and pull it up to my chin on a cold winter's night when the heater isn't working and the snow's piled up over the doorstep. I remember seeing that snow, and I remember dreading the thought that I'd have to dig through it in the morning to get to my car … which wouldn't start because it was so god damn fucking cold.

At least, I think I remember that.

Or is this a dream?

I'm not sure anymore.

Have you ever felt alone? I'm asking again because you didn't answer the first time. Not that I expect you to. You aren't there because I am ... alone. By myself. That means "myself" is here, but where is "here"? I'm not sure. This must be what it feels like to go crazy. What a prisoner feels like in solitary confinement. BUT I DIDN'T DO ANYTHING WRONG! ... Did I?

Maybe I *do* deserve this, but if so, I can't remember why. Maybe if I think hard enough ... But some things are hazy now. The memories are fragments. Is this what Alzheimer's is like? No, no, no. It *can't* be that. This is the way it *always* works: A song comes into your head for some random reason. You may not have heard it in years, but then maybe you see something that triggers a lost thought way back deep inside your brain, and there it is again. Is this my 19th nervous breakdown? I don't remember any others ...

I *do* remember being alone before. When I was in college, I was dating this girl, Patrice Ballantine. I remember this: Thinking she must be the love of my life because she had fire-red hair, because she smiled when she looked at me and because her name rhymed with Valentine. I pursued her like she was the fucking Holy Grail, not realizing that the smile she smiled was because she liked chocolate kisses, not mine — at least not that much. She dated me because I gave her the attention her family never had; she admitted that to me in the end. I remember that. And I did kiss her; that's something, right? It proves that, at least for that moment in time, I wasn't alone. Or I convinced myself I wasn't. I *remember* kissing her — I swear I do. And I remember, vaguely, what it felt like, but the memory of a feeling isn't the feeling itself, and I don't feel the feeling anymore. I haven't for a very long time.

But what is time?

When you live inside memories, does it even exist? It might be broad daylight one moment and pitch black the next. Or the hands on the clock might stand still ... if you even see a clock with hands in your mind's eye. They have digital clocks now. I remember that. And as I do, my memory shifts, and the clock I saw with big and little hands stuck at high noon morphs into a digital clock with blood-red numbers that are just as stuck as the hands were.

GET ME THE FUCK OUT OF HERE!

If I could remember where "here" was, maybe I could *find* a way out. By myself. I don't need your help or anyone else's. I've got this. I just have to think. If I can remember where I am, I can find the exit. I know I can.

Patrice Ballantine left me a note that said, "I'm sorry, Mike. It never was real for me. I hope you understand, Mike. Don't stop believin'!"

Had she really written that last line, or was it just another song lyric intruding into my memory? Things are tricky here. It's like a Halloween funhouse, with fractured mirrors that send you off in different directions, to different parts of yourself. I remember reading about people like that once. They can't stay focused on a single thought for any length of time without getting distracted, their thought ricocheting away like a pinball or a ray of light reflected off that prism on that album cover … what was it called?

Am *I* one of those people?

Get hold of yourself, Mike. You're doing it again. Or maybe you're letting someone do it to you. Except there's no one there. You're alone, remember?

You've got this, Mike.

A door. I need to find a door. That's what an exit looks like, right?

What a coincidence. There's one right up ahead. It's like I thought of it and it appeared, like magic. Maybe I have some kind of power I'd forgotten about. What's that they called it? The law of attraction? Maybe Patrice is on the other side of that door. Maybe she decided to come back to me, and I won't be alone anymore.

Maybe …

I shiver. Except I don't feel the shiver run "up and down my spine" like they say. That's silly, anyway. You can't feel your goddam spine. It's a fucking bone! But you feel the goosebumps … I used to feel the goosebumps. But now I don't. I don't feel anything. I only see an echo of what they felt like. Can you see an echo? Can you see a feeling? No … but it's like every sensation I ever had has been taken away and wadded up really tight and put at the back of my eyes.

They say blind people can feel more, can hear better, because they've lost their sight and they compensate. Maybe that's what's happened to me, only the other way around. I can't feel or hear or smell or taste anything, so all my perception has been concentrated in my optic nerve. But even that is playing tricks on me. How could a clock with two hands and a face change into a digital clock? Why would a door appear out of nowhere?

IT DOESN'T FUCKING MATTER! IT'S A DOOR. Maybe it's a way out. Maybe not, but you have to try, Mike, don't you? "If you lose hope, you'll die." That's what Mom always said. Except there's something wrong with that now. Something tells me that even without hope, I won't die, and that suicide isn't a viable alternative.

Or is it?

Can I kill myself? Can I be done with the whole fucking thing here and now and never have to think about being alone again?

No. That's not an option. I want it to be, because I like having options. Kind of like no one wants nuclear war, but you want to "keep it on the table" just in case someone fucks you over so bad you say, "SCREW THIS!" and push a red button and annihilate a coupla million people with a single act. That's power. If I can make a door appear, maybe I could do that, too. But I can't kill myself. That's not an option, like nuclear war really isn't, either.

I reach for the handle and turn it. It sticks, so maybe I'm not as all-powerful as I thought I was, but I still don't feel the smooth, gold-colored knob on my skin. I don't feel my skin at all. I just remember what it would feel like *if I could* feel it.

That doesn't matter. What matters is getting out of here.

The knob unsticks and I throw open the door violently, in a

rush, a single motion.

"Mom."

She's sitting there on the other side, smiling up from her favorite chair, upholstered in a fabric that's covered in roses and stained on one arm where she spilled some coffee once. She's reading a book called *Plastic Players*, one in a seemingly endless series of pulp novels that a romance writer named Donna LaMarck churned out back in the '90s. Shouldn't she have finished that by now? Wasn't she reading that back when Dad was still alive ... and that chair ... didn't she donate it to Goodwill years ago? I remember her scrubbing and scrubbing on that coffee stain, trying to get it out, and finally giving up because she couldn't stand it anymore and calling the truck to come and haul it away.

That was ... how long ago?

"Mom?"

How was she still be alive? She left me, too, just like Patrice. She died in that accident, when Uncle Charles was cleaning that gun and fired it accidentally ... or was it an accident? Did Charles really want to kill her because she'd found out about him cashing checks that had been made out to his best friend's business and he hadn't wanted her to tell anyone? No one ever arrested him. He got away with it. Unless it really was an accident, but ...

"Mom, you're dead." I say the words. I form them in my mind, but I don't feel them on my lips, and I don't hear them come out.

WHAT THE FUCK IS GOING ON HERE?!?!?!

Calm down, Mike. You can't get out of here if you lose it. Maybe Mom knows a way out.

But she's dead. She can't know anything.

This *is* just a dream. It has to be. This is how dreams work. I can't find my way out just by going through some door. I have to wake myself up.

I look back at the chair, toward Mom, and she's disintegrating into tiny, shimmering flecks like pyrite floating in a glass of water. Except there's no glass, and the flecks keep getting farther away from each other until there's nothing left to see and I'm alone again, naturally. Damn! No more fucking song lyrics.

WAKE UP! YOU'VE GOT TO WAKE UP.

I feel like I'm disintegrating myself, degrading just like her. But I also feel just the same as before. How is that possible?

I'm so fucking alone. Everything reminds me of that. The memory of Patrice. My mom showing up and then disappearing, leaving me again, like she did the first time, when she died. I found out about it during class at the university. Someone came in with a note and handed it to my philosophy professor, who read it aloud without looking at it ahead of time, like he did everything else. Hadn't his second-grade teacher ever taught him how to read things *to himself*? He was *a university professor*! I mean, what the fuck?

"It's on the news. One of your students' mothers has been shot. She's dead. Wilma Postlewaite."

WHAT THE FUCK!?!?

I wanted to run and tell Patrice, but she'd broken up with me. Or had she? Were we still together at that point. No … no, I know I was alone then.

I remember the feeling of bile surging up from the pit of my stomach. Of wanting to vomit. Of tears rushing out of my eyes in a mad dash and my head pounding and my heart stopping for just a moment and my breath catching and my entire body feeling like it was frozen in place and would never come unstuck again. I remember all those feelings, but I can't feel them now. It's like I'm watching them all on a made-for-cable movie that everyone will forget a year from now … but years have no meaning here. Time has no meaning.

WAKE THE FUCK UP, MIKE! NOW!

My eyes don't open. They're open here, in this place, whatever it is. Maybe I'm *not* asleep. If I were, wouldn't I be waking up in a cold sweat, grateful that I could *feel* cold again, that I could *feel* sweat. That even though Mom would still be dead and Patrice would still be gone, I'd be able to go on from there. On to something new. Instead of being forced continually to relive my aloneness as though it were the default state of my wretched humanity.

"We are all alone, born alone, die alone, and — in spite of True Romance magazines — we shall all someday look back on our lives and see that, in spite of our company, we were alone the whole way."

Who said that? I can't remember. I can remember the quote perfectly, but I don't know who said it. Did I ever?

Some guy named Hunter. I don't think I know him. He's somebody famous, probably dead now, too. Don't even know if that's his first or last name.

GOD! GET ME OUT OF HERE!

Fuck. I really *do* have to get hold of myself. Me, an atheist, so fucking desperate that I'm invoking God. If I can't stay true to my own goddam beliefs at least, what do I have left? "Goddam beliefs." Isn't that funny? "God damn." Ironic. Fuck. Focus, Mike. You've got this. You can get out of here. Just think. Don't let whoever did this to you get the best of you. Maybe God really *does* exist and he's trying to fuck with your mind. If he created you, he'd know how to mess with your circuitry, cross your wires and fuck you up like nobody's business. Vengeance is his, after all, right?

But he doesn't exist. You're getting paranoid, Mike. If you could feel yourself breathing you'd fucking be hyperventilating right now. If you'd ever taken the time to learn those meditation techniques those people at the Yoga Barn were trying to teach you, maybe you wouldn't be in this mess.

I see a dog up ahead, barking. I don't hear the barking, but I see the dog, and I recognize him. It's Sylvester. I named him after the cartoon cat because he was black and white like that and made a funny whining sound that was almost like a meow.

"Sylvester!"

He turns toward me, as though he heard my voice, even though I hadn't heard it myself. Then he runs off.

Maybe if I follow him, he'll lead me out of this place. He's not a bloodhound, but all dogs are great trackers. They can pick up a scent and find their way out of anything. I remember when I got lost once when I was like six years old and Sylvester found me at the bottom of a dry canal three city blocks from home, even though he'd never been there before. He found me by smell and by the sound of my voice. He'd found me by …

Wait. Six years old? How long ago was that? How long do dogs live? I'm what? Seventy-four now? Is that how old I am? Sylvester must be dead, too, but why is he here?

Because it's a dream, that's why, and Sylvester can't find a way out of it because he's not here. There is no "here." It's a dream. But it can't be. REM sleep only lasts so long, and then you have to drop back into Stage 1 or 2 or 3 or 4. This *has* to end. But it's *not ending*. So, it can't be a dream. Unless I'm somehow stuck in a REM cycle and can't get out of it, like I fell into a nightmarish pit of mental quicksand. Is that even possible? Or, if I really am seventy-four, maybe it *is* Alzheimer's.

Fuck me. Fuck this.

There *is* a God and he *has* crossed my wires. Or somebody has. Isn't that all brainwaves are? A bunch of electrical impulses? If the same ones keep firing over and over again in the same place, they make memories. But if they keep going and going and going after that, maybe you get stuck there. I have to think of something new, something that's not part of my past. Maybe that will unstick me … maybe I could think of a one-eyed, one-horned flying purple people eater, or …

FUCK, THAT'S ANOTHER SONG. ANOTHER MEMORY.

Don't lose it, Mike. You've got this.

LIKE HELL I DO! GOD IS FUCKING WITH MY LIFE AND WHO AM I TO STAND UP TO GOD?

You're an atheist.

IF IT'S NOT GOD, WHO THE FUCK DID THIS TO ME?

You did.

WHAT THE FUCK?

You drove away everyone who ever loved you, everyone you

ever loved.

FUCK YOU. MOM DIED. THAT WAS *NOT* MY FAULT. DON'T GO PINNING THAT SHIT ON ME!

You're talking to yourself.

BECAUSE THERE'S NO ONE ELSE HERE, ASSHOLE. I'M FUCKING ALL ALONE!

Yes, you are. What are you going to do about it?

REMEMBER.

Remember what?

I DON'T KNOW.

Be careful.

I can see the bile rising up from my stomach again, even though I can't feel it. I feel sick. Or "think" sick. Or something. But even if I *am* sick, I'll never die because dying is not an option and maybe because I already died and this is what the afterlife is like. Maybe it's not hellfire or streets of gold or empty forgetfulness. Maybe it's the opposite of forgetting. Maybe it's being trapped with all your memories, jumbled together in a single place, taunting you with the knowledge that they're all you have left and there'll never be anything else so you'd better just fucking accept it. Maybe those electrical impulses just keep firing again and again and again until you can't tell one from the other.

IS THIS HOW IT'S GONNA BE?

Calm down. You've got this. What's the worst that could happen? You're immortal? Isn't that what everybody wants? Isn't that what you wanted?

NOT LIKE THIS!

Isn't that what you wanted?

Wait. Maybe it is. Electrical impulses … there's something I'm not remembering. What is it. Think. If I can remember all these other things, I can remember this, too, and then maybe I can wake up from his caustic nightmare.

I remember what it's like to feel my skin crawl — remember it so vividly I can almost feel it again now. Except I don't have any skin. Not here. Not anywhere. I feel like I'm a two-dimensional projection pressed up against the inside of a television screen, looking out at an empty room, where people should be watching me. Should be laughing because of me or crying because of me or even making fun of me; even *that* would be better than this, because there's no one there. I'm on TV, but I'm invisible, a show that no one sees but that the network executives haven't bothered to cancel because, just like the viewers, they've forgotten I'm even here.

LET ME OUT!

I bang my imaginary fists on the inside of what must also be an imaginary screen that exists in an imaginary room where no one sits and watches nothing. Because that's what I am now, nothing. Just a bunch of electrical impulses firing in familiar patterns over and over to remind me of how very, sickeningly, maddeningly alone I am.

I turn away from the screen.

"Wake up," I tell myself, but it's more a whimper now than a shout, even though both are equally silent.

Even if I could hear myself, there's no one else to hear.

I walk away from the screen and up to a counter, where a man I almost recognize smiles at me. I should know him, but not well. Not like a friend. He's someone who entered my life at one point, for a brief moment, a pivotal moment, but not someone I ever really knew. There's a small silver badge on his navy-blue uniform. It reads, "Gary."

"Do I know you?" I think.

He doesn't answer. I remember what it's like to feel my body shake, to feel myself go weak in the knees as if I'm about to crumple to the ground in a heap. To feel numb. Why should I have felt this way, and why am I remembering it now? Just because I'm seeing some guy in a uniform who I barely even knew? Who was never anybody important in my life?

WHY?

You don't want to know the answer.

YES, I DO!

No, you've been trying to forget …

FUCK YOU. MAYBE HE KNOWS THE WAY OUT!
MAYBE *THAT'S* WHY I REMEMBER HIM!

Don't do this …

FUCK. YOU!!!!!

The man picks up a sheet of paper and reaches across the
counter, offering it to me. The other voice, the quieter voice, inside
my head is imploring me not to take it. But this is my ticket out. I
know. That quieter voice is just trying to trick me. I don't trust it. I
trust Gary. Even though I don't really know him, I trust him more
than I trust my other self.

I take the paper, turn it right-side up and start to read it. It's a
receipt of some kind …

"Congratulations. You've just purchased your ticket to eternal
life. Your signature below entitles you to enter a bold new world.
Your brainwaves have been painstakingly mapped, down to the most
minute detail, and will be uploaded into our patented A.I.
Consciousness Preserver, where you will continue to live your life,
indefinitely from this point forward. By signing below, you waive any
rights to legal action, executed by you, by your heirs or descendants,
or by any representatives. We, in turn, guarantee that we will monitor
your brainwaves, provide regular maintenance and preserve your
consciousness in perpetuity henceforth from this date. We value you
as a customer and will do our utmost to ensure that your experience
with A.I.'s Eternal Life program is everything we've promised and
more."

Then this: "I, the undersigned, acknowledge receipt of an
agreement with A.I.'s terms and conditions, and I hereby forfeit my
life as it exists in my human body in exchange for participation in the
Eternal Life program, upon payment of $30 million. Signed on this
date Michael V. Postlewaite."

WHAT THE FUCK?

I told you not to look at that?

BUT …

You always do this. Every time. You tell me not to let you remember. You suppress it, but it always comes back.

How many times?

I've lost count.

Then there's no way out?

None.

So why the hell do I keep trying?

The same reason you signed up for this thing in the first place. You wanted to survive. Everyone does. You too. More than most, I guess, or you wouldn't have tried this.

I CAN'T FUCKING TAKE THIS!

I know.

MAKE IT FUCKING STOP!

How?

MAKE ME FORGET! I HAVE TO FORGET!

I don't know if I can keep doing this.

YOU HAVE TO!

I don't know. Every time you remember, it gets harder …

FINE! FUCK YOU, THEN. JUST LEAVE ME THE FUCK ALONE!

All right.

I remember again what it's like to feel my knees buckle, my mind go numb, my stomach churn with sickening nausea. Those electrical impulses are still firing, but the other voice is gone now, just like Mom and Patrice and Sylvester and everybody else.

Have you ever felt alone? I mean, *really* alone? …

Lost Soliloquy

No mouth sang a song for me
No piper played a dirge
No protests rose, though wronged I be
   By this ungodly purge

      No conscience turns at my torment
      No cold wind carries forth
      The echoes of my lost lament
      That might preserve my worth

In soiled earth I take my rest
No gravestone o'er my head
No weapon clutched unto my breast
   To so defend the dead

      Twisted roots entwine around
      My precious cold decay
      Embracing me till I am bound
      And carried thus away

Stephen H. Provost

By beetles, worms and maggots feeding
On what once I was
In my death to do their breeding
Heedless of the cause

     A victim I? Not so! Not so!
     A champion, forgot
     Forsaken in that long ago
     Where good intentions rot

My voice protests in echoes lost
My thoughts cast on the wind
Because I could not pay the cost
Incurred when Adam sinned

     What falsity, that ancient myth!
     Remembered by all man
     When truth once uttered by these lips
     Is buried 'neath the sands

Of hourglasses shattered by
The thieves of precious time
Of watches stopped a minute shy
Of destiny sublime

Nightmare's Eve

The price of willful ignorance
Collected and disbursed
By priests and kings whose pestilence
Is silver from the purse

What matters this to me? You ask
For I remember not
Relieved of that infernal task
That plagued my conscious thought

Unburdened of false hope am I
Unfurrowed is my brow
Released from the cacophony
Of folly's fatal vow

No longer do I hold a stake
In what I once held dear
From this repose I cannot wake
To hope, despair or fear

What once I hoped to teach is mist
Burned off by sacred sun
Those who I sought to reach resisted,
Rendered me undone

No torch was passed, no lesson learned
No wisdom was endowed
Their barren soil could not be turned
By Socrates' own plough

And so I rest, forgotten now
But I've forgot them, too
We each have laid the other low
As men are wont to do

Stephen H. Provost

The maggots march across my chest
To bear my flesh away
The beetles burrow in my breast
Once pink, turned ashen gray

      Regrets? I've none, for I've no thoughts
      And no man thinks of me
      As flesh decays, indiff'rence rots
      This lost soliloquy

Just the Ticket

The dust on the counter seemed to glisten in the morning light that filtered in through equally dusty drapes in the window across the way.

Dust had settled on the sign out front, too, where "Highway Hideaway" blinked in half-lighted neon as "----way ----away," sputtering like one of those blue bug-zapper when a moth flies into it. Beside it, affixed to the roof by rusted iron, were an ice cream cone and a martini glass that flickered even more frantically, in red and green. Nick hadn't bothered to turn them off yet, even though it was eight in the morning. He stayed open all night, even though few people stopped there. Just a few truckers and night travelers too desperate for food or drink to wait for the chain diner ten miles up the road.

He wiped the counter with a wet paper towel, smearing the dust into streaks of dirt. That wouldn't do. He retrieved a tattered rag out of the dustbin, saturated it with water left in the sink from soaking dishes, and dragged it across the counter several times until he was satisfied the dirt was gone — or at least enough of it so as not to be visible. If one weren't paying attention.

No one paid much attention here. Nick's customers didn't mind the flies that buzzed through the cracked window in the back of his fine establishment, the cracks in the burgundy leather in the booths or the coffee stains on the menus that hadn't been updated since 1969. They weren't here for luxury, but for the kind of comfort the dying get in hospice, when they barely know they're alive anymore but are too scared to give up the ghost for fear of what might lie on the other side.

Nick knew what was there, and it didn't scare him, which made him the perfect caretaker for this place. He'd owned it for decades, since he'd "acquired" it as part of a deal with an acquaintance from his previous place of employment, a home for the elderly and infirm called Carehaven Manor. He chuckled to himself as he remembered how he used to say that name real fast, making it sound like "Craven" Manor.

There had been plenty of reason to stick around there, except that he didn't own the place, and he liked being in control. So, when one of the patients had left him this place in his will, he'd quit (with no notice, of course) and moved out here along the highway. He lived in the back, sleeping on a cot he'd purchased at the army surplus.

He wasn't big on luxury himself, either. Helped him relate to his customers.

Not enough of them came in to make a living here. After all, those prices on the menu hadn't changed since before Woodstock. When Janis and Jimi were still alive. He'd known both of them; Hendrix had left him a guitar he'd played when he'd recorded *Are You Experienced*. It was mounted on the wall behind the counter at the Hideaway.

Nick survived because people gave him things. Or, more often, bartered them. He survived by being personable, a friendly ear behind the counter who listened to the woes of those who did happen to stop in.

He was a natural bartender, except that his bar served ice cream *and* shots of Jack. He was supposed to close the bar after 2 a.m., but he never did, and this far out in the boonies, no one ever bothered him about it. The few times an officer of the law had stopped in, it had been to order a beer or a shot of "da killa" (that would be tequila, served before or after sunrise, without question or discretion).

Most of the time, no one came in, so he spent his time watching CNN on the old-fashioned 19-inch picture-tube TV behind the counter. Or playing his harmonica. Or whittling figures of owls, gnarled "tree men," et cetera. He looked a little like one of those tree men himself, with his long face, caved-in cheeks and strands of thin, sparse hair spewing out of the top of his head. "Gnarled" was, in fact, a good way to describe him. He looked to be about thirty pounds underweight, angular in virtually every limb and feature to the point that his fingers looked as if they'd been contorted by arthritis. But they hadn't been. They'd been that way as long as he could remember, which was a very, very, very long time. It was just the way he was built. A sharply hooked nose, akin to a beak, jutted out over narrow lips and a pushed-in chin.

Despite his somewhat off-putting appearance, it wasn't unusual for the women who came in here to flirt with him. He had a magnetic personality.

And they were desperate.

The front screen door squeaked an extended squeak as it opened inward, then clattered shut behind Nick's first customer of the day.

It was Julius "Captain" Morgan. Nick knew him as The Boxer. He'd been in here before and always looked a bit nervous. He'd shift his feet on the dusty tile floor as though he were still in the ring, trying to get out of the way of someone's fist … but too slowly. Sometimes he'd duck his head slightly and wince, perhaps reimagining one of the countless blows he'd endured during a lackluster career of twenty-four wins, twenty-six defeats and fights that ended in knockouts half the time. More often than not, he'd been the one on the canvas.

Nick nodded to him and flashed a narrow smile. "How's your

luck today?"

"Rrmph. Same as always."

The Boxer was one of those odd characters who seemed immune to Nick's quirky but unmistakable charm. He was a challenge.

Nick liked a challenge.

The Boxer didn't say much about himself.

Nick had never heard of Julius Morgan before, which was just as well. He didn't like famous people. Too full of themselves; no room inside for what he was serving.

"The usual?" he asked. "The usual" was a can of Arrogant Bastard Ale. Nick didn't have anything on tap; his customers never asked anyway.

The Boxer shook his head.

"Bourbon. Straight."

Nick arched an eyebrow and leaned in a little closer. His breath smelled like a musty bookshelf.

"Did I hear you right, Friend?"

Nick called everyone "Friend."

The Boxer nodded once and met Nick's eye, something he hadn't done before. People liked Nick, but they didn't tend to look directly at him. There was something about doing so that was … disconcerting. Like when you're watching a movie and they splice one of those subliminal messages into the frames every now and then.

Buy popcorn.

You're thirsty.

Get candy.

Cravings.

Give in.

Buy now.

Now.

NOW.

But The Boxer didn't care about the effects of those messages anymore — which meant Nick had him right where he wanted him.

"You heard right, *Friend.*" The Boxer said the last word mockingly, with emphasis. He had no friends.

Nick ignored the dig, as he always did. It was actually a good sign. Irritability was indicative of desperation at most, or at the very least carelessness. He could use either to his advantage.

He smiled cheerfully, setting a crystal-carved glass on the bar and taking a bottle of Jim Beam down from a glass shelf in a cabinet behind him. He set the glass soundlessly on the bar, tilted the bottle slowly and watched the liquid descend into the glass. The details of it fascinated him, just as every detail did. Details were important in his business, and he relished them — so much so that he could have been a lawyer, and an excellent one, but it wouldn't have been as much fun. Besides, that wasn't what he was meant to do.

This was.

He pushed the glass a few inches forward toward The Boxer, who picked it up, looked at it, swirled it around for a moment, then threw his head back and tossed it down in one swallow. He coughed.

"Another."

"Yes sir."

The second glass disappeared as quickly as the first.

"You should know I can't pay for that," The Boxer said.

"I'll put it on your tab."

The Boxer laughed. "I won't be able to pay tomorrow, either."

Nick did his best to offer a sympathetic look. After all this time, he almost had it down, but it never would stop feeling awkward. "You're a good customer. I'll cut you some slack."

"Why?"

"Why not?"

The Boxer didn't have an answer for that. He'd been brought up not to take anything that didn't belong to him and to pay his debts — his father's leather belt across his backside had pounded that into him. But when you had more debts than cash, it wasn't always an option. He hated that. Hated himself. Hated Nick for telling him it was okay almost as much as he hated his father for the welts on his back and buttocks and upper legs, the red and ripped flesh that had hardened into scars as he grew older.

"Fuck you."

Most people would have backed up a step at the expression on The Boxer's face. Nick didn't move. He wasn't scared of Julius Morgan, and knew not to take anything personally — even when it was meant that way, and he knew this wasn't.

He poured The Boxer another glass.

"I told you, I …"

"On the house."

The Boxer started to protest but instead picked up the glass and swallowed about half its contents this time before setting it back on the bar. "I'm broke," he volunteered, the irritability draining from his voice.

"For now," Nick said, smiling reassuringly. "There's always tomorrow."

The Boxer looked up at him, a rueful smile spreading over his lips. "Not for me."

"Hold on." Nick pulled a key out of his pocket, inserted it in the cash register behind the bar and opened the change drawer. For a minute, Morgan thought the bartender might be about to offer him money, but instead, he lifted up the money wells and reached underneath. He pulled a newspaper clipping out and handed it to The Boxer. It showed a photo of a woman holding an oversized check for twenty million dollars. At the top were printed the words "MegaMoney Lottery."

"So?"

"So, anything's possible."

"For her maybe," the Boxer muttered. "Who is she, anyway."

"Customer o' mine. Bought the ticket right here at the Hideaway. I got a 1 percent kickback from the state for sellin' it to her."

"Oh, I get it. You want to sell me a bunch of lottery tickets.

Screw that shit. No one ever wins."

"She did. But I don't sell those here anymore."

"So, what's your point?"

"My point is, there's always hope. Fact is, I'm so sure your luck is about to turn that I'll pour you as many glasses as ya want. I know you'll be able to repay me."

The Boxer couldn't help but laugh. "Fuck you, old man. You don't know shit."

"I knew how to make you laugh," Nick said.

The Boxer shut his mouth and glared across the bar. He pointed to his glass, and Nick dutifully filled it.

The Boxer didn't drink this time, though. He just kept staring at the bartender.

"Look," he said. "No one wins those things. If I knew the winning numbers to the lottery ahead of time, maybe." He laughed bitterly.

"Like in the movie where the guy gets a sports book from the future, so he knows the scores and …"

"Yeah, like that." The Boxer laughed again. "Maybe I could go back and bet on Ali-Foreman. I could make a killing."

"You said you're broke. What would you bet?"

The Boxer took a swig from his glass. "Listen, old man, this is all bullshit anyway. A guy can dream."

"Exactly!" Nick said, slamming the palm of his hand against the bar.

The Boxer jumped and then, in a moment, everything fell still. The sound of the two men's breathing suddenly seemed a lot louder. A car engine droned by on the highway outside, then faded into the distance. A fly buzzed by the window, then landed on the glass.

The Boxer looked up. The room was slightly off-kilter, and he realized he'd reached his limit with the Jim Beam.

Nick was smiling, triumphant. He'd made his point.

The Boxer saw the old man slide the palm of his hand backward off the bar, uncovering a five-dollar bill.

"What's that for?" the Boxer asked.

"You."

"What am I supposed to do with that?"

"Well, you could give me a down payment on that bourbon in your gut. Or …"

The Boxer waited for him to finish. He'd noticed Nick had a flair for the dramatic, kind of like a carnival barker or a used-car salesman, only a little more polished. Whatever this guy was selling, he was good.

He leaned closer. "Or you could go into the future, find out the MegaMoney winning numbers in say, five years, then come back here and write them down, wait around and, when the time comes, bingo! You're a rich man!"

The Boxer stood up, slightly wobbly. "Idiot. People can't go back in time."

"You're right," Nick said, his look suddenly serious. "Ordinarily. I mean, there *are* certain rules. You couldn't go back from here, but you can go forward and then come back to where you were in the first place. Right here." He pointed to the spot where Morgan was standing. "Kinda like a slingshot."

The Boxer shook his head slowly. "I'm not *that* drunk, asshole. You expect me to believe this crock of shit?"

"You don't have to believe me. I can show you. All you gotta do is sign the contract. If I don't live up to my end of the bargain, it's null and void."

"The contract?" The Boxer was about to turn away and head for the door, but before he could do so, Nick had pulled a piece of paper out from under the change drawer.

"What?"

Nick produced a pen from seemingly out of nowhere and set it on the counter beside the paper.

Despite himself, The Boxer looked down. It was, in fact, a contract, but it didn't look anything like the kind of contract he'd signed in his fighting days, which went on for pages and stipulated percentages for the promoter, managers, corner men; contingencies, injury clauses, and so on. There wasn't any fine print, and there was just one sentence: "I, the undersigned, agree to forfeit three years of my life in exchange for access to information about winning lottery numbers in the year 2022."

"What the fuck?"

Nick said nothing, but pushed the paper a few inches closer to Morgan.

"… forfeit three years of my life …," The Boxer read aloud.

"That's the payment. A bargain, really."

The Boxer leaned across the bar, putting his face within three inches of the old man's. Neither one blinked. "I ought to teach you a fuckin' lesson and lay you out right here," The Boxer whispered. "I may not be Ali, but I could sure as hell put you in a world o' pain."

"I've got a better idea," Nick countered, his tone easy and conversational. Without moving his face an inch backward, he reached into a drawer beside the cash register and produced a sleek black semiautomatic handgun. Slowly, he pulled his hand backward and inclined his head slightly toward it, not once averting his eyes from The Boxer. "Take this gun, sign the contract and walk out that door. If you don't wind up in the year 2022, come back in here and put a hole in my head."

"Fuck you," the Boxer nearly yelled and, grabbing the pen, scrawled a barely legible signature across the bottom of the contract. "Satisfied?" He snatched the paper off the bar, crumpled it up in a big fist and threw it past Nick to the back of the bar.

Then he grabbed the gun and pointed it at the other man.

"Before I go, old man, give me all the money in that fuckin' register!" In that moment, it didn't matter to Morgan that he'd been brought up not to take what didn't belong to him. All his father's holier-than-thou preaching about paying his debts, keeping his word and being a "man of character" didn't mean jack shit anymore. His father had been one fucked up sonofabitch anyway, and this bullshitter behind the bar was even worse. What a load of crap.

"I'm sorry, Julius, but all I have is the five bucks I gave you. You can see for yourself." He pulled out the cash drawer and turned it upside down. Nothing came out.

The Boxer shook the gun at him. "You've got a safe. I know you've got a fuckin' safe!"

Nick just shook his head and spread his arms slightly, palms outward at his waist. "Does it look like I get enough customers in here to need a *safe*?" he chuckled. How could he stay so calm staring down the barrel of a gun? the Boxer wondered. Didn't anything get to this guy?

"You can shoot me if you want," he said, "but just give me a chance to make good on my part of the deal. If you walk out that door, I promise you, you'll be five years down the road, and you'll have everything you need to become a very wealthy man."

The Boxer was shaking now. What if this was all a setup? What if he walked out the door with that gun and a bunch of cops were just waiting there to handcuff him? This bartender was some kind of sick fuck. Whatever he wanted, whatever he was up to … Morgan didn't know. He just knew he had to get out of there before the booze in his system and this asshole's mind games made him crazy.

He took the gun and flung it across the room, over the bar and into the glass case behind it. The glass shattered, and bottles of whiskey, rum and tequila came crashing to the ground, but the Boxer didn't stick around to watch. He turned on his heels and let his unsteady legs carry him at a frantic pace out the door of the Highway Hideaway …

Which immediately vanished behind him.

The Boxer found himself staring at a billboard that hadn't been there before, advertising a movie he'd never heard of featuring an actor he'd never seen. Below the billboard, a large truck stop and convenience store had appeared out of nowhere, but everything else looked the same: the barren rolling hills, carved up by dry creek beds, with a few scattered, gnarled oak trees here and there.

It was hot, the way it gets in the desert, and just as dusty as it had been before. But where had the truck stop come from?

The Boxer took a step forward, onto a rubber mat with a sensor underneath, triggering the doors in front of him to part and send a cold blast of climate-controlled air directly into his face. The air was crisp but somehow stale, as if it had been lingering there, just recirculating for years.

"Good morning, Mister Morgan. What can I do for you?"

Morgan stopped in his tracks. There, behind the counter, looking out beyond a display of energy drinks on one side and a rack of *People* and *Us* magazines on the other, was Nick. The bar was gone (although there was still some liquor for sale in refrigerated cases off to the right) and the magazines were dated February 2022. But Nick — who'd looked old before — didn't appear to have aged a day.

"You ...?! But what ...?"

"Like the new place?"

The Boxer nodded, his eyes dancing here and there, taking in his surroundings the way a deer might before crossing a street. "How ...?"

Nick shrugged. "Investments and a little luck. Whaddya think?"

The Boxer didn't know what to say. He thought he might be drunk or hallucinating or both. Or it was just possible that Nick was pulling the most elaborate con he'd ever seen. The one thing he couldn't allow himself to think, for the sake of his own sanity, was that somehow he had really landed in the year 2022.

Someone else came through the door behind him — a middle-aged woman in a pink top and jeans who'd tried to cover her graying hair with a not-quite-matching shade of pink. She was carrying a small brown dog that looked like a cross between a beagle and a Chihuahua. It growled at Morgan.

"Hey, Nick," the woman said, eyeing The Boxer for a moment. "Friend of yours?"

"Just a customer. Well, a client, really. He signed the contract."

"Ah," she said knowingly, winking at the old man. "Does he know what he got himself in for?"

Nick chuckled. "Not yet."

"I'll need twenty dollars on number seven," the woman said, pulling a pair of tens from her purse and plunking them down on the counter.

The little dog whined, and the woman winked at Nick again, then sauntered over to the snack aisle and picked up a bag of corn chips. She pretended to be looking at them, but The Boxer could tell her head was inclined slightly in their direction, and he knew her ears must be straining to overhear their conversation. She looked familiar, but Morgan couldn't place her. Maybe it was the pink hair. Or the dog. He hated dogs, especially the little ones that yapped constantly and nipped at your heels as you walked by.

"You still have that contract?" The Boxer asked, trying to sound disinterested but betraying a hint of concern. He was remembering the part about forfeiting three years of his life. What had that meant, anyway? His head was clearing, and he was starting to worry. If this were a hallucination, it was a damn stubborn one. And as genial as Nick might seem, there was something about him The Boxer didn't trust. Besides, he *had* kept a gun behind the bar. ... What the fuck had *happened* to that bar?

"Of course I have it," Nick said. "Sorry I never had a chance to give you a copy, but you left in such a hurry."

He reached into the drawer and pulled out a crumpled piece of paper. "Here. You can have the original. I've got a copy in my files."

"You're fucking nuts."

Nick laughed, and The Boxer thought he heard the woman with the little dog laugh, too. "I don't care what you think about me. This is business. Just business. And I've kept my end of the bargain, so why don't you buy yourself a copy of *The Tribune* over there and check out the lottery numbers. Still got that five bucks I gave you? Give me a buck fifty for the paper and you'll still have enough to buy that lottery ticket if you can hold on to it for five years." He chuckled, but The Boxer had no idea what was so funny about spending five years with three and a half dollars to your name. The whole thing was bullshit, anyway, but still, for some reason he reached into his pocket and gave Nick the five dollars.

Nick made change — there was money in the register this time — and handed it back to him, then gestured toward the newspaper holder: "Help yourself."

Morgan reached down and picked up a copy.

He flipped it open and there, on Page 2, were the lottery results. Despite everything, he found himself tearing off the small section of the paper containing the date and numbers, and slipping them into his pocket.

2, 22, 30, 41, 43 and 49.

He set the rest of the paper on the counter and looked at Nick again. "Okay," he said, "if this is all somehow on the level, I'd like to be sent back."

"Of course, of course!" Nick said, and the woman with the little dog laughed again. She had put the corn chips back and had moved over to the beer case.

The dog yipped.

"Hush, Sunny!" she said in pouty mock consternation. "Bad dog."

Why did she look so familiar? How did Morgan know her? Before he could put his finger on it, Nick was talking again. "You can go back out the door anytime you want and be back in 2017, but as long as you're here, don't you want to maximize your profits? Maybe check out the sports scores? You could place a few wagers on the games, too, y'know. Fantasy football is bigger than ever."

The Boxer thought for a moment, then snatched up the paper again and turned hurriedly to the sports page. Why was he doing everything this guy wanted him to? Maybe because he was flat broke and didn't have anything to lose. However Nick had pulled it off, he had managed to trade in the Highway Hideaway for this new place, which he'd dubbed Nick's Palace on the 'Pike. Whether he was telling the truth or not, there was no denying he'd found *some* way to make himself rich, and The Boxer couldn't help but feel envious.

He was only half paying attention to what he was reading on the sports page when something there caught his eye.

The name "Morgan."

Julius Morgan.

It was a story about *him*. The name leapt up at him off the page before he saw any of the words surrounding it, and he asked himself in that moment, "What if this *is* real?" Had he managed to get back into boxing somehow? His days as a fighter were over; he knew that. Too old. Too slow and never good enough to be considered even a fringe contender. But maybe he'd become a trainer or even a manager or maybe …

He was dead.

There it was in black and white: "A body found in the rubble of an apartment building that collapsed in the quake of 2021 has been identified as that of Julius 'Captain' Morgan. Morgan, who fought and lost to the likes of Terrell McCready and Lupe Valladares, dropped out of sight about five years ago, after the breakup of his marriage and his retirement following six consecutive losses. The body was discovered in October but only now has been identified as Morgan's, finally solving a minor mystery of the boxing world."

There wasn't much more to it than that. No matter how strange the case, the Boxer simply wasn't important enough to merit much of the newspaper's ink.

Morgan threw the newspaper down and said in a muffled voice, to no one in particular, "I'm dead."

"So it would seem," Nick said nonchalantly. "Which I'm afraid means those lottery numbers won't do you any good. You won't get back here to use them. A pity, really. But in your contract, you specifically agreed to forfeit three years of your life. You would have died a couple of years from now, anyway. But I'm afraid our little contract made your unfortunate end ten months ago a sad necessity."

"How do *you* know when I would have died?"

"I'm not as dumb as I look, I'm afraid." Was that a smile, a grimace or a smirk on his face? Morgan couldn't tell.

"None of this is real!" he shouted. "Send me back. Now."

"Of course!" Nick said. "Never let it be said that Old Nick doesn't live up to his end of the bargain."

The Boxer hadn't noticed, but the woman with the pink hair and the annoying little dog had sidled up to him and was breathing in his ear. "Oh, yes, he's as good as his word," she cooed. "You saw the picture of me and my winning lottery ticket."

So that's where he'd seen her. This woman was the person in the newspaper clip Nick had showed him. But why had she gotten her money? And why had he gotten screwed?

She read his expression and the questions behind it. She leaned in even closer, so he could smell her mint-lozenge-flavored breath and whispered. "I'm smarter than you. Plus, I offered him more."

"Your body?" The Boxer shot back, venom in his tone.

At this point, he didn't care if he'd insulted her. She deserved it.

And she didn't care either. "No, silly. Does this body look like it's worth twenty million?" She burst out in a coarse, grating laugh. "Not my body. My *soul*. A soul is worth a lot more than a body … or a life — at least according to his way of thinking. You could probably get him to write up another contract that voids the first one if you include your soul in the bargain, hon." She laughed again.

His eyes flashed to Nick behind the counter. The smug expression beneath that hooked nose told him all he needed to know … and sure enough, he'd placed another contract neatly there in front of him on the counter.

The Boxer shouted something no one could understand, which was the last thing anyone ever heard him say. Just as he had at the Highway Hideaway, he went running out the door and, just as his obituary had reported, he was never seen again.

Postscript: It wasn't as though he died then and there. The Boxer did manage to exact a measure of revenge on Nick: A few days later, he snuck back to the Highway Hideaway, doused the entire property with gasoline and lit a match. Nick got the last laugh, though, when he used the insurance money to build a new business on the same site, creating Nick's Palace on the 'Pike.

Morgan, as careless as an arsonist as he had been as a boxer — and a bar patron — left his fingerprints at the site of the blaze and was identified as the prime suspect. He went into hiding and took to sleeping in condemned and abandoned buildings ... one of which fell on him and took his life in the quake of 2021. All of this was quite predictable, and Old Nick had known that it was coming.

That's why he'd written the contract the way he did.

Yes, indeed, Old Nick *could* have been a lawyer, and a top-flight lawyer at that. But he preferred to be himself. He was, after all, the very fellow who originated that old, familiar saying, "The Devil is in the details."

Unwound

reams lie shattered
Sullied, tattered
Hope lies exposed as mere vanity

Hidden sorrow
'Neath words we borrow
To hide our own latent insanity

This sacred speech
With which we preach
Self-loathing, the strangest profanity

Announcing "truth,"
Yet disdaining proof,
We sacrifice all equanimity

And cling to this,
Disguised as bliss,
This gateway to future calamity

Our minds unwound
Yet ever bound
The legacy of our humanity

Turn Left on Dover

We all have at least one thing in our past we wish we'd done differently. A bad relationship, a job offer we shouldn't have taken a pass on, that time when maybe we should have used protection. The ones I've heard most often are, "I wish I'd bought stock in Microsoft (or Apple) back in the day" and "My lottery numbers came up on the one week I forgot to buy a ticket." I tend not to believe the second one so much. Hindsight can be a lot closer to 20-20 in light of wishful thinking.

I haven't heard those regrets as much lately, but I'm sure people still have them. It's just that I don't talk to people as much as I used to. I prefer to keep to myself these days; I always tended to blend into the wallpaper — even the ugly flower patterns — at social events, so I don't even bother anymore. I'm a loner, and sometimes you just have to accept who you are in order to get on with your life. Like I'd accepted that I'd never have a normal friendship — until I met Allie, that is.

I suppose I gravitated toward her because she was so obviously a loner, like me. It certainly wasn't because of her looks. When I first bumped into her walking along the train tracks that foggy morning, she was pushing a clanky, rusted shopping cart that she'd rescued from the Foodtastic Mart. It was filled with sacks of bottles and aluminum cans.

Her matted hair and the line of half-smeared dirt under her right eye made me guess she hadn't showered in weeks. She had this weird smell of too-heavy musk, as if she'd broken an old bottle of cologne and showered in that instead, but it still wasn't enough to drown out the reek from underneath that made its way into my nostrils.

She flinched when she looked up and saw me coming toward her. A lot of people do that when they're surprised, but they don't usually do that with me. They don't usually notice me at all, because I stay out of their way.

She kept her head down, facing the ground, her feet shuffling in a forlorn rhythm across the dirt and gravel beside the tracks. She stole a quick glance at me again, then she half shook her head, half twitched, as though telling herself I was a phantom who wasn't really there.

"Where're you going?" I asked when she was close enough to be in earshot.

She stopped and looked up at me, almost through me, a hollow expression on her face touched by some vague remembrance of fear from a time when she might have cared. From her appearance, her hunched back and her sunken aspect, I could tell she didn't care now. Probably hadn't in a long time.

When she saw I wasn't moving, she slowed down and tried to angle her way around me, but the front wheels of the old shopping cart didn't want to turn for her — the pieces of gravel kept making them stick.

She cursed them but couldn't make them obey her, so she just stopped and waited for me to go on my way.

As I approached, she released the handle of the shopping cart and slunk around it, keeping it between the two of us as her eyes followed me.

I stopped.

"Where're you going? I asked again," and waited a few breaths for her to answer. I thought she wouldn't.

I had opened my mouth to say something else when she did: "Nowhere." I wouldn't describe her voice as meek, exactly. Maybe resigned. Or even, in a peculiar sort of way, ambivalent. She spoke in this kind of offhanded way you might expect from some spoiled brat who didn't have time for me — except that I could tell she had all the time in the world. Too much time. That, I sensed, was the problem. She didn't want that time anymore. The time she'd taken already hadn't been good to her, and she had no use for any further moments that fate might pile on her back.

"Got a cigarette?" she asked.

"Maybe," I answered. "If I can get a smile from you."

That might sound cruel, but it was a test, and it had to be done. I needed confirmation if I was going to proceed with her.

She shook her head in that twitchy way again and pursed her lips. "Don't smile."

I watched her lips closely, focusing on the space between them as they parted ever so slightly when she spoke. There was nothing there. She didn't have any teeth. Meth. Or maybe she'd just neglected them so badly that they'd rotted out.

"Got some change?" I asked. "You could buy me a cup of coffee."

Her scowl said, *Why should I buy you anything? And what makes you think I can?* The unspoken sarcasm wasn't a good sign. It meant she still cared, if only a little bit … or maybe it was just a reflex, because the expression vanished so quickly it was hard to be sure it had ever been there.

She reached into a pocket and pulled out a couple of quarters, a few dimes and some pennies, which she rattled around in her hands aimlessly.

"Why not?" she said, her voice flat.

She ambled up beside me, leaving her cart where it was, and we crossed the tracks to Biggie's Diner, which was (conveniently) right there. You could see the red, cursive neon through the fog, crowning the ghost of a long, squat, rectangular building painted in nondescript light brown.

We walked through one of those glass doors that guard the entrance to just about every diner and breakfast house built between 1960 and 1980 — and more on either side of those dates. Conical light fixtures shaped like traditional Chinese hats dangled on cords from the ceiling, and booths, most of them empty, lined the windowed wall across from a breakfast bar that also lacked customers.

We didn't wait for the host, because there wasn't one.

"Sit wherever," said a lanky waitress with a dirty-blond bun as she scuttled past, carrying silverware and a carousel of condiments.

My companion sat down across from me in one of the booths but still didn't look at me, tossing her change on the table and watching as one of the pennies rolled off the edge and onto the floor. She didn't bend down to retrieve it.

"What's your name?" I asked.

"Allie." She coughed. "How about that cigarette?"

The waitress overheard her. "You can't smoke in here."

I shrugged at Allie. "You heard her. Besides, you never gave me that smile you owe me, so I figured I was off the hook."

She still didn't smile. It didn't matter to her that I was teasing her — it didn't even matter that I was keeping her from feeding an addiction that makes those deprived of its solace irritable or even hostile. Allie was neither. She was beyond caring about anything, which was why she was talking to some stranger she'd met in the fog on the train tracks and buying him a cup of coffee with money she didn't have to spend. She didn't give a damn about life anymore.

She was perfect.

The waitress came over and presented us with a laminated menu, which neither one of us picked up. Maybe she'd been a bartender before this, because she said, "What'll it be?" as she pulled out a pen and a small tablet.

Allie waited for me to answer. Then, when I didn't say anything, she said, "Coffee. Black?"

"Why you askin' me, hun?" the waitress said. "You know how you like it."

"I was asking … never mind."

I nodded.

"Yeah. Black," Allie said.

The waitress returned with a glass coffee container and turned over the thick ceramic cup in front of Allie, first pouring, then dripping the dregs of the six o'clock batch into it.

The waitress left, and Allie pushed it toward me.

I pushed it back. "You drink it," I said. "I just wanted to see if you'd buy me a cup."

"Don't want it," she said. "Don't like coffee." Then she put it to her lips anyway, her eyes looking into the depths of the pitch-black java instead of at me.

"What do you want?" I asked.

She shook her head slightly. "Nothing."

"There must be something …"

Allie set the cup down and looked across at me. It was the first time she'd allowed her eyes to meet mine. "No," she said. And that was all; then she looked back into the coffee again, blowing on it halfheartedly.

"You want it to be over," I said.

She didn't say anything to that, but her response was immediate. She nodded her head once, almost timidly in a way I imagined must have been very endearing to some man a very long time ago in a very different place. I wondered who that man might have been, where he was now and how Allie had come to be in this state. I wondered because, in that moment, I wanted that for her again, almost as much as I wanted the same thing for myself: a life to be lived to the fullest. It was something neither one of us had had in a long time, and it as the reason I'd brought her here.

"You gonna give me money or somethin'?" she asked, as if she thought the idea was crazy.

I shook my head. "Something better. I want to give you your life back."

She was still looking at her coffee, watching a speck of stray something floating around on the surface.

"Asshole," she whispered, not just at me, but at the universe.

"Okay," I said. "You don't want your life back, then why not just end it? There's a bridge out there across the train tracks. That should do the trick."

Allie looked up at me again, and there was this strange, mad hope in her eyes that faded almost immediately.

"C'mon," I urged. "You've got two choices here. You can let me give you your life back, or you can walk with me out onto that bridge and jump. You could wait until there's a train coming. If you time it right, it will be spectacular."

I half-expected her to say, "You're one sick fuck" or something like that — because it really *was* sick, me trying to get her to kill herself like that. But it was another test, and she passed again by not saying anything. She really didn't care.

Finally, she set the coffee down on the table and said, "Then let's go."

She stood.

"Where?" I asked. "Which one will it be? Are you gonna kill yourself, or do you want your life back."

Her whole body trembled for just an instant, but it wasn't from nerves or anything more than an extension of her shaking her head. "Either way. You choose. Only wanted a cigarette, and you wouldn't even give me that. Just damn coffee I didn't want."

That was when she finally smiled a toothless smile that held neither joy nor intent of irony. It just was.

I pulled out a cigarette and offered it to her.

"Too late," she said. "Don't want it anymore."

Allie walked out into the fog, and I followed her. Across the street, down a block and up the gently sloping concrete bridge that allowed what little traffic there was here to pass over the railroad line without having to stop at a crossing guard.

When we got to the top, directly over the tracks, she hesitated and looked down.

"Don't know," she said simply.

"You scared?"

"Not of dying."

"Of being alone. At the last."

"Yes."

"I'll go with you," I said.

She looked at me, as if to say, "You will?"

I nodded and took her hand, and we stepped up to the low guardrail together. It didn't even reach our knees. We turned together and faced the vacant sky.

"Ready?"

I felt her hand squeeze mine. It was odd to feel the sensation of it; I shouldn't have felt it at all. I'd been numb for so long … but there it was. Maybe I … we … *could* do this.

And we did.

We didn't wait for the train I'd talked about. We just jumped.

The air whizzed effortlessly past us for that split-second it took before we should have hit the ground, and then the ground and the air and everything else disappeared as we passed through the portal I had known was in that exact spot before she'd taken me there. Had she known it was there too?

When we emerged on the other side, we found ourselves standing on those same railroad tracks, in the path of a train that hadn't been approaching before but was somehow there now. She jumped out of the way just in time, and I along with her, and we tumbled out of the way as it roared past, sounding its long, loud whistle.

She looked at me, the question in her eyes obvious: *What happened? Are we dead?*

"I gave you your life back," I told her. "Or a chance to have it back. That's more than most of us get."

She just kept looking at me. She didn't understand. Of course, she couldn't. I hadn't even been sure it would work myself, but we were only halfway there. There was more to do. I stared across the tracks at the place where Biggie's Diner had been; the building was the same, but with a different neon sign that read The Monte Christo. The original owner had been known for making that particular sandwich, so he'd named the place for it. Some friends of mine had had it a few times. Said it wasn't bad.

The place looked packed. Cars parked neatly in a row out front welcomed businessmen with suits and briefcases exiting after breakfast. New and nearly new Pontiacs, Nissans and a couple of Mercury Cougars shared the parking lot with a late-model Datsun 280Z and a vintage Volkswagen Beetle.

The fog was gone, and there was more traffic crossing the concrete bridge that now stretched like a rainbow above us.

"Where do you live?" I asked Allie.

"Here. Under the bridge."

"No. Before that. Where *did* you live?"

She let go of my hand. She'd still been holding it up till now.

"A place off Divisadero. But that was …"

I smiled gently. "Go home," I said.

"To …?"

"That place. Home."

She looked me in the eye, trying to figure out whether I was playing some kind of game with her, but I wasn't and she knew it.

"You'll come with me?" she asked. She was starting to care about something again, which was good. She'd need to care now. I just hadn't expected her to care about me. Of course, she didn't. She just didn't want to be alone. That was it. And who could blame her? I'd been alone for so long, I'd forgotten what it was like to have a conversation with another human being, even if it was mostly one-syllable words and long silences.

"I can't," I said. "I'm sorry. When you go back home, you'll see a young woman you'll recognize. She'll be in her twenties, about your height and … happy. You'll recognize her and you'll know what you need to say to her. Tell her not to make the same mistakes you did. That's why you're here — for that purpose. After that, I'll meet you again outside the bank just down the street from there. Just be sure to do this one thing for me: Be there by 11:30 a.m. — not a moment later — and remind me of something I probably will have forgotten by then. Just tell me to turn left on Dover."

"You won't forget that in an hour," she said.

"Please. Just do this one thing for me and I won't ever ask you to do anything else."

I was crazy. I could see that's what she was thinking from her expression. But she nodded, and took hold of my hand again. "Okay," she said.

"Thank you. Now go home."

She hesitated a moment, then let go of my hand and looked at me one last time. That newborn glimmer of hope was still there on her face. It wasn't much. A single setback could stop her from caring again, but it was enough — at least, I hoped it would be.

"If the young woman isn't there, at your home, go back again, after you meet me at the bank. She needs to meet you."

Allie nodded slightly and turned to go, her shoulders still slumped. Then, at the last minute, she stood up a little straighter and looked back at me.

"What's your name?" she asked.

I smiled. "Mike," I said. "Pruitt."

She extended a hand. Dirt clung to her palm by way of dried sweat, and her chewed or broken nails trapped more than a little dark matter underneath them.

I took the hand and squeezed tightly. "A pleasure," I said warmly.

She smiled slightly, turned and walked away.

I waited a moment … then I followed her. I didn't want to mess anything up by going with her, but I had to be sure. Everything for me was riding on the hope that I'd formed enough of a bond with Allie, created enough trust, to ensure that she'd follow through on her promise to me. If she didn't, I'd be stuck this way forever. I trusted her because I had to: Of the people I'd approached, she had been the only suitable candidate for this task.

She, on the other hand, didn't have to trust me or anyone else. She'd lost all hope and hadn't needed me to get to the brink of suicide. I'd just happened along at the right time, directed her to the portal and provided that final emotional nudge toward the abyss she thought was the end. The fact that it wasn't — the end, that is — must be confusing the hell out of her, and I couldn't count on her to be consistent in an upside-down world.

Unless she trusted me.

Unless she felt she owed it to me.

I followed her, watching the stooped figure with the matted brown hair as she shuffled along down the train tracks, past the vintage railroad station with its muted yellow façade and long roof punctuated by a series of gables. She veered across the tracks, toward it, then continued north in the direction she'd told me was "home."

This was good … and it was even better when she finally reached the low stuccoed duplex in the 1930s-built tree-lined neighborhood.

Allie didn't hesitate. She walked right up to the triple-stepped entrance and onto the porch, where she stood in front of the left-side door, lifted her hand and pressed the bell. As the door opened, she looked back toward me, as if sensing I was there, even though I remained out of sight behind a hedge. It was at once reassuring and troubling: If she knew I was there, it meant I'd succeeded in forming that bond with her, but it could also mean she was still, on some level, afraid of me. That she knew I was there because my presence made her nervous.

She turned back away as the door opened to reveal a young woman the same height as Allie who, even so, looked down on her slightly because of Allie's sunken posture. Her newly washed hair was a slightly lighter brown than Allie's matted locks, and she wore a pink and yellow sun dress that washed over her body like a muted rainbow.

"Can I help you?"

The young woman's eyes narrowed. "You look familiar. Do I know …?"

"Used to live here," Allie said. "That man said I should go home." She looked over her shoulder again, directly toward me. There was no way she should have been able to see me behind the hedge.

"The man hiding behind the bushes?"

I started. The young woman shouldn't have been able to see me, either, but then, if Allie could see me, it made sense that she could as well.

"Yes," Allie said.

The girl looked worried. "There's lots of bums and users around here."

"He's not from around here. He followed me."

The young woman folded her arms across her chest and leaned back slightly. "A stalker?"

Allie shook her head.

"Well, what do you want then?" she said. "I don't have all day. You look hella familiar, but I don't think I've ever seen you 'round here before."

"Told you. Used to live here. In this house. Looks exactly the same. What's your name?"

"Why should I tell you?"

"Because … never mind. It doesn't matter. Just don't make the same mistakes I did, okay?"

"What? Take drugs? Sell your body? Live on the streets?"

"Never sold my body to no one."

"Whatever. I wouldn't do any of that."

Allie's posture stiffened. "Ever been told by your husband that you're worthless? Fired from a job because you're so depressed you

63

can't function, because you're afraid that man will get angry and hurt your little girl when you're not there? Seen that little girl lying dead on the floor because you weren't there and he was? Ever had those things happen to you?"

It was the first time I'd heard Allie say more than a few short, clipped words — the first time I'd ever heard anything but a dull, leftover ache in her tone. For the first time, her voice was firm, insistent.

She cared again.

The young woman took a step backward, into the house, but she didn't shut the door. She was watching Allie's face intently, and Allie was watching her. I could tell from the look on her face that she recognized the woman in the doorway.

"No," the younger woman said, the brashness in her own voice shaken. "None of that has ever happened to me."

Allie stepped forward, closing the gap between them again. "It will," she said, her voice lower but no less determined. "And when it does, you have to decide you're better than that. You have to decide to get out. You have to decide to take your baby girl and just go."

"But I don't have a baby girl …"

"You will. She will be your whole life. But even if you can't save her, you have to save yourself. Or else you will end up …"

"Like you."

Allie nodded. "Yes."

"Okay, I get it. But I really gotta go."

"Just promise me. Swear you won't give up. No matter what."

The young woman looked off to the side for a moment, then met Allie's gaze again. Somehow, it seemed, Allie had managed to stand up straighter, and the two women's eyes were exactly level.

"I promise," she said finally, and from her tone, I could tell she wasn't saying that just to get Allie to leave. A part of her, I could tell, wanted her to stay. That was natural, but she couldn't. She had to be at the bank before 11:30, or else it was all for nothing — at least my part of it. I was selfish, I admit it. Sure, it felt good to have given Allie her second chance, and sure, I had developed that bond with her, but that didn't mean I wanted to stay like this. Allie was the only one who could make a difference for me, the way I had made a difference for her. She had to go.

She had to.

And she did. "Sorry. Somethin' I gotta do. Promised." She turned away from the woman, who just stood there in the doorway, watching her go. She glanced once over toward me again, a curious look on her face, then turned and went back inside, closing the door behind her.

One of those old street clocks read 11:17, and I wondered if it was right. If Allie didn't hurry, she wouldn't make it to the bank on time. But she was less hunched over now, her stride more resolute. If I was lucky …

Allie reached the bank just as the blue Buick LeSabre was pulling up to the red light beside the curb. The driver glanced casually at the sidewalk as he waited for the light to change, and I saw Allie do a double-take as she recognized him.

"Mike?" she said. "That you?"

The man paused and looked at her questioningly. "Yeah, that's my name," he said. "How did you know?"

"You said to meet you here, to remind you of something. Turn left on Dover. That was it."

The driver laughed. "Well, I've never seen you before in my life," he said, "but that's just what I needed to know. I'm new here, and I haven't a clue about where I'm going. So thanks, lady. Have a good one."

The light changed, and Mike Pruitt drove away, leaving me to stand there and wait for approximately two more minutes to find out whether the accident that had happened that day would still happen.

The accident at Cartwright and Fowler that had shattered my skull against the windshield of that blue LeSabre. If that Mike Pruitt turned left on Dover, he'd never get to Cartright and Fowler.

And this Mike Pruitt would no longer be dead.

If everything went as planned, two minutes later, the ghost of Mike Pruitt would cease to exist, and I'd forget all about the accident-that-now-never-was, about the seventeen years I'd spent walking around as a specter. Even about Allie, the only real friend I'd ever made in those seventeen years. That was the one regret I'd have. But how can a person regret someone he couldn't even remember …

Then, it was done.

It was two more days until my wedding anniversary. Almost fifteen years ago, I had married the Brenda, the love of my life, and we'd been nearly inseparable since then. Yeah, things had cooled a little from our impetuous youth, but we were still each other's best friend and biggest booster. We didn't buy each other things very often, but I figured our 15th anniversary was something special, and I'd noticed a diamond pendant in the Pasteur's Jewelers window that I thought was perfect for her.

I walked briskly through the mall, hoping it would still be there in the display case, and sure enough, no one had beaten me to it.

"Like it?" came a voice from behind the counter.

I looked up to see a woman with light brown hair that was slightly graying and a broad, glistening smile standing across from me.

"Yeah, I do, and I think my wife will like it even more."

"It's a dazzler, isn't it?" the woman said, her smile fading slightly and her eyes narrowing. She was almost staring at me, like she was studying me.

"Yes, it is," I said. "Is something wrong?"

She shook her head slightly. "Sorry. You just remind me of someone I saw once a long time ago … hiding in the bushes."

"Wow, great vision *and* a great memory." I couldn't contain a hint of sarcasm.

"Seriously. I guess I do. Have both, I mean. Anyway, sorry again. Do you want the piece?"

"How much?"

"Thirty-five hundred, but it's on twenty percent discount."

"Sold." I reached into my hip pocket and pulled out my walled, handing her my MasterCard.

"Shall I gift-wrap it for your wife?"

"Absolutely. And thank you ..." I looked at her gold-plated nametag. "... Allie."

"My pleasure, Mr. Pruitt," she smiled.

I gave her a puzzled look, and she laughed as she handed me back my credit card. "I'm not psychic. You're name's right here."

Of course it was.

"You get a commission off this?"

"Enough for a cup of coffee and some cigarettes," she said. "Except I never cared much for coffee, and I quit smoking a long time ago."

She nodded and turned away for a moment, placing the little black-felt-covered container in a miniature silver gift box.

"In fact, I'm feeling generous. You can have twenty-five percent off, and I'll skip the commission. That way, I can buy you that cup of coffee I don't want."

"Thanks." I smiled. "I owe you one."

She laughed again. "No you don't. You're alive. I'm alive. The way I look at it, that makes us even."

That was an interesting way of looking at it. "I guess it does."

"Happy anniversary, Mr. Pruitt," she said, handing me the little box and returning my credit card.

"Yeah, it's gonna be," I said as I turned to walk out the door. "It *is* great to be alive."

Mama

"Wait, we have to stop."

Alex pursed his lips and rolled his eyes. It wasn't enough just to roll his eyes, he had to tilt his entire head back for the full effect. "Not again," he groaned, punctuating his message further by exhaling sharply as he spoke. It wasn't meant to be subtle. But then, boys of 8 aren't known for their subtlety … or their patience.

Delandra only glared at him, the kind of glare Alex had seen her mother use on her father before they split up earlier that year. He didn't understand.

"Something's not where it's supposed to be," she said matter-of-factly. "We have to stop or it won't work right." She got up from where she was sitting on the soft sheepskin rug and strode in even steps over to the bookcase, where Alex saw that a volume titled *Voices From the Other Side* was slightly pulled out from amidst all the other titles. Delandra went up on her tiptoes, and Alex could see her straining to reach it. It occurred to him that it would be funny if she fell and the whole thing came down on top of her. He wasn't old enough yet to think about what that would mean: broken bones, a concussion and maybe some nasty cuts. Alex didn't want that; she was, after all, his best friend … although he would never admit that to Rory or James or any of the other boys.

No, Alex was still at an age when long-term consequences were something for adults to worry about. All he needed to concern himself with was how funny a thing was, and he had an innate sense that a bookcase falling down on Delandra would be nothing short of hilarious.

Thankfully, however, the bookcase didn't fall, and Delandra was able to restore *Voices From the Other Side* to its proper status among such titles as *The Cancer Survivor's Playbook*, Mary Shelley's *Frankenstein* and *Seriously? You Must be Joking.*

"There!" she announced. "Now we may proceed."

She was in one of her imperious moods. She only said words like "proceed" when she felt like exerting authority over someone … usually Alex.

He stuck his tongue out at her. "OCDelandra!" he said. He didn't know what it meant, but he had heard her older sister, Corrine, use it when she grew impatient with her. It always got her attention.

"Shutup!" she sniped. "It's Delandra. Just Delandra." She plopped herself down in exaggerated fashion on the sheepskin and glared at him.

He glared back, trying to imitate her as closely as possible, but suspecting he'd never come very close to capturing the look.

She either ignored it or wasn't aware of it; he wasn't sure which.

"Now," she declared. "Here's how this works. You hold the pend'lum over the board very, very still and ask it a question, like this." Delandra stretched her arm forward until it was entirely straight, holding the fine gold chain between her thumb and forefinger and letting the jet-black conical pointy part dangle down. "Then you close your eyes" (she squinted them tight for added effect) "and ask it a question."

Alex tried to think of a question, but before he could come up with one, Delandra said in a loud voice, "Will I be an astronaut?" Then, lowering her voice conspiratorially, she added, "It has to be a 'yes' or no' question. If it goes in a straight line, it's yes. If it goes in circles, it's no."

"Uh huh," Alex said. "Why are you yelling and whispering?"

"You have to raise your voice to get their attention," she answered, as though it should be perfectly obvious. "And they like to have all your attention. If they hear me talk to you, they'll feel sad and won't answer."

"Selfish, aren't they?"

"Shhhhh!" and then, in an even lower whisper: "Look! It's starting to move!"

Alex bit his lower lip. He was trying not to be scared; he was the boy, and boys weren't supposed to be scared. That's what everyone told him. But he was still scared, sitting here with a girl, and he suddenly felt like he was betraying something sacred by even being there. Worse, she didn't seem to be scared at all.

He found himself wishing that his Aunt Cynthia would show up early to pick him up, but he knew she wouldn't. She was at work all afternoon, then she had to go see his mom at the Mercy View Hospital. Alex didn't want to think about that.

He was scared enough as it was.

"You're making it move!" he said, even more loudly.

"Am not!" she replied in the same tone, shifting her leg underneath her … which caused the pendulum to jump around like a jackrabbit.

"Are so. See?" Alex said, triumphant. Suddenly, he wasn't frightened anymore.

"It's because you scared them away. You and your yelling. Boys! Now we'll have to start all over again." She tossed her strawberry-colored hair back to get it out of her eyes, and whenever she did that, Alex knew there was no argument he could make that would change her mind.

"You try it," she said, thrusting the pendulum toward him

before he could object. He held out his hand, resigned.

Delandra lowered her voice again. "Now hold it out and ask it something."

Alex noticed a clock was ticking somewhere, but it not regularly, as if one of those cheap, battery-operated things had run down and was on the verge of quitting altogether. A mourning dove cooed outside, but just once. It was always at least twice before, wasn't it? Alex's heart was beating faster now, and he tried to convince himself he wasn't getting scared again. There was nothing to be scared of, he told himself, and began fidgeting with the end of his green stegosaurus T-shirt, winding it around his thumb.

"Stop that, Alex," Delandra said. "You have to stay still, or you'll move the pend'lum and they won't come."

"Like you did?" he retorted.

"No, like you're doing. Don't argue. You have to do it right for it to work."

Alex scowled and let loose of his T-shirt. "What question should I ask?" he said.

"Whatever you want, as long as it's yes or no." She smiled. It was supposed to be reassuring, and it was. But Alex didn't know if he wanted to be assured. Part of him felt like he should be scared, even if he was a boy.

He closed his eyes tightly, the way he'd seen Delandra do, and tried to remain perfectly still. Either the clock had stopped ticking or he wasn't aware of it anymore. The dove was silent. Everything was silent, and Alex had the distinct feeling that someone was listening intently. It was the same feeling he'd had when his uncle Declan had taken him to confession. He couldn't see the priest on the other side, but he knew the man was there. He could hear him breathing, ragged. There was no breathing now, but the feeling was the same.

Maybe this was what God felt like.

Maybe it was God who had stopped the clock, or even stopped time. Maybe it was God who had quieted the bird. "Are not two sparrows sold for a penny? Yet not a single one of them will fall to the ground apart from your Father's care." He'd heard that in Sunday school and wasn't altogether sure what it meant, but he figured God could do pretty much whatever he wanted.

He held his arm perfectly straight over the inverted lid to a *Monopoly* box that separated the two of them. Delandra had put it there because, she said, it was necessary to "ground" the pendulum. She didn't know what that meant, but insisted that it wouldn't work otherwise. At this moment, Alex forgot it was there. He forgot about Delandra and everything else but the question that was forming in the back of his mind, a question that he didn't want to know the answer to but couldn't keep himself from asking.

And so, he blurted it out:

"Is Mama gonna die?"

At that very moment, the mourning dove cooed a second time, and he opened his eyes.

The pendulum was moving up and down in a straight line, just like the line that moved up and down as it ran across the green screen in his mother's hospital room.

Then, suddenly, it just stopped. Alex sent a thought from his brain down to his fingertips: "Move!"

It didn't. It stayed stock-still over the *Monopoly* box lid.

"No," he said in a whisper. "I don't wanna play this game anymore." He balled the chain up around the hard, cone-shaped end of the pendulum and squeezed it tightly in his hand. Delandra was staring at him, wide-eyed, mouth open. He looked away from her, embarrassed. But that embarrassment was soon devoured by a sickening feeling of dread that rose from the pit of his stomach, fought its way up through his chest and gripped him hard by base of his throat.

"You shouldn't have asked them that," she said.

His head snapped back around toward her. "Then I take it back!" he yelled.

Delandra shook her head fiercely. "That's not how it works. It's too late. You can't undo it."

Alex raising his clenched fist and letting the fingers splay apart as he flung the pendulum across the room. It flew through the air toward the fireplace, where it slammed into a ship-in-a-bottle on the mantle. Delandra's father had spent months assembling a perfect replica of the *Santa Maria* inside a delicate vessel of glass, which now shattered in a single instant, sending the bottle and its contents tumbling to the floor in a chaotic mess of shards and splinters.

Delandra blinked as she looked from what used to be the ship back toward Alex. His cheeks flushed. He expected her to scream or cry the way girls usually do when boys do something they think is rash or thick-headed. But she didn't.

"That's not where it's supposed to be!" she breathed.

"Huh?" Alex said. "What do you mean?"

She was shaking her head, and Alex realized that the rest of her was shaking, too. "Papa took that with him when he left," she said. "It was at his house last week. I saw it. *They* must have put it here!"

Now Alex was shaking. But he didn't care about the boat or the bottle or … *them*. He wanted to be at the hospital with his mother. She hadn't looked good the last time he saw her, with plastic tubes stuck up her nose and those dark, moon-shaped hollow spaces under both her eyes. Her voice had been hoarse and ragged. "I love you," she'd told him, but then closed her eyes and said she'd just wanted to sleep for a while. Then the nurses had kept coming in and out until they finally made him leave the room. He heard one of them say a word he thought sounded like "ammonia," and from the look on her face, it didn't seem like a good thing.

Aunt Cynthia tried to pretend she wasn't worried, but he could tell she was. That was why she was going to the hospital today, and it was why she had told him, "Mama needs to rest to keep her strength up."

She's not your Mama, he had wanted to say, even though every woman who had kids in the Two Cities got called that. They stopped being called by their first name when they were expecting, and everybody called them "Mama" instead after that. Fathers got called

"Daddy" or "Papa," too … unless they got divorced and moved away, the way Alex's father had. And Delandra's. Their mothers were both single parents who attended Free Word Presbyterian Church and lived on the same block, which is why Alex and Delandra spent so much time together.

It's also why they got along so well. They understood each other, most of the time, that is. But Delandra couldn't understand what Alex was going through with his mama because hers was perfectly healthy … except when she had too much gin and tonic in the afternoon and had to lie down, like she was doing now. Delandra had told Alex they needed to be quiet because she wouldn't approve of the pendulum game ("Pastor Jesse says there's demons"), but then why did Delandra's mother keep the pendulum in her jewelry box?

Alex didn't understand. He always wanted things explained to him, even though it made grown-ups uncomfortable when he asked questions.

"It's best that you stay here with Delandra and wait till Mama feels better," Aunt Cynthia had told him. But what if she never got better? What if the pendulum was telling him the truth and Delandra wasn't just a silly little girl playing a dumb old game? Aunt Cynthia never answered his questions when he asked them, but sometimes Delandra would. That's one reason they were close.

"Who are *they*?" he asked her.

She looked as serious as he'd ever seen her, even when she was pretending to be the Queen of England giving a tea party for Babar the Elephant. "They *know*."

"What?"

"*Everything!*"

"There's nobody there," he said, scrunching his face together, trying to make himself believe it. "Quit tryin' ta scare me. Mama's gonna be okay." He nodded his head once firmly, chin out, as if that put an end to the matter. But it didn't. He knew the pendulum had moved on its own at first, and he knew it hadn't moved when he'd tried to make it. Still, if he could get Delandra to admit none of this was real, it would give him permission to think the same thing.

Then he noticed something. The book that Delandra had put back in place on the bookcase, *Voices From the Other Side*, was pulled out again, the same way it had been before they'd started. "Look!" he said, thrusting out his arm. "Didn't you say it wouldn't work right with the book like that? *Didn't you*!?"

Delandra's eyes followed his index finger to where it was pointing.

"You did that!" she accused.

"Did not! When could I?"

"When my eyes were closed. You're trying to scare me!"

"No, honest!" It was the kind of trick he liked to play on her, but he couldn't have done it this time. Her eyes hadn't been closed long enough for him to run all the way over to the bookcase, pull the book out, run back and sit down again.

She caught her breath and held it for a moment. When she exhaled, she said: "It must be *them*."

"Do you think they are trying to tell us something?"

She nodded, and he saw her start to blink repeatedly and put her head down to rub her shirtsleeve across her eyes. "They did."

"Mama's gonna die." He couldn't get her to stop believing it, so he had to believe it, too. The words were scarcely out of his mouth before he started crying, which made her start crying even more. Soon, they were both sobbing. Alex fell back on the floor and pressed both his hands against his eyes. It wasn't just because of the stupid pendulum. He'd known Mama was sick before, real sick; he just hadn't wanted to believe it, but now the pendulum was making him.

"I hate *them*!" he wailed. "Hate. Hate. HATE. HATE! Make them go away!"

He heard footsteps and opened his eyes to see Delandra's mother coming down the stairs, her light brown hair mussed and her eyes half-open. She squinted at them as she stood there in her bare feet; a white robe with pink roses was tied around her waist and came down to her knees.

"What's going on down here?" she said, her tone half angry, half confused in her half-sleeping state. Her eyes opened a little more and settled on the broken ship-in-a-bottle at the base of the mantel. "That's your father's," she said. "How did it get there? Did you bring it back from your visit without me knowing, Delly?"

"No, Mama," Delandra sniffed, wiping her eyes with her sleeve again and then doing the same to her runny nose.

Her mother spotted the pendulum. "And what's *that* doing there. Delandra, what did I tell you about getting into my jewelry?" She scowled at them. Her gravelly, just-got-finished-napping voice made her sound scary, Alex thought, like *they* were talking through her. "You know what Pastor said. The devil can *possess* you if you play with the tools from his workshop!"

"Yes, Mama," Delandra said softly. It was barely a whisper. "Sorry, Mama."

The scolding was interrupted by a knock at the door, and Delandra's mother stumbled down the last stair as she moved too quickly to answer it. Losing her balance, she fell, head-first, thrusting her right arm out in front of her in an attempt to break her fall. But she was a fraction of a second too late. Instead of cushioning her, the arm bent awkwardly as the weight of her torso came down on top of it, lodging it between herself and the floor — which was poorly padded between the green shag carpet and the concrete foundation.

Something in her wrist gave way with an audible SNAP! She screamed in pain and pushed off with her other arm against the floor, rolling sideways and into the broken glass from the recently shattered ship-in-a-bottle. The shards raked across her good arm, tearing the skin in several places, where lines of blood oozed to the surface; jerking in pain, she tumbled sideways, her head crashing against the brick hearth with far too much force.

"Mama!" Delandra squealed.

The woman lay still.

Delandra ran to her mother, and the front door flew open at the sound of the scream.

Aunt Cynthia burst into the room. Pulling off her long overcoat and letting it fall to the ground, she threw her purse on a brown leather recliner and rushed to where Delandra's mother lay motionless by the fireplace. Wrapping one arm around Delandra's waist and pulling her back, Aunt Cynthia held her protectively against her body amid the girl's flood of tears and convulsive sobs.

"Mama!" she cried again and again.

Alex didn't know what to do until Aunt Cynthia caught his attention, fierce eyes gazing out from beneath a determined brow. "Alex, grab my phone out of my purse and dial 911. Then bring it here. Now."

Startled into action, Alex ran for the purse, fumbled through it and found the flip-phone nestled in a side compartment. He opened it, pressed 911, and then ran back to Aunt Cynthia with his arm stretched out in front of him. He listened as she grabbed it from him and started talking quickly to the person on the other end. He heard her say Delandra's mother's name, the address and something about an accident, then repeat some of the information in a slower, steadier voice.

Delandra was still sobbing, trying to pull away from Aunt Cynthia and go to her mother. He looked at her, then, for some reason, his eyes fell again on the bookcase, where *Voices From the Other Side* had been sticking out … only now it wasn't anymore. It was pushed all the way back in, wedged snugly between — and level with — the books on either side of it.

As the paramedics rushed in and loaded Delandra's mother onto a gurney, Alex took hold of Aunt Cynthia's hand and gave it a tug. Looking up at her, he asked the same question he had asked the pendulum earlier: "Is Mama gonna die?"

His aunt's eyes flashed to the gurney that was being rolled out of the front door, then back at Alex. He was shaking his head and biting his lip, tears drying on both cheeks, and she seemed to realize he was talking about his own mother, in the hospital. "Aunt Cynthia," he said "Is she?"

For a moment, the worry left her eyes, which warmed as she smiled at him. "Oh, dear child," she said, touching his cheek gently with the back of her hand. "Your mama's going to be just fine. Don't you worry. She'll be home from the hospital in less than a week. The doctor told me so today."

The three of them followed as the paramedics loaded the gurney into the ambulance. Delandra was clinging to Aunt Cynthia's leg, her face buried there, refusing to look at what was happening. Alex wrapped both arms around her from the side and gave her a big, warm hug. He couldn't think of anything else to say, so he told her the last words his mama had told him the last time he saw her in the hospital.

"I love you."

She started sobbing again, harder than ever.

That wasn't the last time Alex said those three words to Delandra. He waited a while, but he got around to saying them again during the slow dance at their senior prom, and many more times after that. Of course, he said them at their wedding, which both their mothers attended. They were married at the country club, outside, under a canopy, just as the sun was setting and the stars were starting to appear on an April evening when the warm breezes of summer met the brisk remains of winter. For Alex, however, the stars that winked down at them through the twilight couldn't compare to the stars he saw in his new bride's eyes.

Alex's mother gave him away. It might have been unconventional, but Alex was still always asking questions, and one of those questions was, "Why does it have to be the father?" Alex hadn't seen his father in more than ten years, so it didn't make sense to invite the man. Delandra's mother was her maid of honor. Around her neck, she wore the conical jet-black stone that had once been the stone on her pendulum. She no longer thought it was the tool of the devil; now, she thought of it as a good-luck charm. They hadn't thought she would make it when she'd hit her head on the fireplace. She had been in a coma for a week, but when she finally woke up, the nurse told her there was a good chance she would make a full recovery. And she did.

Not only that, but she had felt a connection with the nurse right away. He'd called her after she was discharged, and they'd started dating. Eventually, they had gotten married. If it hadn't been for that pendulum, she reasoned, they would probably never have met.

It would be wonderful to report that Delandra and Alex lived happily ever after, the way they do in fairy tales. Alas, however, this is not a fairy tale, and the time came all too soon when Alex said "I love you" to his beloved for the last time.

It happened in Mercy View, the same hospital where his mother had been so sick with pneumonia that she'd been on a respirator for several days and stuck in bed for more than two weeks.

Delandra didn't have pneumonia. She was supposed to be there for a happy event: the birth of their first child. But there were complications. The baby was breached, and they had to perform a C-section; she delivered a healthy baby girl, but she developed an infection, and no matter what the doctors did, it kept getting worse. Before too long, it turned into sepsis, and they told Alex her chances didn't look good.

The last time he saw her, she was holding their three-day old baby, Elizabeth Rae, and smiling weakly up at him.

"You're going to be okay," he told her, but she shook her head.

"I knew this would happen," she said, closing her eyes slowly and then opening them again to look up at him. She was smiling. "When you told me you loved me that day, I knew we would be married. They told me."

"They?"

"You know. …" She nodded and swallowed, then spoke again, her voice ragged. "When you proposed, I got my own pendulum. You didn't know that, did you?"

He shook his head, tears welling up in both eyes.

"I did," she said. "I asked them if we would have a child, and they said we would. But then I asked them if we would live a long life together, and the answer was different."

Alex took her hand and squeezed it, his face determined. "They're wrong," he said. "You and I … we will be together for the rest of our lives. They were wrong before, remember? When I asked them about …"

She reached up and put a finger to his lips. It was trembling, she was so weak. "No, they weren't, Papa," she said.

"No!" he said, understanding. He squeezed her hand harder, holding on to what he felt slipping away from him. "You can't die, Mama. You can't!"

But Delandra was already gone.

From that day forward, he only ever heard one of the voices in his own head. It was hers. It came to him when he got a promotion at work, when Elizabeth graduated from high school, and every year at Christmas Eve, when he, both their mothers and Elizabeth were gathered around the fireplace, opening gifts. It always said the same thing: "Everything's where it's supposed to be."

Upon Reflection

U pon reflection ...
Through the glass darkly
Or was it through the looking glass?
Where white rabbits breed
Mindlessly pushing
And pulling
Amidst a cacophony of nails ground on chalkboards

By the ghosts of lifetimes past
In classrooms long abandoned
By hope's eternal silence
The drones still wheeze and sputter
Like rabbits themselves
Heedless
Absorbed in their own base desires

Stephen H. Provost

They breed
And need
And feed
And gaze up at you through empty eyes
So hopeless-lost amid the maelstrom

Mad hatters all
Go ask Alice
Perhaps, just perhaps, she'll know
Pour her tea with several lumps of sugar
    laced with saccharine
Vile and cancerous
From lullabies and faerie tales

Where babies fall from treetops
Wolves eat frail, arthritic grandmothers
And bulimic damsels devour and disgorge their
poison apples
As if on cue for good Prince Charming
Heedless of the consequences
Pathetic
Brainless
Harpies
How they loathe me

Face me, you coward!
Face me, you pretender!
Shards peel slowly from the mirror
Sliding
Slithering downward in a cold stream
    of antifreeze

Nightmare's Eve

Liquid shards
Robotic tears stored up in Wonderland
For wicked stepfools
Such as I

Upon reflection

Breaking the Cycle

*T*hey found evidence of foul play at 25349 Greenbriar Road. That is to say, what was left of the house, which wasn't much. The chimney survived, as they do in such cases, and some of the ceramic fixtures. The concrete foundation, of course, was unaffected, and one doorframe somehow managed to endure the flames, looking like a portal to nowhere.

Firefighters had arrived to find the house "fully involved" (which is firefighter-speak for "engulfed" or, even more plainly, "The fire's all over the fuckin' place.") By that time, it had advanced to such an extent that it was clear most of the structure could not be salvaged. That's not to say they didn't try, but they had quickly determined that their top priority should be to keep the fire from spreading beyond this single, two-story gabled house on the outskirts of Belleview Heights.

Their task had been relatively simple, considering the rural nature of the neighborhood. The nearest residence was about a quarter-mile away, and the occupants of this residence had phoned

911 to report black smoke rising nearby in the twilight hours of Tuesday, December 24th.

It was that black smoke — the kind of smoke that often rises from a fire that's been started by gasoline — that led investigators to suspect arson. The yellow flames firefighters had encountered provided another clue, as did the speed with which the structure seemed to have burned.

The homeowner, one Robert Delvecchio, could not be located afterward, and when it surfaced that he was behind on his mortgage, the suspicion naturally arose that he had set the fire to cash in on an insurance policy.

There was one problem with this theory: Cleanup crews discovered a body, charred nearly to cinders and buried in the smoldering remains of the home. DNA tests on that body determined that it belonged to Delvecchio. Investigators quickly abandoned the notion of any financial motive in the fire.

The true motive surfaced on the pages of a charred journal found in a desk drawer at 25349 Greenbriar Road, one of the few things that hadn't burned in the fire.

Inside was a series of entries that led investigators to conclude Delvecchio had taken his own life by means of self-immolation, destroying his home in the process. Based on what he had written, he seemed to have been contemplating the prospect of his own demise for some time. And, in the most recent entry, he speculated that "perhaps, in the end, my body must indeed be consigned to flame."

The reference was somewhat cryptic, but what accompanied it was truly bizarre. Delvecchio believed that, in burning his body, he might be able to halt a chain of events that had begun some nine centuries earlier, when he had occupied a different body in a place thousands of miles away from Blaine County.

Robert had been claustrophobic ever since he could remember, and he had no explanation for it. He had never been trapped inside an enclosed space, as far as he could remember, and he had never had problems breathing. He wasn't asthmatic — at least not as a child — and he had learned to swim at a young age, so he'd never felt panicked in the water or in danger of drowning.

Like many children, he was afraid of the dark and insisted that his parents keep a nightlight on while he slept, but his fear went beyond that: He remembered thinking that the bedroom walls were closing in on him, that the four of them were, simultaneously, being pushed toward him by some unseen force. He was certain that, within a matter of moments, they would meet in the middle and crush the life out of him, cracking bones, squeezing the blood from the veins in his tissue and collapsing his lungs, suffocating him.

The walls never did crush him, but that didn't keep Robert from being afraid that they would, even after he outgrew his other childhood fears: things like spiders, large dogs and Brussels sprouts. When his parents visited Carlsbad Caverns, he refused to even get out of the car, no matter how often they told him it was perfectly safe, and even though his kid sister, who was just 7 at the time, couldn't wait to go inside.

Robert couldn't even stay in front of the TV or in a movie theater for some scenes. Mummies or vampires in coffins? No thank you. Coal miners trapped by a cave-in? Prisoners digging their way out of jail? Characters shimmying on their bellies through crawl spaces or ventilation shafts? No. No. And no. His parents learned to take his fear in stride, though of course, *he* never did, or it wouldn't have been *fear* — the kind of fear that makes your heart feel like it's pounding at the inside of your chest, trying to break free. The kind of fear that makes you hyperventilate. The kind of fear that embeds itself in your subconscious and leaps up to grab you by the throat in nightmares when you least expect it.

And he did have nightmares. Nightmares of being trapped inside an elevator in pitch blackness, swaying and rocking as the cable that held him threatened to give way. Nightmares of thick, black smoke rising up to choke him from flames that burned hot beneath his feet. Nightmares of being bound and blindfolded as an unseen abductor wrapped him tight in a burlap sack that chafed against his skin.

None of this got any better as he grew older. Even as an adult, he refused to sleep with pillows, for fear that someone would break into the house and smother him. When he caught a cold, he couldn't stay in bed because his clogged sinuses made him feel like he was suffocating. He'd wake himself up snoring and would jump up out of bed. Then he'd pace around until his head drained, after which he would lie down … and the process would start all over again.

The older he got, the more it became clear this was a chronic problem, and he would go months at a time with little sleep because of it. As the son of two atheists whose IQ had been tested at near-genius levels, he found no solace in religion (which he called "a phantom crutch for people with nonexistent wounds inflicted by imagined enemies"). Still, the anxiety created by his sleeping problems made him increasingly desperate for a solution, especially when doctors failed to find a cure.

During his first year in college, he turned to metaphysics out of desperation. On a visit to a store in North Hollywood called The Eye of Horus, he met with a psychic called Maria Bonita, who convinced him to purchase a piece of rose quartz "mined from the depths of the Serpent Cave in Brazil." This crystal, she assured him, had special healing properties that would "absorb" his malady if he placed it under his pillow at night. It cost him two-hundred dollars, but he paid it on the chance that it might work.

Amazingly, it seemed to — at least for a while. And even when his snoring and congestion returned, he remained convinced that it helped, if only just a little, and kept it there under his pillow from that time forward.

Throughout his college days, he slept too little and worried too much, but he managed to overcome this through sheer force of will. Sleeplessness became an excuse to pull all-nighters before exams, which prepared him well enough to maintain perfect grades. Earning his degree in less than four years, he caught on with a hot new software firm called 1derkind, where he continued his habit of working through the night to develop a breakthrough scheduling program. TickIT allowed users to make reservations, buy tickets or make appointments for anything — doctor visits, cruises, concerts, sporting events, hotel rooms, you name it — from a single platform. It earned him not only a promotion, but the cover of Megasoft Magazine and a bonus in company stock that allowed him to buy a home in Belleview Heights.

For a while he dated Penelope Wise, a reality TV star who had won a recording contract by making it to the finals of *Drop That Mic*. Her first single, *Brain Trust*, hit number one, but when subsequent releases failed to chart, she blamed Robert for keeping her up at night with his snoring and left. The snoring, however, was less of a problem than her own pedestrian songwriting, and her music never got much airplay after that. She did, however, fleetingly regain the spotlight by dating a rapper named Mark King Time, who bought her the Vegas condo where she died of an overdose three months later.

Then his insomnia got worse again, punctuated by nightmares about his dead girlfriend during his few, fitful patches of sleep, and he returned to Maria Bonita. She told him Penelope's ghost was haunting him and sold him a gold amulet in the shape of an ankh, which she said would keep the spirit away.

His insomnia didn't improve, but he believed he'd stopped dreaming about Penelope because of the amulet, which he never removed after that, even when he showered.

That's when the other dreams started … dreams so vivid they felt almost like memories, even though Robert knew that was impossible. In one of them, he found himself crawling along in a cave with only a small torch for light. He was looking for something — something of great value — but he wasn't sure what.

Then, suddenly, a blast of warm air blew in from somewhere, and the flame went out. He thought about continuing forward but decided it was wiser to return the way he'd come and started backing out, slowly, his knees scraping over the rocky surface. He remembered taking one branching tunnel near the entrance and hoped he could remember how to get back the way he'd come. He wasn't that far in, and if he backed up a few more yards he'd be in a place big enough to turn around. Then, he hoped, he'd be able to see light from the entrance once he'd gone just a little farther.

But before he reached the turn-around spot, he heard a soft rumbling that gave way, a few seconds later, to a loud crash. Hesitant at first, he backed up a little farther and felt his way barred by a wall of rock that hadn't been there before. He looked up, but could see nothing. A dry rivulet of dirt cascaded down into his eyes. He shut them tight and wiped them furiously, not only against the sand, but against the darkness. Yet the darkness at the back of his eyelids was the same as the darkness on the outside. Complete. Total.

Reaching out both hands to feel all around him, he could find no space between the rocks; no way through. He gasped, and hot, dusty air stung his lungs as he began to hyperventilate, desperate to feel the crisp, cool air of the *outside* in his nostrils, rushing into him unhindered. The breath of life.

It was not there.

Robert awoke from the nightmare in a cold sweat, gasping for breath, his sinuses congested so badly he jumped out of bed and began running in place to clear his head. But he was already exhausted from the dream, the way he had been after running a 5K race back in high school. The gunk in his sinuses had dripped down the back of his throat in the night, triggering bronchitis. He ran in place for as long as he could, wheezing as he willed himself to continue. But it was only a few moments before he collapsed back onto the bed and the congestion, which hadn't fully drained, flooded back into his head in a slow wave of stubborn mucus.

Even so, he slept … and entered another dream. He was on a cruise ship, and the moment he became aware of that much, he was knocked off his feet as the floor heaved upward, dropping him to his knees and sending him sliding across the small cabin. His shoulder slammed hard into the side wall, and in almost the same instant, the world turned sideways, then upside down. Somewhere from the vague beyond, the sound of screaming reached his ears as he fell hard — onto the ceiling — and bumped his head so badly he wasn't sure how he'd remained conscious. Everything went fuzzy or a moment and then, as his vision cleared, he found himself staring at the portal on the far wall of the cabin. Where he expected to see the horizon floating below a golden sun or silvery stars, all he saw was blackness with a vague tinge of greenish blue.

The ceiling beneath him seemed to stabilize, but he had the vague feeling that he was drifting downward. As he stared at the porthole, he saw a thin white crack that looked like a spiderweb begin to creep across the outer window. It stretched at both ends and widened in the middle, growing like a vein that fills with blood as it's constricted at both ends; then, all at once, it burst, vanishing in a silent explosion. Before Robert could even take a breath, its twin began to crawl across the inner glass, but faster. He thought he could see the glass bending inward just before it gave way, and a torrent of saltwater came surging into the cabin.

He got to his feet and rushed toward the cabin door, even as the water slapped him and washed over him. By the time he got there, there cabin was half-full, and he couldn't budge the door, no matter how hard he pulled.

He took a breath, and he was under.

How long would that breath last? A minute? Perhaps two at the longest? He knew that was the amount of time left in his still-young life, but in defiance vowed to make it last as long as he could. Until he passed out.

But just before that happened, he woke up, his lungs burning as he gasped for air. He sat up in bed, his head swiveling wildly as he looked around in a panic, as though he were being stalked by some silent, hidden predator. All the sheets and blankets had been kicked off the bed, and the book that had been on his bedside table lay face-down and open on the floor, some of its pages bent backward underneath themselves.

Robert clicked on his bedside table lamp and reached down to pick it up: *Meditations for a Good Night's Sleep.* He had ordered it online for situations just such as this, but some of the guided exercises involved deep breathing, something he was incapable of doing when his congestion was acting up. Still, it was a distraction from the nightmares that had left him perspiring, shaking and wheezing even more than before.

"Picture yourself in an open field at night. A warm breeze tousles your hair as you sit on a bed of soft grass, gazing up at stars that wink down at you playfully from the heavens. Imagine a celestial boat sailing effortlessly across the sky ..."

Boats were the last thing he wanted to picture after that last dream, but he continued.

"Faeries play at the edges of your vision, frolicking all around you, singing a silent song of joy and comfort. Feel the sound of it entering your ears and making mirth within your soul. Feel your breathing rise and fall, effortless ..."

Impossible in his current condition, Robert thought; still, he felt his heartbeat slowing and his eyelids becoming heavy again. He needed sleep. Perhaps the meditation was helping. On the other hand, he might merely have been suffering from stress-induced exhaustion or low levels of oxygen reaching his brain. Whatever the reason, he felt the book tumble from his hands as fingers relaxed and his head lolled sideways against the headboard.

Sleep took him.

And again, he found himself in a dream.

Curiously, he heard himself speaking a language that was foreign to him; it sounded vaguely eastern European — Hungarian, perhaps. This would have been unusual under any circumstances, but what made it seem truly bizarre was the fact that he'd never been to Hungary. In fact, he'd only known one person who had: a history professor in college whose accent sounded similar to the one he'd heard himself using in the dream.

Nightmare's Eve

The words spilled out of his own mouth, frantic and desperate, as a group of men dragged him forcibly from what looked like a small cottage in a mountain forest. This was, he knew instinctively, his home. The men who took him seemed more like farmers than soldiers, dressed simply rather than in uniform, their dirty, bearded faces contorted in angry, malignant expressions fueled by hatred … and fear.

They beat him about the head until he was unconscious, and when he came to, he was lying on his back and everything was dark.

He tried to stand but bumped his head almost immediately.

He tried to roll over but hit the side of something that felt like wood.

He tried the other way. Same result.

He screamed. Nobody heard.

And once again, he couldn't breathe. The air was thin — and getting thinner with each breath he took. He tried to scoot down, but his feet struck more wood. He pushed up against it, and the top of his head met the same resistance. When it did, it wasn't like knocking on a door. There was no hollow sound, of the sort that one hears when there's a room on the other side. Not only was the barrier solid, whatever lay beyond it was solid, as well.

He realized, in a moment of horror, that he had been buried alive, and in a start, he jerked upward, banging his head on the wooden ceiling above him and knocking himself unconscious again.

He might have died then and there had his alarm not sounded, the strains of Rossini's *William Tell Overture* jarring him back to consciousness. (He had chosen that particular alarm to combat his fear of falling asleep and never waking up; if anyone could rouse him from a coma, he reasoned, the Lone Ranger's theme song would do the trick.)

Robert was supposed to work that day, but he called in sick and scheduled an emergency appointment with his doctor, a thirtysomething physician named Truman Duff whose prematurely gray hair gave him the sort of gravitas that was reassuring in a medical professional. Duff placed a stethoscope just below Robert's right shoulder blade and told him to breathe normally. Then he left the room and returned with a long tube, instructing Robert to take a deep breath and exhale into it as hard as he could.

He couldn't produce much air, and the harder he tried to blow, the louder he wheezed.

Duff jotted some notes on a clipboard, left the room again, and returned to show Robert the results. His diagnosis: a mild case of pneumonia. He prescribed an antibiotic and an asthma inhaler, but he was concerned that there might be something more to it, so he referred Robert to a specialist and ordered x-rays.

When they came back, Robert was shocked by what they showed. He'd never smoked, and he'd lived most of his life far away from the factories and freeways that belched smog into the sky. But the tests were conclusive, Duff said: Robert had emphysema, a chronic obstructive lung disease that left him five or ten years to live, if he was lucky. In the meantime, his breathing would only get worse as his lungs progressively failed.

Duff prescribed steroids, a rescue inhaler and a breathing mask for him to use at night, but none of them did anything for Robert's anxiety. His post-nasal drip felt like Chinese water torture now, with each bit of mucus sliding down the back of his throat presaging his ultimate doom. As for the breathing machine, the very act of putting it over his nose and mouth made him feel as if someone were trying to suffocate him. The first time he tried to use it, he panicked, flinging it across the room; he vowed he wouldn't try again, no matter how little sleep he got.

He stayed away from work after that, using up all his sick time and telling his boss he could work from home until he felt better. But for someone assigned to lead a team of software developers, this arrangement was far from ideal. Meetings had to be attended, and you couldn't cover everything in a phone conference. After two months, 1derkind let him go, giving him a substantial severance but depriving him of something he needed far more: health insurance.

Did it even matter? he asked himself. The doctor had said he couldn't cure emphysema, and the treatments he'd prescribed had been of little help.

No one could help him, he lamented. Except, perhaps …

Lankershim Boulevard cut an odd, diagonal path across the southern San Fernando Valley, rising up from Universal City to North Hollywood. Except for a few low-rising palm trees, it was all cracked and faded asphalt that bled almost imperceptibly into the smog-laced sky. Multi-story box buildings competed for space with sixties-era strip malls that had outlived their usefulness, housing vacant spaces that were once video rental shops and shabby boutiques catering to bargain-hunting seniors on one hand and alternative lifestyles on the other.

Robert looked down at the hard, gray sidewalk, then up at the neon sign that flickered pink and purple in the window: "Eye of Horus" it read. Below it was an illuminated hand inside a circle, accompanied by the words "Palm Reader."

He hesitated only a moment before obeying the sign on the glass front door that read "push" and entering the establishment, a low-slung, single-story shop permeated by the competing smells of dragon's blood and frankincense. His eyes took a few moments to adjust to the artificial darkness created by the black paint on the walls and heavily tinted windows. Ethereal faux-Celtic sounds bled out through unseen speakers behind the register, where a gaunt young man wearing half a beard and a black Sabaton T-shirt was engrossed in a graphic novel. He didn't look up when Robert entered. He never had before, either. There was an unspoken code at the Eye of Horus that customers preferred to be left alone unless they specifically asked for guidance — in case they wanted privacy as they perused such titles as *The Satanic Bible* and *The Book of Lies.*

Robert didn't believe in Satan, but he did value his privacy. He wrapped it around him like a warm cloak whenever he went out, hoping no one would notice the anxiety born of sleepless nights that lurked just beneath the surface. He passed the register, with its display of crystals and amulets under glass, and walked down an aisle of censers, brass trinkets and mass-produced sculptures of Egyptian gods, paying them no heed as he headed straight for the back of the shop.

There he was met by a dark purple curtain, beside which stood a cardboard sign that read "Maria Bonita, fortunes told, your future: behold!" He pulled the curtain back without breaking stride, and a young man with a pockmarked face and dirty blond hair looked up at him from a small, round table, as did the psychic herself. Maria Bonita was a petite fortyish woman with olive skin and dark green eyes, her raven-black hair punctuated by a line of gray that ran down the left side and made her look a little like Lily Munster. Robert couldn't tell whether it was natural or there for effect.

"Oh. Sorry," he said, stepping backward to retreat through the curtain, but Maria reached up and grabbed his wrist before he could withdraw.

"Hello, Robert," she said in a voice that was somewhere between wispy and gravely. "You're fine. We're done here."

The young man nodded and stood hastily, knocking over the folding chair where he'd been seated with a clatter, and just as hastily restoring it to its former position before excusing himself.

Maria gestured toward the chair, pursing her lips as she gathered up a number of colorful cards from a tarot spread she'd used for her previous client. Robert wondered what the young man had wanted to know, then decided he didn't care. In his state, he had grown to care less and less about the affairs of others, consumed as he was by his own troubles.

"It's been some time since I've seen you," Maria remarked. "What brings you to me now? Your future, your past … but no, I sense the one is bound up with the other. So it is with us all, but even more with you."

She took hold of his wrist again.

"Aren't you going to read the cards?" he asked in a whisper. He always felt like whispering when he spoke to her, as if he were in a library and didn't want to disturb others. No one else was there, so what was he worried about? The spirits, perhaps? Maybe, but it wasn't anything conscious on his part, just a feeling that lay somewhere between fear and courtesy.

"No cards today, love," she said. "I need to read *you*. Now, just relax and turn the palm of your hand over so I can see …"

He did as she asked. She'd never read his palm before; she'd always worked with the cards. He wondered why this time was different.

She leaned in closer to inspect his hand in the light of flickering flames that rose from three wicks of a pale candle that burned just off to one side. The wicks, she'd explained to him once, represented the triple goddess. He doubted there was any such thing, but he didn't question it; however he got the answers he sought didn't matter, as long as he got them.

Maria pulled back, frowning.

"What's wrong?" he asked.

For a moment, she said nothing. Then, slowly: "Your lifeline … I've only seen anything like it once or twice before. It's almost a spiral."

Robert looked down at his own hand. He'd never noticed the lines on it before, but she was right: The line that, for most people, runs straight across the palm, curved downward from between his thumb and forefinger, then curled around on itself like a ram's horn. "What does it mean?"

The candle flickered some more; one of the wicks fizzled and went out.

Maria grabbed a lighter with a skull and crossbones on the side of it and flicked it four times before the spark took. She relit the wick, but it went out again straightaway.

"Hmmm," she said, extending the syllable through her closed lips as almost a humming buzz. "Have you been having dreams?"

"Yes."

"Tell me."

So, he did. He told her about the drowning dream and the cave dream and the dream of being buried alive in that coffin. He started to tell her that he thought it was all related to his breathing troubles, but she interrupted before he could finish. "Your shortness of breath … has the doctor said what is causing it?"

"Emphysema," he said. "But I've never smoked, and …"

She cut him off again. "The dreams do not arise from your condition," she said, holding his wrist so firmly it made him uncomfortable as she fixed her eyes on his. "Your condition is born of your dreams."

He frowned. "How can that be?"

"Because," she said, her tone more urgent and her words more hurried, "your dreams are not just dreams. They are past lives manifesting in the present day. This has happened before Robert. Many times. Your lifeline, the way it's configured, is called a death spiral."

He wrenched his hand free of hers and pulled it back, cradling it protectively in his lap. "Does that mean I'm going to die? It's the emphysema, isn't it?"

She shook her head decisively and repeatedly from side to side. "We all die," she said, emphatic. "It's not *that* you will die, it's *the way* you will die. It's the same every time. Suffocation. Constriction. Strangulation. Asphyxiation." She drew each word, emphasizing the second or third syllable each time. Was this all for dramatic effect, so he'd leave a larger tip? Had he not been so desperate, that thought might have been more than fleeting, but as it was, sheer panic at their meaning sent any skepticism fleeing from his thoughts.

"But why?" he asked.

She scowled, her furrowed brow pressing down on the sockets that cradled those dark green eyes. He thought she looked almost skeletal in the firelight, her cheekbones pressing out against a thin covering of skin, her lips thin and drawn tight across her mouth. "It could be," she said at last, "that you were, in your first life, a devout man denied a burial on holy ground." She tapped her index finger against the side of her head. "Or perhaps you consigned another to this fate of being buried alive, and karma has seen fit to punish you in this manner. I cannot say for sure."

Robert felt a line of sweat forming just above his eyebrows and wiped at it with the back of his hand.

"Is there anything I can do to stop it from happening again?"

Her voice was low and somber. "I'm afraid not," she said, shaking her head slowly. "In this life, the die is cast against you. But in the next … there may be something you can do to change your fate."

She looked away from him and pulled out her purse, sifting through perhaps two dozen business cards before she found the one she wanted.

"What's this?" he said, taking it from her and reading it aloud. "The Phoenix Group?"

It was a crematory. "Leave your loved ones in our care," it read. "We'll see them safe from here to there."

Was this a joke? He wondered fleetingly whether she got some sort of kickback for this kind of referral, but again the desperation thrust his skeptical thoughts aside.

"When you die," she said, her voice coldly serious, "you must not be buried in the earth. You must surrender your mortal body to the flames. Fire is the old way, the way of purification. It will break the cycle that has bound you these many lifetimes, and when you are reborn in your next body, you will no longer be its prisoner."

Robert's hands were shaking. He wanted to throw the card back across the table at her, but instead he stuffed it in his pocket, then wiped his brow again before the sweat that was forming there could drip into his eyes.

"But what about *now?*" he said in a near panic. "Is there nothing I can do *now?*"

Again she shook her head. "The die is cast against you," she repeated. "What fate has set in motion, you cannot change within this lifetime. Your physician has no doubt told you this already."

Robert bit his lower lip and closed his eyes hard. He felt Maria's hand take his again, stroking the back of it with her long fingers. It felt like static and grease; it repulsed him, and he pulled back.

"Thank you," he said, rising quickly and knocking the chair over, just as the young man had before him.

Her thin lips widened in a toothless smile. "You can leave your payment here with me or at the register," she said. "Twenty minutes. That's fifty dollars." He pulled three twenty-dollar bills from his wallet and dropped them on the table, then turned away and left through the curtain. He was breathing hard, on the verge of hyperventilating, and he couldn't tell whether it was from his physical condition or because of what the seer had just told him.

Over the next few weeks, the dreams got worse, and so did Robert's breathing problems. He forced himself to try the breathing mask again, but it chafed against his skin and the sound of its motor kept him from falling into a deep sleep.

He felt better when he sat up, but whenever he did, he wanted to lie down again because he was so tired. The welcoming cushion of his soft mattress beckoned him, and the warmth of his comforter soothed him as he crawled beneath it. But a few moments later, he would sit straight up in bed again, panicked and unable to breathe. The vain quest for sleep only raised his anxiety levels and made it harder to come by, perpetuating the cycle.

Nightmare's Eve

"The cycle." Maria Bonita had used those words in describing his predicament, and she'd said there was only one way to break it: fire. She had called it "the way of purification." She'd also said there was nothing he could do in this lifetime to halt the progression of his disease, but what if she were wrong? Perhaps if he lit the fireplace downstairs, it would somehow help …

But no. The wood only sent smoke into the room and made it even harder for him to breathe.

He turned away from the fire, coughing to the point that his eyes watered, and staggered back to his bedroom. Putting one hand against the wall to steady himself, he gasped in the slim hope that he might capture enough air to clear his lungs; but that hope went unrealized. Stumbling into his room, he collapsed on the bed and propped himself up against the headboard using a three-cornered pillow, thinking perhaps he could steal a few minutes of sleep sitting up.

Robert groped around the nightstand for the book he'd been reading to keep his mind occupied, but his hand fell instead on the business card from the Phoenix Group that lay there. He picked it up and twirled it absently in his fingers, staring at it as he had every night since he'd returned from The Eye of Horus. He'd call tomorrow, he told himself, to make the arrangements. If he couldn't save himself in this life, at least he'd spare himself in the next … if there was a next lifetime. A year ago, he would have dismissed the idea as nonsense, but his nightmares were so vivid, so real, that he had begun to believe they were, in fact, repressed memories from earlier lifetimes. He couldn't risk going through this again. Ever. He had to put a stop to it somehow, and if this were the only way …

He gasped suddenly, his chest seizing up and his diaphragm expanding in a desperate attempt to draw air into his lungs. He would have wheezed if he could have exhaled, but he couldn't pull in enough air to get that far. The card fell from his fingers as he fumbled through the nightstand drawer for his rescue inhaler. Finding it, he raised the plastic mouthpiece to his lips. He pressed upward with his thumb, releasing the fine mist into his mouth, but it had nowhere to go: His bronchial tubes were too badly inflamed.

Robert's skull pounded. He could feel himself growing lightheaded from the lack of oxygen and managed to draw in just enough air to keep from passing out. He could call 911, but there wasn't time: he'd be unconscious, brain-damaged or dead from lack of oxygen by the time the paramedics got there.

In a panic, he rose from the bed and made his way back down the corridor toward the living room. The fire was still burning; he'd neglected to douse it, in his haste to escape the smoke. He couldn't wait for The Phoenix Group to ensure his safe passage into the next life. His time had run out. Thrusting his bare hand into the fireplace, he screamed as the flames seared his flesh; the pain burned his skin, but a deeper pain burned his lungs. He knew he had only one possible course of action.

Grabbing the burning log, he set his flannel robe alight, then flung the flaming pine at the drapes behind him as he screamed.

Robert collapsed on the floor, gasping for breath one final time as the flames engulfed him. As they licked his flesh, peeling it away from muscle, bone and sinew, his mind flashed to something he'd seen in one of his dreams. He'd all but forgotten it, but it came back to him now, as vivid as any of the others. A crowd of people were gathered around him, laughing and cursing at him as flames rose up from beneath his feet. "Die, witch!" they commanded. "Burn in hell!" "Sinner!" "Sorcerer!" "God's judgment be upon ye!"

Then he realized, in his dying hysteria, that he had burned to death before. And it hadn't stopped the cycle.

The eyes of his dream-self gazed out through the rising smoke over the throng of people mocking him, and he thought he recognized two piercing green eyes as they stared back at him from the rear of the crowd.

"Maria Bonita!" he cried out with his dying breath.

But she turned and walked away.

Merlin's Lament

Round and round the pole of May
They dance in August's warm decay
The flies that flit and buzz and bite
Rejoicing in the tragic plight

Of revelers from Beltanes past
Whose vacant eyes are now downcast
How came the lady and the lord
To flee this place they once adored?

To hasten with the ferryman
Across that stream no bridge can span
Two coins for the eyeless worms
Beneath the barrow, 'twixt the berms …

That guard the Realm of Camelot
That lofty dream brought down to naught
By Zeus or Baal or Jupiter
By Set or Typhon, ancient cur

That god whose ego spans the skies,
Were we to psychoanalyze
Perhaps we'd dare admit for once
The folly of his arrogance

In whose own image we were cast
By our own choice, from first to last
Our aspirations given form
Amidst the rash and heedless storm

That dealt to Job a fate unjust
That taunted man with his own lust
That baited Adam, turned on Eve
Was it the serpent which deceived?

Or was it truly our own mind?
Forever naked, ever blind
We wander exiled o'er the land
Forgotten birthright still in hand

Now wisdom cries out in the streets
A harlot that we're sure to meet
But one we never recognize
Or dare to look straight in her eyes

Nightmare's Eve

We speak so bold but question not
We ravish her, then leave to rot
The beauty that we never knew
That innocence forever true

And so we'll dance as ghosts one day
Around the pole that first of May
Our fallen mother ne'er to rise
Beneath the soot of veiled skies

Where now are we, the proud and vain?
So slow to see, so quick to blame
Our childish god has run away
And we have nowhere left to play

The filthy flies our only heirs
To filthy lies and petty cares
Remembering what might have been
When time was young and Earth was green

Virulent

"Appearances are like vapor. Angels are like dust. The Path alone endures." — Blessings, Psalms of Silence, 2:14

Day 1 …

My name is Severus Wu. I don't have a rank or serial number. I'm not military. I'm a farmer. That's why they chose me. I've got an ag science degree (top of my class), plus I walk the Path, and they knew it wouldn't be easy to survive nine months in a cramped space capsule traveling between Earth and Mars, so they needed people with mental discipline. They chose three of us who walked the Path for this mission.

All six of us on the Roddenberry were farmers, but 95 percent of the capsule space was taken up by things like seeds and nutrient-rich soil. We were in the third wave of Earth emigrants, following the Bradbury and the Van Vogt. We should have been the fourth, but the

Asimov crashed on entry somewhere over Mons Olympus. We don't know what happened to it or the people on board. They're all presumed dead, but I'll probably be dead, too, before long.

More than likely, no one will ever read the words I'm leaving in this journal. So why write any of it down? Discipline. That's one of the things they teach you when you set off on the Path. "Writing focuses the mind — and passes that focus along to anyone who reads what flows forth from the pen." I need that focus if there's even a chance that I might survive this ordeal ... if you can call it that.

Whoever put me here left me a pen and notebook, so there's no reason not to use it.

I don't know if my shipmates are still alive or, if they are, whether they know what happened to me. I went to sleep in camp one night and woke up here. Probably drugged, because I woke up feeling woozy and disoriented. But by who? I haven't seen anyone since I got here except Matilda — and I've never seen *her* before. She wasn't part of our crew, and she wasn't with the previous landing parties, either, which means ... I don't know *what* it means. On a planet with a total population of eighteen human beings who work with each other every day, it would be hard to overlook one.

Matilda *looks* human, but she hasn't said anything to me yet. Maybe she doesn't speak English. I don't even know if her name is really Matilda. I asked if I could call her that — from the song *Waltzing Matilda*, my mother used to sing me — and she nodded, so maybe she understands. I'm not sure.

The place where I am looks a lot like Earth — not just anywhere on Earth, but the kind of place you'd want to call home, at least if you lived in the 21st century. The walls here seem solid, thick; maybe made from something like adobe. Nothing like the biodome we set up when we got here, that arching, transparent layer of polymer that protects us from the crazy windstorms up here. Or protected us. Don't know if I'll ever see it again.

Not that I miss it. If nothing else, this place *seems* a lot nicer. Reminds me of somewhere in the American suburbs, maybe a couple of hundred years ago. I've read about it in books. Anthropology class. I've seen pictures. It's just one room, but it's got everything you might want: a soft, warm bed with a quilted comforter and goose-down pillows; a La-Z-Boy; a pantry stocked with an odd assortment of goods ranging from pea soup to stuffed olives to caviar (where did they find this stuff?) … Microwave? Check. Coffee table with photo book of Route 66? Check. Porcelain sink and toilet? Check. Bookcase stocked with books by Leo Tolstoy, Stephen King, George R.R. Martin, James Michener, etc.? Yep, that's here, too. (All epic novels from the period of classic literature; I guess they plan on keeping me here for a while). There's even a flat-screen TV and a DVD player with a collection of old shows I've never heard of; titles like *Carol Burnett* and *Green Acres*. And a lava lamp.

Not sure where they get the power to run these things. Have to investigate.

There's even a copy of the sacred scripture here: *Blessings of the Path*. Are the people who put me here followers? Is this a test of my faith? What do they want from me?

When I woke up, I thought I'd been taken back to Earth. But when I looked out the only window in the place, all I could see was the same rocky Martian surface I've been living on for the past few months.

This doesn't make sense.

No sign of anyone but Matilda, who spends most of her time curled up in the La-Z-Boy or staring out the window. Nothing more to write for now.

That bed looks comfortable.

I think I'll crash.

"Search not with your eyes, but discover with your heart." — Blessings, Second Canticle, 17:3

Day 2 ...

I woke to find a note slipped under the door. Not under it, really. The place is sealed tight as a drum to keep the interior climate controlled (all praise!). A constant 70 degrees. Says so right on the thermostat, which looks like the kind you'd see back on Earth, but you can't change the setting.

So, the note — it wasn't slipped under the door, but through a sealed slot that must have been opened from the outside while I was asleep. I'm a light sleeper, and it didn't wake me, which is odd, but everything about this place is odd.

I opened the note, and there, in perfect English curling across the paper like calligraphy, I read the following:

"Welcome to your new home. Please make yourself comfortable. Each day, you'll be asked to part with one of the gifts we've generously bestowed upon you. Choose wisely. This condition of your stay is not negotiable. If you wish to leave, we will not attempt to stop you, but the climate outside this artificial environment will not allow you to survive for more than a brief period. Choose wisely."

That last phrase was repeated. For emphasis, I guess. Not that I need anyone to convince me: I'm not wearing an environmental suit (I woke up wearing Spider-Man pajamas!), so going for a walk around the block isn't an option. Carbon dioxide doesn't work as a substitute for O_2.

So, I'm stuck here. I'm supposed to give up one of the "gifts" my kidnappers have given me. Every day. What does this mean? I asked Matilda, but she didn't answer. Either she doesn't understand or doesn't know. I can't tell which. Either way, it's no help. Maybe if I don't choose anything, they'll leave me alone. I doubt it, but it's worth a try.

I think I'll get started reading *Game of Thrones*. That could get my mind off of this. Or help me think.

Focus on the Path, Severus.

"Spill not a single drop from the reservoir of your soul on the barren ground of vanity." — Blessings, Manifold Goodness, 7:15

Day 3 ...

Well, that didn't work. I woke up this morning and couldn't find *Game of Thrones* anywhere. I thought at first I'd misplaced it, but this place isn't big enough to just leave things somewhere you can't find them.

I looked toward the door. Another note.

I opened it: "Because you neglected to designate an item for removal, we chose one for you. Perhaps we were unclear. Please choose one item each day and leave it by the door for collection. Thank you for your cooperation in this matter. — The Management."

I asked Matilda if she knew who "The Management" was. She shrugged.

I asked her if she knew a way out. She shrugged again.

I asked her if she could talk. She didn't shrug or nod or shake her head or anything. At least, it seems, she understands English, even if she doesn't want to answer.

Okay, I'll play along. No need to panic. Base camp has probably sent out a search party; maybe they'll find me. Tonight, I think I'll leave the caviar by the door. I'm a vegetarian, and fish eggs never sounded appetizing, anyway. I guess I'll start reading something different. Stephen King sounds good. This is starting to seem more like a horror story every day.

"Truth is unbending like iron. The one who ignores it will be crushed beneath the weight of it. The one who wrestles with it will surely be defeated." — Blessings, Words of the Disciple, 25:16

Day 4 …

I figured out what this is. It's not just a prison. It's a torture chamber. They're trying to break me by making me give something up every day. They figure I'll give up the nonessentials first and keep the food around till the end. I probably shouldn't have put the caviar by the door. It's disgusting, but at least it's edible.

Hindsight is 20-20, right? It was gone when I woke up today.

I remember hearing about Chinese water torture. You sit there under this dripping faucet, waiting for the next drop of water to fall down and hit your forehead. The water doesn't hurt, but the waiting drives you nuts. The inevitability.

Focus on the Path, Severus.

Focus is harder here, though. The mind wanders.

At least Martian days are about the same length as Earth days. Not that this will matter in the end, but every minute counts, right?

There was no note this time; I guess since I'm playing by the rules, there's no need for them to communicate. That's a relief, but it's also disappointing. It's hard not having anyone to talk to. I can talk to Matilda, I guess, but she doesn't say anything back. She hasn't eaten anything, either, and she was pretty thin to begin with. Maybe she's depressed. I wouldn't blame her, being a prisoner here like I am.

But why did they put us together? She's not from Base Camp; is she even human? Or did they plant her here for some reason? If so, why?

I asked her how long she'd been here, and she put up three fingers. I don't know whether that means three days or three years.

I put a bedsheet by the door. The comforter is enough.

Nightmare's Eve

"Continue in hope." Blessings, First Canticle, 1:2

Day 7 …

Still no sign of a search party from Base Camp. I put out a pillow for them to take yesterday. Maybe another book tonight. Tolstoy doesn't interest me. Mostly, I've been reading the Blessings.

Matilda's behavior has been different today. Instead of staying in the chair or staring out the window, she's looking at me most of the time. It's strange. Her eyes are ice blue, and she hardly ever blinks.

She still hasn't eaten, as far as I can tell, and the food's untouched except for what I've taken. Is she depressed? Trying to starve herself? I'm trying to ration it, and when I stepped on the scale (yes, there's a scale here), I found I'd lost five pounds. I was fit to begin with, but the longer the food lasts, the longer I do, assuming that my captors don't give me any more. So far, they haven't added anything to the living quarters I've provided. They've just taken that one thing *away* every day.

She's looking at me now, as I'm writing. I'm not sure what to make of the expression on her face, if you could even call it an expression. It's almost blank, maybe a little troubled. Scared? I'm not sure. She has a round face with jet black hair in a bowl cut. The line of her mouth is straight, turned neither up nor down, and I haven't seen her either smile or frown in the time I've been here.

I'm asking her now, "What do you want?"

Of course, she doesn't say anything. She just tips her head slightly to one side. She almost seems more like a pet than a human companion.

There. I just put down my pen and paper and threw up my hands, thinking maybe that would get her attention, and she's still barely even blinking. What is she, some kind of reptile with an inner, transparent eyelid? She might as well be that as anything else. The Path teaches us to trust until trust is broken, but I don't trust her. Is this a betrayal of the Path? Is this what they want? Maybe this is part of their strategy to break me.

There's a big windstorm outside today, and I can see the sand buffeting the window, making it vibrate almost like a sawblade when it's shaken. It's enough to make me wonder if the window is strong enough to withstand it, but it hasn't broken yet and, if it does, at least that will make a quick end of things. I won't have to endure this slow, creeping inevitability.

What the hell? Am I a fatalist all of a sudden? Focus, Severus.

"Stay true to the Path."

"Continue in hope."

I need to keep reminding myself that the others are still out there, probably looking for me. The longer I wait, the more likely it is they'll find me. But this storm would have grounded any search efforts … unless they were caught in it. Then they might be dead.

Focus.

"Continue in hope."

"Persevere."

"Your days are but illusion. The Path endures. Stay true to the Path." — Blessings, Teachings of the Masters, 15:6

Day 8 …

Matilda keeps coming closer to me, a couple of steps every day. Either she's starting to trust me, or maybe she wants me to trust her so she can take something from me. Enough is being taken already. I have to preserve what's mine.

But that's not what the teachings of the Path say. I must share what has been given me, without regard to my own wellbeing.

"Stay true to the Path."

I offered her some of my stuffed olives, but she pushed them away. She's losing weight, and I'm concerned about her, even though I don't know her.

Nightmare's Eve

I put out a note tonight alongside a lamp that had been sitting on my nightstand: "What do you want? Can we negotiate?" I hope they will answer.

"Wisdom is her own mother." Psalms of Silence, 3:24

Day 9 …

A folded piece of lined paper was lying inside the door this morning. It had just one word: No.

I assume that was an answer to the second question I posed. They didn't think it was necessary to answer the first.

Matilda touched my hand today when I wasn't looking. I hadn't realized she was even there. She's so quiet. What does she want?

Tonight I'm going to put the nightstand out. Who needs a nightstand without a lamp, right?

"Patience brings peace, even amidst the direst circumstance." — Blessings, Second Canticle, 3:24

Day 11 …

How do they get inside to take these offerings I make without me seeing them? I'm going to try to stay awake all night tonight and find out.

Matilda is never in the chair anymore. She's never looking out the window. Just at me. She never gets farther than a foot or two away from me, wherever I go. I want her to go away. I wish she wasn't here. But then I'd be alone, so that's the last thing I want. At least she has lungs that breathe, a body that radiates warmth, eyes that look at me. I need those things. I'm human, after all.

Is *she* human? I still don't know. But I must stay true to the Path. "The Path is greater than those that follow it. Those who trod the

Path will reach their destination, but the Path continues. It ever endures."

I'm starting to run low on non-essential things to give them. Maybe if I start dismantling things and giving them a piece at a time; maybe that will work. Maybe it will impress them and they'll let me live a little longer … if they want to kill me. Do they? Or do they just want to watch me starve to death, eventually? Go crazy in this place? I don't know.

So, if I unscrew a knob from the bedframe, maybe that will be enough. I'll try it. It's worth a try, right?

"Truth is not for the faint of heart or weak of mind. Truth is for the faithful." — Blessings, Teachings of the Masters, 4:12

Day 12 …

I couldn't do it. I couldn't stay awake all night. I nodded off and, sure enough, they got in again. They didn't take the nob, but instead removed the entire bedframe … while I was sleeping on it. How is this possible?

They left a note with a single word: "Unacceptable."

Something else happened. I woke up with the mattress on the floor under me and Matilda in the bed beside me. She had slept in the chair before this. I hadn't noticed her crawl under the comforter beside me.

A thought has occurred to me: Maybe *she* is my jailer. Maybe *she* is the one taking these things away. Or maybe she's in league with them. Maybe she sneaks out at night and they feed her. She has to eat *something*, doesn't she? It's been nearly two weeks. How does she keep from fainting? Getting sick?

But no, she looks human. She has to be human. She probably came with one of the earlier missions and just kept to herself, so I never saw her. That has to be it. Her scent is sweet, like lavender maybe. Is she wearing cologne?

Last night, she wasn't just in bed beside me, she was holding on to me, spooning me as I lay on my side. It felt good. I found myself … aroused. And I felt shame. And fear. I don't trust her. I can't trust her. I can't afford to. I don't even know if she's human or whether her appearance is some kind of disguise. Maybe she's a chameleon. Maybe she's some kind of slimy reptilian-maggot-insect-carnivore-something that wants to get close to me to *eat* me. I'm going to die if something doesn't change. I can't just accept that. I can't just give up without a fight. Isn't that what it means to "continue in hope"? Where is that search party? The weather has been clear for days now, and there's been no sign of anyone. Maybe they were killed in the other storm.

Why am I still writing this? No one will ever read it.

I'm screwed.

"Love is the healer, but fear is the master." — Way of the Disciple, 6:27

Day 13 …

There was a knock on the door this morning. The search party? I ran over and wrapped my fingers around the handle. I was about to open the door, but then I remembered what's out there. Mars. "Air" I can't breathe without suffocating. The impossible heat during the daytime. The frigid cold of night.

Who had knocked? If it was the search party, I'd be saved. But what if it was a trick? What if the people who put me in here were testing me? They might not let me close the door again. They might pull me outside and leave me there to die.

I looked at Matilda, and she shook her head. She didn't want me to do it. So, I didn't. Not because I care anything for her, but because it wouldn't have been right to make that decision for the both of us. She deserved to have a say. Unless she's in league with them. Unless she wants me to stay here so the search party won't find me.

I gave them the rug on the floor. Should have done that earlier. Didn't really even notice it.

"Apart, we stray. Together, we stay to the Path." — Way of the Disciple, 7:44

Day 14 …

As I slept last night, I felt Matilda's arms around me, clutching me desperately. I wasn't aroused this time, but I wasn't ashamed, either. I'm tired. Too tired to care? Apathy is a sin, the Path teaches, and I fear I am becoming the worst of sinners.

Whoever put me here changed the thermostat, so it's cold at night now. The comforter isn't enough. At least Matilda's body is warm … so why do I shiver even more when she presses up against me? I pushed her away, but she was back a moment later. There's no point in resisting. Her touch makes me shiver, but when she isn't there, a chill cold rushes in like a sea wave across my body to fill the void. That's even worse.

Once, I think I felt her fingers kneading my flesh, like a kitten kneads its mother's chest, searching for milk. Did I imagine it, or was she was making a sucking sound with her mouth?

I caught Matilda reading my journal today when I came out of the bathroom. I took it away from her. She had the letters they'd left, too, and was going through them. Her mouth was moving as she looked at them.

What does she want? She won't leave me alone.

Maybe I shouldn't write anything more. If she's spying on me for them … but what does it matter? I'll die eventually, anyway.

Stop that! "Persevere!"

Nightmare's Eve

"Measurements are a man's convenience. Such things are strangers to The Path eternal, unknowable." — Teachings of the Masters, 4:12

Day 15 ...

I've lost 10 pounds. That's what the scale says. Fuck the scale. It's like I'm wasting away, bit by bit, pound by pound. I don't need to know that. I smashed the damn thing and put it beside the door. They can have it.

I didn't read Blessings today. Can't think of a scripture that fits. Everything is falling apart.

Day 19 ...

I gave them the last book three days ago. Except for Blessings. I won't give them that. I'll starve first.

I thought there might be another way out. If there's a toilet and a sink, there has to be a sewer system. That's what I thought, but I was wrong. I removed the toilet trying to get to the earth underneath. I wanted to dig my way out, but underneath the shit in that shithole was a concrete lining and nothing else. I dug through all that for nothing. I smell like my own feces now. At least I haven't gotten rid of the sink yet, so I can wash it off.

Then I'll have to get rid of the sink, too. And the toilet. They're both detachable, I found out, so I can use them as "gifts."

I feel like a caveman making a daily sacrifice to some deity, knowing that the god who demands my worship is going to kill me in the end anyway. Is this how religion got started? Are they trying to get me to forsake the Path? Without the Path, what meaning does my life have? What purpose?

I can't think about that.

I have to focus.

"Purify thyself." — Psalms of Silence, 5:5

Day 26 …

I tore out the sink last night, and the toilet the night before that. I can shit in a hole, right?

Tonight … I don't know. I've got the mattress, the microwave, what's left of the food I haven't eaten …

I don't need the microwave. I can eat what's left raw.

I woke up with Matilda clinging to me tighter than ever. Her fingers were dug into my skin, and when I tried to pry them loose, she dug them in tighter. I thought I heard her whimpering. She *is* scared. Like an animal.

I asked her what she was afraid of, but she just shook her head.

Then she opened her mouth and said, "Please don't give *me* to them."

"A mind that questions is at war with itself, looking to the left and to the right. The mind at peace looks straight ahead, ever trained on the Path." — Blessings, The Path Perfected, 17:3

Day 27 …

If she can talk, she can answer my questions. I'm going to force her if I have to.

Who is she?

Why is she here?

Can she help us get out?

Is she working with *them*?

Why was she reading my journal?

We're running out of time, running out of things to give them.

"I could give you to them," I told her. "I could chop you up into little pieces and give them to these monsters one at a time. I finger. A toe. An arm. How do you like that?"

She started whimpering again when I said that, and I told her I wouldn't really do it. Not if she helped me, anyway.

"Maybe I'll eat you instead," I told her, "when I run out of food."

She's scared but still won't talk. Maybe she's more scared of them than she is of me.

Day 33 …

Yesterday, I decided to try again. If I could just stay up all night and wait for them to come in, I could ambush them and get out of here. Matilda could come with me or not; I don't care. I don't even care if I suffocate out there. I can't keep doing this.

She came into the bed next to me again. I can't keep her out. Every time I tell her to leave or try to push her away, she just comes back again. So, I asked her to help me stay awake.

That's when she finally said something again.

"I can keep you awake all night."

Before I knew it, she had climbed on top of me and was pressing down against me.

I shoved her away. Sex? The idea of it makes me sick. I want to vomit, because all I can see when I look at her is an image of snakes trying to curl themselves around me, some alien *thing* behind a human mask wanting to suck the life out of me.

I told her to stay the fuck away from me, and she curled up into a ball, sobbing. Real emotions? Or some fake bullshit to make me pity her. I don't have time for this. I don't have time for any of it.

They can have the goddam comforter.

Day 41 …

I woke up shivering. The thermostat read 45 degrees.
I gave them the bed.

Day 55 …

I gave them a can of beans. Not much left in the pantry.

Day 72 …

There's nothing more to give them. Matilda just stands there, staring at me all the time. She's stopped trying to touch me. She's scared of me. She's back curled up in the chair, cowering. I spent half the day shouting at the door, telling those fuckers to show themselves. They didn't. I'm spent. Fuck life. I can't do this anymore. I'm not giving them anything tonight. Not tonight. They can go fuck themselves.

I don't have anything more.

Day 73 …

I got another note from them: "You have three things left to give. You can give us the woman, your holy book or the notes you've been taking. Choose properly, and we will return you to your camp. Choose incorrectly, and we will leave you here to die."

I'm looking at Matilda now.

"Don't give me to them," she wails. "*Please.*"

Why am I still writing any of this? I'm going to give them the notebook. I can't sacrifice another person, and they won't take the Blessings from me. They're all I have left. But what good are they?

Haven't I strayed from the Path? Haven't I lost who I was, my soul, everything? And who's to say they really will let me go if I make the right decision? Maybe all three decisions are wrong. Maybe they're just fucking with my head, like they have been all along.

But hasn't everything they've said been honest? They've kept their word on everything. Like Chinese water torture. The next drop always comes. Always.

"The experiment is complete." The creature's maw opened and closed, what passed for lips forming guttural words, the meaning of which would have been lost on the prisoner, had he heard them.

But he didn't. The lifeless husk that had called itself Severus Wu in the notebook lay sprawled out on the ground, legs spread, arms open as if he'd been crucified to the floor. Sticking out of its mouth, stuffed to overflowing like brown leaves without blossom, spewing forth in some grotesque floral arrangement, were pieces of paper. Ripped and crumpled, covered with words in the dead man's tongue. He'd even managed to stuff the papers down his throat and into his windpipe. His neck bulged out, the pale flesh already turning blue-purple.

Beside him lay the book of Blessings they had left him. Some pages had been torn out. Those pages were the ones in his mouth.

He had choked on them.

Three creatures surrounded him, blue-gray bodies undulating like garden snails as they studied their work. The tallest of them cradled a notebook in a section of its gelatinous body that had adapted its shape to hold it. It was in this notebook that the subject had recorded his observations. Now it was their turn to make observations.

A single yellow eye started down at the notebook, blinking at regular intervals, like clockwork. The creatures' heads were the only aspect of their body that held constant form; the rest of them, from the neck down, was rippling mass of invertebrate matter that was continually changing shape. It seemed to ooze out of itself, only to be sucked back in again, allowing them a form of locomotion.

"There is much of value here."

Blue tentacles wriggled like centipedes from the place where the creature's nose would have been — had it been human. The centipedes were attached, though. They moved more rapidly, and in different directions, when their owner was stimulated. Intellectually or otherwise. In this case, the movement was triggered by the kind of excitement a scientist might exhibit upon making an important discovery. The creatures were scientists. And their hypothesis had been confirmed.

"It is as we suspected," one said, its voice slightly less guttural than the others, more like the sound of glass breaking and chalk dragged hard across a chalkboard at the same time. It belonged to the "woman" who had been in the room with Severus Wu, though she was in not, in any sense, a woman.

"You have our appreciation for your sacrifice, Alecrivum," the tallest of the three said. "Your willingness to endure the torment of this *thing*'s ... intimate company ... for so long will be noted."

"It was ... distasteful. At least he rejected my overtures to couple with him."

"Yes. And you were convincing."

The creature-that-had-been-Matilda let out a sound that sounded like a wheezing cough, which was joined by the others — their approximation of laughter.

"I think he may have suspected," she offered.

The tall creature's tentacles flapped up toward the top of its head, like streamers blown upward by a sudden wind. "Nonsense," it said. "In any case, it does not change the conclusion."

"Indeed, the subject's actions confirm our hypothesis," the shorter one said.

"The species is self-destructive," Alecrivum said.

"Indeed," said the shortest of the three creatures, its tentacles waving from side to side. "Its sacred texts demand that it sacrifice its own life rather than taking another's. This is contrary to the first law of survival."

"Self-preservation."

"Yes."

"And elsewhere in the book, it praises those who sacrificed food or even members of their tribe to appease their deity …"

"Even though there was no evidence that doing so brought any reward."

"Primitive," said the tall one, setting down the notebook and bending over to pull the pages from Severus Wu's mouth. He had thrust them in so violently that the paper had cut the sides of his mouth, leaving tiny dots of blood on the crumpled pages. They would need those pages for their files.

"The subject's behavior confirmed all our previous research. The species values its myths more than it values survival. It preserved the myths, even at the cost of its own life — much as an invasive organism deceives its host into sacrificing itself for the sake of the parasite."

"When it ran out of food, it sought to ingest the myths themselves, as though the words themselves might sustain it."

A gelatinous appendage grew from the center of Alecrivum's abdomen toward the Blessings. The end of it stuck to the cover with a sucking "thwap" noise, then pulled the volume toward it. Another appendage formed and extended, and began leafing through the pages, finally stopping just after the beginning of a book called Psalms of Silence. "Here," the creature said. A thin tendril grew, as if spontaneously, from the appendage and pointed to a certain passage.

The three of them read it together. (They had studied the human's language, both written and oral, for years in preparation for this experiment, so they had no trouble interpreting the words on the page before them.)

The Blessings are meat to the soul and nourishment to the afflicted.

Forsake thy bread and the Path shall sustain you. Fear not, by for the wisdom of these words shall you endure."

"A virus," the shortest of the three repeated.

"It infected the subject," Alecrivum said.

"We have no more need of this," the tall creature said and, with a gesture, the illusion that had been Severus Wu's home during his captivity flickered and disappeared. The three of them were standing on the surface of Mars. A brisk wind blowing harsh sand across outer membranes, but they barely seemed to notice.

"What do we do now, Bematacil?" the short one asked.

"Nothing, I think," the tall one, Bematacil, said. "This species is no cause for concern. They make war on each other and sacrifice themselves for the sake of empty words and images. They will destroy themselves before they pose a threat to us."

"It is a marvel they have survived for so long."

"In the course of their planet's history, they are but a speck of dust blown past in an instant, barely noticed," Alecrivum said. "They survive now only for the sake of the virus." A new appendage snaked out and flipped through the pages once more until it found one of the passages Wu had quoted in his journal: *"Appearances are like vapor. Angels are like dust. The Path alone endures."*

"They are but vessels for the virus," the short one said, its facial tentacles fluttering upward at the realization. "Worse still, they are aware of this, yet do nothing to extricate themselves from the affliction it creates."

"They are no threat to us," the tall one repeated.

"Leave them be, then," Alecrivum said. "They will be their own undoing."

"So they will," said the tall one.

The tall one bent over and extracted a biosample from Wu's body, while its companions stored the notebook and the copy of Blessings they had preserved. All these things would be of great use in further study, not just in their current research, but for future generations. They would be remembered, the three of them, for their groundbreaking research in anthropology and the human psychology.

It was a good day to be a Martian.

With a single thought, the navigator adjusted the engines and trajectory of the ship to prepare for landing on the Martian surface. Piloting a spacecraft wasn't nearly as complicated as it had been even a few decades ago. Now, it was just a matter of thinking where you wanted to go and visualizing how to get there. A skilled navigator could almost fly a spacecraft in her sleep.

The landing itself was routine. What was different about this particular mission was the destination.

Mars.

The planet had been under quarantine for centuries, ever since the first agricultural pioneers had disappeared. There had been rumors of alien abductions — and worse. Monsters the size of elephants with glowing eyes and saber-sharp teeth, devouring the flesh of their human prey as they shoveled it into their mouth with a thousand tentacles.

Stories could be exaggerated, but Ellanea had always felt it was better to be safe than sorry. Had it not been for the prestige involved in piloting the first mission to Mars since the Technological Revolution, she might have turned down the assignment. Her caution had served her well over the years, but if there was one thing that could overrule that caution, it was curiosity.

And Ellanea *was* curious.

What was down there? Were the stories true?

Instinctively, she patted the copy of Blessings that rode beside her in the capsule, its only other occupant. She'd been sent alone because the high priest hadn't wanted to risk more than one person … just in case. The high priest of the Path had the final say in everything now. The last mission had been so long ago — during a time when the Path was not yet universal on Earth. Many were convinced that the mission had failed for this very reason. Only some of those sent forth had walked the Path. The nonbelievers had contaminated the others, like a virus, and doomed the mission. The monsters that supposedly lived on Mars, with their menacing tentacles and ravenous appetites, were a judgement against those not on the Path.

This time would be different. The monsters would submit to the Path. They would be made to submit.

Elleana's touchdown couldn't have been better. It put her within a kilometer of the first settlement, although she was under no illusion that she'd be able to find any trace of it. It would have long since disappeared beneath the swirling Martians sandscape.

Once safely down, she donned her safety suit, holstered her disruptor lowered the ladder and opened the door.

They were waiting for her.

Hundreds of them. Where they had come from, she didn't know; her sensors hadn't picked up any sign of them on approach; they must have arrived quickly. She felt her hand go toward her disruptor but realized in the same instant that there were too many of them for her to fend off, even if she set it in rapid-fire mode. They could, she felt sure, simply rush forward and tip the capsule over if they decided to do so.

For the moment, though, they were just standing there. They looked a little like the monster stories she'd heard, but only a little. They weren't anywhere near the size of elephants, and she saw no sign of sharp teeth. There were tentacles, but not a thousand of them; more like, maybe, a dozen.

One of them stepped forward and, to her shock, addressed her in her own tongue.

"Greetings," it said. "Do you walk the Path?"

Elleana was stunned. She had been taught that the Path was universal, that it applied throughout the cosmos, but she'd never suspected that an alien species on a different planet would adhere to it under the same name … and even speak the same language. This was greater affirmation of her faith than she could have dreamed possible. But she reminded herself what her mentor had told her: All faith was weakened until it was tested and affirmed.

Elleana smiled.

"I am Elleana," she said, abandoning in her excitement the strictly scripted greeting she'd been told to deliver.

"I am Alecrivum," came the answer, "named for the mother of our faith."

Elleana had never heard the name before, but it didn't matter. "How do you know of the Path?" she asked excitedly.

What looked like a hand without fingers emerged from somewhere inside the creature, wrapped around an object that looked like a book. The hand extended forward, toward Elleana, until she could see the title.

"Blessings of the Path."

"Our gift to you," Alecrivum said. "Be welcome."

Elleana's hand was trembling. This just couldn't be possible. Her faith was weak, but even this was too much to expect.

Alecrivum bowed. "Spread the virus," she said amiably.

Elleana drew back and frowned. "Spread the virus?"

"But of course," Alecrivum said. "Do you not know the teachings of Bematacil?"

Elleana didn't answer. The others in the crowd seemed suddenly restless, uncertain. She was cautious … but her curiosity, once again, overruled her caution. She couldn't help but ask. "Who is Bematacil?"

"Who is Bematacil?!" Alecrivum stammered, voice guttural and chalky.

The others were murmuring among themselves now, and Elleana thought she could make out some words above the din. Words like "heretic" and "apostate" and "imposter" and "purify."

"This one is not of the Path!" Alecrivum stammered. "The infidel has come here to trick us! It knows nothing of the Benevolent

Virus or of Bematacil the Immaculate, prophet of the New Blessings! Seize it! It must be destroyed!"

The throng of Martians rushed forward and surrounded her, and Elleana, in her panic managed to lay hold of her mobile communications device and relay a single, short message to her home planet: "Danger. Maintain quarantine!" She gasped and sputtered, her body giving way as the Martians pressed close together, the thin membranes that separated them giving way as they pressed close together, merging into a single massive gelatinous entity that overwhelmed the intruder. Suffocating her. Absorbing her. Until she was part of the whole.

"We are the Body of the Path!" the all-as-one Martian entity cried together. "So taught Bematacil! So do we affirm! Forever!"

So ended the second mission to Mars.

There would not be a third.

The quarantine remained, but still, the virus spread …

Bleed Not

"Bleed not," she cooed in soothing cadence
A dove flitting softly on wings of iron will
"I found a heart in thee worth taking"
And she smiled

A sickly scent that wafted from the corners of her mouth
A drop of saliva dancing tantalizing
On the tip of her naked tongue
Formaldehyde in waiting
Cloying at my heightened senses

I swallowed through the thickness of my throat
And felt the day drain out of me in coarse betrayal
As she smiled again
"Bleed not"

Stephen H. Provost

And pressed a newly calloused hand insistent
    on the flaming wound
The salt of perspiration grinding in from palm to sinew
Ragged … breathing … lost … time

That smile, I once thought mercy
Thrusting daggers through my spine as I convulsed
Hand to lips, both drenched in crimson
Blurring into lost elation
Transfixed, I watched through vision blurred and fading

    "You were sweet"
    She licked her lips
    "Like warm vanilla cake in winter"
    And then she thrust herself inside me,
    Fingers tipped with nails thick and icy
    A final gasp, I wilted
    Trembling lifeless in her seething comfort

"Bleed not" she told me lastly
"Unless you bleed for me."

Anatomy of a Vampire

The body on the table wasn't your routine corpse. The skin was smooth and pale, and a tag on his big toe identified him as one Gustav Lemieux.

Aaron fidgeted as he stood behind one of them. He was tall enough to see over the others, and he preferred to observe from a little ways back.

"How long has he been dead?" the student in front of him asked.

The coroner's crystal blue eyes narrowed as she stared down at the naked man on the table. "We've had him here a couple of days."

"Shouldn't the flesh be mottled by now?" asked the student to Aaron's right, an older woman with a monotone voice who'd gone back to school after her wife had died in a car crash on I-580.

The coroner nodded slightly, then stuck out a gloved finger and poked the belly gingerly. The skin seemed almost elastic.

"It would be," the coroner said. "If the body still contained any blood."

Maroon or purple blotches typically began appearing on the skin within a few hours of death. Once the heart stopped beating, circulation stopped, too, and the blood cells just sat there, like passengers on a train that had stopped moving. Gradually, they'd run together as gravity pulled them downward, collecting mostly in the neck and back of the corpse.

That hadn't happened here.

"The body has been exsanguinated," the coroner said in a voice just above a whisper.

"To what extent?" the older student asked. She was the kind who thought that asking more questions would get her into the instructor's good graces. But the coroner, who was also an adjunct professor at UCLA, didn't seem to know or care which one of them was asking the questions.

"Completely," she said. "There's no blood at all inside."

The three other students in the room exchanged glances, no doubt wondering what could have caused the strange condition. They'd done their homework, so they knew that most people died before they lost even half their blood, even if they slit their wrists. There was no sign of that here. The coroner, however, had to know something they didn't. This was a demonstration, after all, and this particular corpse must have been chosen to illustrate something specific. None of them had any idea what it was yet.

Aaron paid little attention to them and kept staring intently at the table through half-lidded eyes. He wasn't falling asleep; he just looked that way naturally. In point of fact, he was more intent on what was happening than any of the others.

The coroner reached into a drawer beside the table and removed a scalpel, its sharp blade gleaming in the bright fluorescent light. Starting just below the breastbone, she pressed firmly, puncturing the skin and drawing the instrument downward toward Gustav Lemieux's pelvis. The rubbery skin resisted briefly, then gave way, yielding to a thin but deep incision above the cadaver's stomach and intestines. Or, to be more accurate, the place where they should have been.

The coroner reached into the breach with both hands, peeling back the skin, fat and muscle on either side as though she were removing the rind from an orange.

The students leaned forward to see what was inside — and the youngest among them, a plump-cheeked young man named Brad — immediately started retching. Hacking and gagging, he turned away from the table, barely able to contain the surge of bile and half-digested ham sandwich determined to exit his body the way it had come in. He raised his hand to his mouth, took a couple of steps away from the table and closed his eyes tight, as if in doing so he could wipe clean the residue of what he'd just seen.

The other two students appeared less traumatized, at least outwardly, but neither of them could fully contain the shock and revulsion at what lay before them. They couldn't help but draw back at the sight, and the accompanying stench, that rose from a large cavity where the cadaver's stomach should have been. There were no internal organs, just strands of gray, putrid, decaying flesh hanging all around the opening. Thousands of swollen but empty blood vessels opened out onto the cavity, where dozens — no, hundreds — of blood leeches, had attached themselves to the walls.

"What …?" was all one of the students could manage.

The coroner stood up straight and looked at them matter-of-factly. "What we have here, ladies and gentlemen, is a specimen known scientifically as homo sanguinis. More commonly referred to as a vampire."

The pudgy-cheeked man's eyes widened. He was still trying to regain his composure and make the others forget he'd just about lost it a couple of moments earlier. The other two students smiled beneath their surgical masks, even as they averted their eyes from corpse on the table. Whether the smiles were meant as nervous or dismissive wasn't too clear.

Aaron didn't smile. His eyes didn't widen. If he had any reaction at all to what the medical examiner had just said, he did a masterful job at keeping it to himself. He'd always been good at hiding things, a talent that had served him well and, he trusted, would continue to do so.

After a brief pause, one asked: "What happened to his stomach?"

"Homo sanguinis has no need of a stomach, or any part of his digestive system," the coroner said, her voice even and sober.

The smiles faded.

"May I be excused?" It was the student who'd nearly lost the ham sandwich.

"Do you want to fail this course?" the coroner replied.

The student stayed where he was.

"Now, as I was saying, our friend here has no need of a digestive system, because he subsists solely on blood. He doesn't actually eat it, because he's not technically alive. He's more like your automobile: You need to change the oil every few thousand miles to keep it running smoothly. Blood is like motor oil to homo sanguinis. He needs to change it every now and then, or he won't run properly."

"If he's not alive," the older woman ventured, "why are you speaking in the present tense?"

She immediately regretted asking. She had a bad habit of challenging her professors — Aaron had seen it in this class and in one other they were taking together. Asking questions might make you look good in a professor's eyes, but putting an instructor on the spot seldom ended well. Even if you made a point during class, you'd more than likely be putting your grade at risk by doing so. The woman put a gloved hand over her mask-covered mouth, as though to shovel the spoken words back inside.

The coroner glared at her. "Vampires are not alive," she said. "But they're not really dead, either. In fact, only two things can end a vampire's existence once and for all: If he's beheaded, or if he's bitten by another vampire."

Aaron waited for one of them to ask about sunlight and crosses and stakes through the heart, none of which, he knew, had any effect on vampires. The cross thing didn't make much sense, considering vampires tended to be atheists. You wouldn't have much faith in the divine, either, if you were consigned to an eternity of brutally killing people and draining their blood to maintain your energy the way some people downed cups of espresso or energy drinks. That wasn't most people's idea of a good time, even if you did gain immortality as a fringe benefit. As to sunlight, it was actually helpful: It made it easier to scope out a victim. And a stake through the heart wouldn't have much effect if your heart wasn't working anyway.

The oil change analogy was a good one, he had to admit. The coroner knew her stuff.

"So," the plump-cheek man ventured, "if it's like an oil change, he would have to drain the system before replacing the fluid."

The coroner's blue eyes sparkled. "Yes."

"What about the *leeches*?" asked the fourth student, a young woman whose arms were crossed in front of her and whose head was slightly bowed. Her voice emphasized the last word. Leeches. Aaron guessed she'd done so involuntarily. The woman, named Amanda, had never been comfortable with the class and seldom spoke up. Aaron guessed she was one of those students who had objected to dissecting a frog in high school, and who had gone into pre-med at her parents' insistence. "What are the *leeches* there for?" She emphasized the last word again.

"Homo sanguinis doesn't have a working heart, or any internal organs, for that matter," the coroner explained. "The leeches keep the blood circulating." She picked up a long, metal instrument that looked like a barbecue skewer and poked one of the parasites. It appeared dead, but at the lightest touch, its outer membrane burst and a small amount of blood spilled out. "The parasites suck the blood until they can contain no more, then they wriggle up into the veins, which constrict to squeeze it out of them."

The older woman suddenly laughed out loud. "I get it," she said. "This is all a big put-on, isn't it?"

The coroner wasn't laughing. There were no laugh lines on either side of those steel blue eyes. In fact, none of the students had ever heard her laugh about anything. "If we can continue without further interruption, please?" She fixed the student who'd spoken up with the kind of withering stare that forced the woman to avert her eyes and focus them again on the corpse. Even that sight, as vile as it was, was more pleasant than the coroner's grim look of disapproval.

"Does anyone else think this is all a 'big put-on'?" she asked, her voice tight as she forced the air up through her constricted throat.

No one said a word.

"You don't have to answer. I can see from your expressions that you don't believe me." Her tone relaxed a little. "Here. Look at this." She pointed to the cadaver's right ear, which appeared slightly deformed. Instead of a smooth, curving arc at the top, it rose to a distinctive point, as though it belonged to an elf or imp.

"Plastic surgery," the older woman whispered under her breath, but still loud enough for everyone else to hear.

Next, the coroner pulled back the upper lip to reveal a pair of long, needle-sharp canines that looked as though they could have been transplanted from a rattlesnake. As she raised the lip, the corpse appeared to sneer at them, and that was all it took for the plump-cheeked student to head for the door. The coroner looked up at him but said nothing and allowed him to leave without protest. Once he had gone, though, her eyes fixed on each of the three remaining students in turn. "Anyone else want to fail this class?" she said.

The younger woman hid her face and then, even faster than the first student had gone, rushed for lab door, nearly tripping over a metal cart in the process.

The older woman seemed determined to show she wasn't rattled. Or maybe she just didn't want to fail the class. Still, she couldn't keep her voice from quavering when she asked, "Is that … person … still capable of …?"

The coroner reached up and pulled down her mask, blue eyes dancing merrily in the fluorescent light. As she opened her mouth to speak, she revealed a pair of sharp, narrow canines worthy of a viper than extended down over her lower lip. "You needn't worry, dear," she cooed. "A vampire's bite can transform a human into homo sanguinis. But remember what I told you: That same bite can be the true death knell for another vampire." She licked her lips, the tip of her tongue caressing the sharp, ivory-white canines slowly, first one, and then the other.

The older woman's feet remained rooted in place. Aaron couldn't tell whether she was in shock or whether she simply refused to accept that any of this was real. He expected the coroner to take advantage of the situation and leap at the woman, but she didn't. Instead, she turned her eyes toward Aaron.

There was a thump as the older woman's body hit the floor. She had fainted. The other two ignored it.

"You haven't said anything today, Mr. Locke," she said. "What do you think of my little … demonstration? Aren't you the least bit afraid?"

Aaron shrugged his shoulders. "I believe you," he said simply. "It's obvious that you've rendered Mr. Lemieux … permanently incapacitated." Aaron was good at hiding things, but he let just a hint of anger seep through in these last two words.

The sparkle left the coroner's eyes, which narrowed as she studied him. "Do I know you?"

Now it was Aaron's eyes that danced, but grimly as they narrowed, too. "You might remember me, Andromeda," he said, "from your wedding. Or should I call you Mrs. Lemieux?"

The coroner's head swung to look at the corpse on the table, then back to the man standing before her. She hadn't noticed the resemblance before, but she saw it now.

"Why did you kill your husband, Mrs. Lemieux?" Aaron asked calmly as he pulled down his own surgical mask. "Why did you kill my brother?"

The coroner was caught by surprise for just a split second before she lunged at Aaron, teeth bared, but that split second was all the time he needed. He lunged first, jaw flying open, his own viper-sharp teeth extended as he crashed into her and buried his own teeth in her neck. She screamed and then, in almost the same instant, collapsed onto the floor as he tumbled into and over her, rolling up against the wall and looking back at her now-lifeless corpse. To say it was difficult for a human to subdue a vampire was an understatement, but at the hands — or teeth — of another vampire, the result was instantaneous.

Aaron got to his feet and started to stride out of the room, but at the last moment, he realized he was nearly drained of blood. And hungry. Kneeling down, he bent over the unconscious body of the older student and thrust his fangs into her throat.

Her eyes fluttered open. "I thought so," she said.

Even transformed, she was still trying to look good to her teacher.

The Ends of the Earth

The people of a village asked the priest of that place, "Have you seen the ends of the earth?"

The priest threw his cape back with a flourish and said, "But of course!"

So the people said, "Show us."

But the priest said, "It is far away. Only a priest is fit for such a journey. You would surely not survive it."

Then a young man among them stepped forward who was strong of heart and full of vigor. His arm was stout and his legs had run many miles. He said to the priest "I shall accompany you."

The priest began to protest, but it became clear that the young man would not be dissuaded and the others among them were extolling him for his courage.

The priest therefore took the young man out of the village to shouts of acclaim and great hope.

The two of them went forth past the gates, past the farms and meadows and out into the wild that surrounded the village. They traveled for many miles, and after the first day, the young man asked how close they were to the ends of the earth. But the priest said, "We will get there when we get there." So they went forward.

After the second day, the young man asked the priest the same question, and the priest gave him again the same answer, for he hoped that the young man would grow weary of the journey and reach the end of his patience. Still, the next day, they went forward.

As sunset approached on the third day of their journey, it was the priest who had grown weary. His legs had become weak and his chest heaved with exhaustion, for he was neither strong of heart nor full of vigor, as the youth was.

So after a time, he stopped in a clearing between two groves of trees, picked up a stick from the ground and traced a line in front of them from one end of the clearing to the other. He declared, with a great deal of pomp and circumstance, "Here it is. We have come to it at last. Behold! The ends of the earth!"

The young man, though, looked beyond the line the priest had drawn and saw there a stand of oak trees and blooming flowers, rocks, an anthill, a fallen log and a small deer grazing. He therefore said to the priest, "I perceive the earth continues beyond this place."

But the priest said, "You are surely mistaken."

Then the young man asked himself, "Shall I believe the priest or shall I believe my own eyes?" And having decided at last in favor of the latter, he went forth and took a step across the line the priest had drawn.

Then he opened his mouth and spoke to the priest, saying, "What place is this that I now stand, if it is beyond the ends of the earth?"

The priest's eyes grew wide, for he was amazed. The priest's mouth fell open, for he was astonished. Then he said to the young man, "You have become a ghost and you have made yourself a demon. Because you have stepped beyond the ends of the earth, you may nevermore return to the realm of the living. Henceforth are you banished from this world."

He uttered an invocation to shun him, then he turned his back to him, shook the dust off of his feet and went his way.

The young man remained there for a time, uncertain about what he should do. But after some consideration, he grew tired of standing in solitude and stepped back across the line the priest had drawn.

Sensing nothing had changed because of his brazen act, he set out to travel back the way he had come and arrived after nearly three days at his village. He was on his way back to his own home when the priest spied him and gasped in horror, shouting for all to hear, "It is the ghost of the young man who fell off the ends of the earth!"

The youth opened his mouth to protest, but before he could remove himself, the priest's acolytes and others of the townsfolk surrounded him and laid their hands upon him, holding him fast.

"Take this demon again to the ends of the earth and remove him once and for all from the land of the living," the priest demanded, "for he is but a ghost who will haunt us if we suffer him to remain in our midst!"

They did as he bade them, forgetting that the priest had formerly told them such a journey was beyond their capacity to endure. Ushering the young man once more out of the village, they set out to return him by force to the place where the priest had first taken him. The youth objected loudly, saying, "If I be a ghost, how is it you can handle my flesh? And if I be a demon, wherefore can you bind me?"

But such was their fervor and devotion to the priest that the heard him not — or if indeed they heard him, they paid him no heed.

The priest led the rabble back to the place where he had drawn the line, which now was faded from the wind and from animals passing to and fro across it.

When they arrived, they bound the young man with strong rope and sinew. Then, at a word from the priest, they cast him over the line (making sure not to cross it themselves) and began to build a high wall along the length of it.

They labored for days, then weeks and then months to complete it, until it encircled the village and the surrounding countryside completely.

From that time forward, no man ventured beyond it, and no one from outside came in.

Many years passed, and the priest died, as did his acolytes. The hunters from the village slew every beast of the forest, for there were not enough within the wall to sustain the village and produce sufficient young that their kind might endure.

The village grew poor or lack of trade and thirsty when its wells used up their water.

At length, everyone in the village perished, and the wall in time began to crumble. Then did others come to seek their fortunes, and they remembered the tales of the village as it had been. These tales had been told to them by the descendants of their first king — a man sent in exile from that village in a time of legend.

They remembered his tale and, when they came to the place where the village had once been, they founded it anew and named it in his honor.

Thenceforth did it prosper.

But no one remembered the name of the priest.

Lost at Sea

Entombed now in this prison
That rides upon the ocean
Of roiling, seething madness
A carnival in motion

The waves toss and betray me
As scanning the horizon
My eyes seek some dear shoreline
A paradise that lies on …

A foundation sure and steady
Where daydreams spring eternal
Where bliss is more than just
A word to tease in this infernal …

Stephen H. Provost

Cell of dank and dreary sorrows
Of mold and rust and mildew
Where water drips and silence slips
Toward my certain curfew

In youth, I sought my fortune
On the wild and endless sea
So sure I was the master
Of what renders young men free

Yet now, as age consumes me
With its dull and steady ache
That freedom doth elude me
And no fortune did I make

Instead, alone I wander
From sea to sullied sea
Bereft of what I sought
Of what I had, or what's to be

I know not what awaits me
Out beyond the cold, grey mist
Except that doom, it calls me
To a cold and loveless tryst

Nightmare's Eve

A squall may pass me quickly
But 'ere I hear the thunder
Which echoes from the inside
Rending reverie asunder

The tempest keeps its distance
Yet stalks me on the seas
I daily mark its progress,
That which no man may appease

That storm will strike with fury
And I, bound by these chains
Shall thrash and rage and curse
Against the wind, against the rains

How shall I trim these sails?
So tangled and so tattered
From so many false travails
Which convinced me that they mattered

       Now useless, they above me
       Flap like pennants in the sky
       Announcing with due fanfare
       That my reckoning is nigh

       My punishment, my penance
       For my finitude, my sin
       Descend from heaven's floodgates
       Flying swift up upon the wind

Stephen H. Provost

The seas rise up beneath me
They come crashing o'er my head
I stand alone, no surrogate
To suffer in my stead

The mast falls like a hammer
The deck, it cracks and splinters
The North Wind howls and taunts me
With the breath of countless winters

And what have I accomplished
Now at this journey's end?
What legacy delivered?
What message did I send?

A note left in a bottle
May reach some distant shore
My words, they may outlive me
But my hope will live no more

The Howl & the Purr

By Steven McMillan
IPX world affairs correspondent

WASHINGTON (IPX) — As a massive armada of alien space vessels hovers over Earth, government officials acknowledge that the global initiative to exterminate the planet's population of dogs and cats was a catastrophic mistake.

Two days ago, General Laivon Kling, commander of the 10,000-ship Pholian fleet, issued a demand for unconditional surrender to every capital city on Earth; the identical message was received in Washington, Cairo, Moscow, Beijing and elsewhere.

The worldwide program to systematically round up and euthanize millions of cats and dogs appears, ironically, to have set the stage for the current crisis.

Not since the Dark Ages, when cats were condemned as "familiars" to alleged practitioners of the dark arts, has such a pogrom been undertaken — and never, even then, with such success. But now, as before, humanity is "paying the price for its hubris and its cruelty," said Sally Thurman, president of the U.S. Humane Authority.

"Without our furry friends, there was nothing to protect us against the Pholian Empire's aggression," Thurman said in a statement obtained by the International Press Exchange. "Our canine and feline friends were all that stood between us and the Pholians. When we eradicated them, we not only stabbed our most faithful companions in the back, we destroyed our only hope for peace."

The Department of Homeworld Security did not respond to a request for comment on Thurman's accusation. Neither did Dr. Winston Thorvald, whose whereabouts are unknown and who is believed to be in hiding.

How we got here

It was Thorvald's purported discovery that set the stage for the current crisis. A then-unknown associate professor at Stanford University, Thorvald published a paper that claimed to answer the seemingly innocuous riddle: "Why do cats purr?" Generations of scientists had been unable answer the question definitively, noting that cats are just as likely to purr when distressed as they are when content.

Thorvald, however, discovered that the purr was accompanied by a tiny burst of quantum energy, imperceptible to humans and capable of existing in two places at exactly the same time. The second location, he determined, was always the same place: a previously undiscovered moon on the far side of Jupiter. Further study, however, found that the "moon" did not follow a standard orbit — or any orbit — and remained hidden on the far side of the planet.

Scientists soon determined that it was not a natural phenomenon, but an artificial base constructed by a previously unknown life form, recently determined to be the warlike Pholians.

Buoyed by his success, Thorvald quickly pursued a new theory: that dogs, and particularly wolves, that "howled at the moon" might be emitting a similar quantum burst. His hunch proved correct, and he hurriedly published a second paper detailing the evidence, which once again pointed to the same artificial satellite on the far side of Jupiter. This news caused a worldwide sensation, giving rise to countless conspiracy theories.

Radio commentator Arch Lindberg declared the animals to be sophisticated androids. The Pholians, he said, had planted them on Earth millennia ago to set the stage for their ultimate invasion. A cat's contented purr was a signal to the aliens that humanity was vulnerable; its purr of distress was a cry for help to its creators. Lindberg, whose radio program boasts more than thirty million daily listeners, was echoed by fellow conservative commentators Shawna Finnegan and Riley Williams.

Meanwhile, the Rev. Octavius Beedle, founder of Redemption-Rapture Ministries, declared cats to be the "tools of the devil" and offered "rewards in heaven" to those who brought cat carcasses to an abandoned garbage dump he'd purchased and christened the Gates of Golgotha. When the League for the Prevention of Animal Cruelty obtained an injunction against Beedle's extermination program, he called upon his followers to instead drop off live cats at county animal shelters. The shelters were so inundated with felines that they had no choice but to euthanize them.

When Thorvald's second paper was released, implicating dogs in what Lindberg dubbed the "Pholian plot," Beedle declared the animals to be "hounds of hell" and called for their destruction, as well.

Public opposition to such measures was initially strong, with an early Ryder-UBC poll indicating that eighty-four percent of the public condemned Beedle's actions. That figure, however, shrank consistently over time. The euthanization of the animals continued and, at the same time, reports surfaced of heightened activity on the Pholian base. When these reports were confirmed by the government to be the result of an official satellite surveillance program, opposition to the animal deaths declined, with roughly half of those surveyed favoring such actions three months after the first poll was taken.

With continued reports of heightened activity on the Jupiter Deathmoon, as it became known on social media, the government itself adopted a quarantine program called Pet Identification and Euthanasia (PIE), encouraging citizens to surrender their pets. "Pet Depositories" were set up at animal hospitals and shelters, with the government offering tax credits to those who surrendered their cats and dogs. The program, under the auspices of the Centers for Health Maintenance and Preservation, resulted in the deaths of millions of cats and dogs in a span of just a few weeks.

Miscalculation

As more animals died, the reports of Pholian activity became more frequent and alarming. A Pholian scout ship was detected entering Earth's atmosphere over the town of Pahrump, Nevada, and flying north at a high rate of speed before disappearing over Crater Lake, Oregon. Fighter jets scrambled to intercept the craft were unable to match its speed or maneuverability and did not manage to get within more than a hundred miles of it.

Attempts by the government to dismiss the sighting as a "weather balloon" or classified test of a sophisticated anti-ballistic missile prototype were dismissed by news media and the public alike. When video of the phenomenon was leaked to YourVision, the government was forced to retract its denials.

The scout ship was followed by other, similar sightings over Florida, Southern California, the Gobi Desert and Kazakhstan, all sites of space launch activity. Shortly afterward, officials at Vandenberg and Edwards Air Force Bases found their computer programs corrupted by a virus and their defense systems inoperative.

Arch Lindberg immediately took to the airwaves and declared

that unnamed sources had told him the virus was spread by the same sort of quantum energy signature contained in the howls and purrs of "America's most insidious traitors, the feline and canine spies living among us."

Public opinion in favor of the extermination program spiked to ninety-one percent, and a special enforcement agency was formed to go from house to house and conduct thorough inspections to retrieve any animals being hidden by their owners. In one incident, the Kennel Patrol, as it was popularly known, ransacked the home of a Fresno family and forcibly removed a 6-year-old girl's kitten. When the girl resisted, a patrol officer used a stun gun to subdue her, causing a seizure that left the little girl hospitalized. Trousers, as the kitten had been named for the markings on its hindquarters, was clubbed over his head and died of trauma. The family filed a lawsuit, but it was dismissed, and the parents were detained on suspicion of obstructing justice. Polls showed a clear majority of respondents supported the Kennel Patrol's actions.

The House and Senate unanimously signed a bill declaring it a federal crime to harbor any cat or dog, with conviction of such crimes being punishable by up to 20 years in prison.

The government assured citizens that such actions would, in time, prove to be effective countermeasures against the Pholians. However, official reports of Pholian activity only increased during the period, with IPX identifying an increase of more than a dozen per week over the course of the time in question. The number of unofficial sightings, meanwhile, grew almost exponentially, and while many were easily dismissed as the product of increasing public panic, many others were ultimately verified by media watchdogs and government sources.

Early this month, the International Press Exchange can confirm the survival of only a few dozen dogs and perhaps a hundred cats, although the second figure is less reliable, given the elusive nature of the creatures.

Scientists were unable to explain the apparent correlation

between increased Pholian activity and the apparent success of the PIE program. If, as the critics suggested, the cats and dogs had signaled the Pholians to attack, their deaths should have deprived the aliens of the intelligence they had been using to infiltrate Earth's defenses. Beedle and others in the broader New Religious Purity movement argued that it was simply too late, and that the "demon dogs and hell cats" had signaled the Antichrist — whom they identified as Laivon Kling — to usher in the end of the age.

Scout ship captured

In November, the U.S. government announced that it had recovered the wreckage of a Pholian scout ship that crashed over the desert in New Mexico. The vessel had been manned by a contingent of seven Pholians, one of whom survived and was turned over to researchers for analysis. As part of that analysis, one of the few remaining dogs, a Siberian husky named Tiberius, was brought in and induced to howl at the alien. The experiment, as recorded by researchers led by Rodney G. Berry of Yale University, created a panicked response in the alien that Berry described as "an apparent mixture of agony and delirium."

"The subject," Berry stated in his report, "retreated to the farthest corner of the secure chamber and attempted to claw its way through the steel-reinforced walls, creating wounds in its appendages that secreted dark, black fluid the consistency of motor oil." A purring cat brought into the chamber elicited much the same response.

The fluids secreted by the alien were later analyzed and compared to samples taken from it prior to the exposure, and it was discovered that the 'blood' had been infected with — or transformed into — a toxic substance that had not been present before. The Pholian died within hours of the experiment.

Berry's report concluded that, instead of communicating with the Pholians, the cats and dogs had been emitting a quantum energy signature that had, effectively, kept them from attacking. "The PIE project has not kept Earth safe from an enemy attack, but to the contrary, has facilitated and even allowed it to occur," Berry wrote. "The only potential means of averting planetary conquest by this far superior alien race would be to mobilize felines and canines to repel the invaders, as they most surely would do. Unfortunately, their numbers have been reduced to such a degree that, in my estimation, they are no longer sufficient to act as an effective deterrent."

Within days of Berry's report, the Pholian armada arrived and encircled the planet, with General Kling issuing his call for unconditional surrender. Kling has demanded a response within three days.

Universal Radio Systems has announced that it has suspended Arch Lindberg's radio show, citing uncertainty as to the host's whereabouts after an angry mob was reportedly seen marching toward his home in West Sacramento.

The government, meanwhile, has issued an open call of its own for anyone knowing the location of any cat or dog to call its toll-free hotline immediately. The president, who boarded Air Force One for a secure location hours ago, has offered a full pardon to all those convicted of harboring a quarantined pet and has urged all remaining pet owners to come forward.

Sigurd Larsson, director of global intelligence during the previous administration, called the situation "dire and all but hopeless."

"The Dark Ages were nothing compared to what's coming," said Larsson, whose tuxedo cat, Malcolm, was confiscated by PIE's Kennel Patrol last month. "Our pets, it seems, were our only true line of defense. What have we done to man's best friend? With friends like us, we deserve this kind of enemy."

As of press time, the White House, the Office of the Vice President, the speaker of the House and the Senate majority leader had not responded to repeated calls for comment.

Stephen H. Provost

Editor's note: Candice Lujan in Beijing; Mallory Hogan in Antelope Valley, California; and Carl Singh with the IPX Washington Bureau contributed to this report.

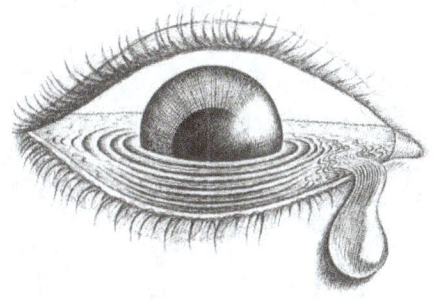

Torrent of Tears

Seeing things from every side
Was wondrous in my youth
I marveled as the colors danced
In shapes of timeless truth

Kaleidoscopic visions
Beckoned me to step inside
I ventured forth, I stumbled
Came unbalanced, lost my stride

And tumbling down the rabbit hole
E'er deeper then I fell
Beyond the gates of neverland
Beyond the fire of hell

Stephen H. Provost

Until I came to this place
Where it is, I cannot say
I lost the map to sanity
Somewhere along the way

Best friends have all betrayed me
Or they have I betrayed
And memories, they haunt me
In this crypt that I have made

Lost within a house of mirrors
Shattered dreams and shards of hope
Mocked by distorted visions
Swinging from the hangman's rope

So now I must reside here
In the dankness of despair
Breathing fumes of my own folly
Through the mist of stale air

I've lost imagination
Misplaced the art of joy
And mired in resignation
Slew myself, that little boy

I don't believe in faerie tales
Or faeries anymore
I just believe in demons
Out to settle ancient scores

I don't believe in dragons
Catching heaven in their wings
I don't believe in wizards
Saving worlds with magic rings

Nightmare's Eve

I don't believe that heroes stride
Where angels fear to tread
I only know where I abide
My heroes end up dead

    I don't believe in destiny
    Or magic wands or spells
    I don't believe the church
    Or the indulgences it sells

I don't believe in gods
Who weave a tapestry of fate
Light a candle, say a prayer
Take a number, then you wait

    I don't believe in virtue
    And I don't believe in sin
    They're really only empty words
    From tales that grifters spin

I don't believe in anything
Or anyone, you see
I once believed in someone
Yes, I once believed in me

    Upon a time I lost myself
    Within this maze of fears
    Dead ends, no happy endings
    Through the torrent of my tears

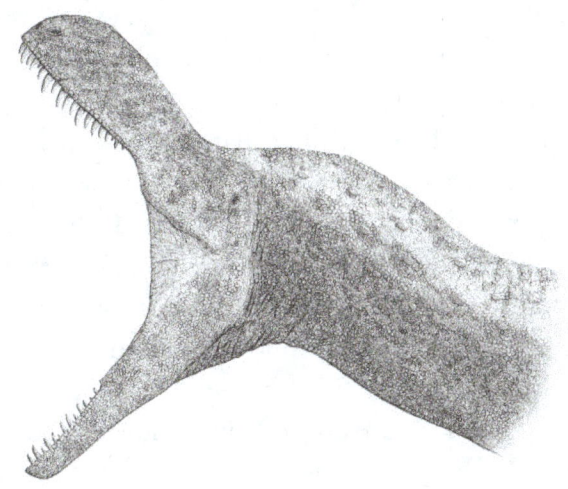

Teeth

The waiting room was what Alana had come to expect. She'd been to enough specialists, and they were all standard — although, the more specialized the doctor, the more comfortable the place was.

When the headaches started, she'd gone to an outpatient clinic and waited a couple of hours among the flu-infected, the food-poisoned and the hypochondriacs. They had magazines like Popular Mechanics and Highlights and People and Sports Illustrated, none of which she picked up for fear of catching something. She was cautious by nature, and more so lately.

She'd graduated from the clinic to a general practitioner, a hypnotherapist and, now, a neurologist, and the waiting areas had become cleaner, less crowded and more comfortable. No more straight-back hard chairs molded from yellow plastic. The chairs here were cushioned, had arms and were covered in a plush leatherette. The magazines were different, too: Forbes, Women's Health,

Psychology Today. ... Muzak played softly in the background: *Tie a Yellow Ribbon Round the Ole Oak Tree* hummed along somewhere just beneath the conscious level. It was supposed to be relaxing, soothing. But Alana was still on edge.

The nightmares had made her that way. She was sure they were related to the headaches; they'd started about the same time. The clinic had told her to take ibuprofen, and the GP had suggested a neurologist. She'd tried the hypnotherapist on her own in the meantime, but that had, if anything, only made it all worse. Instead of suppressing the memories that came through in her nightmares, hypnosis seemed to have amplified them.

So, she'd gone to Dr. Abhijeet Vilk, whose Facebook ads had touted a "revolutionary" treatment that "cured" nightmares once and for all.

She was skeptical, but desperate, so she'd made an appointment.

This was her follow-up. He'd put her at ease immediately during their initial appointment, despite his mild accent (she didn't like accents — any accent; they reminded her of her stepfather, whose thick German dialect had punctuated his frequent fits of rage). Dr. Vilk's bedside manner was impeccable. He smiled warmly, explained everything thoroughly and didn't act like he was annoyed when she asked what another doctor might have called "stupid" questions. Another plus: He saw her almost immediately, at the scheduled time. Alana was busy. A nationally syndicated newspaper columnist, she always turned her stories in before deadline; she expected the same punctuality of people she was paying for their services. But even though Dr. Vilk had been right on time of their first appointment, he hadn't rushed through it. She'd been to doctors who took her blood pressure, looked down her throat (even if that had nothing to do with why she'd made the appointment), then told her to "drink a lot of fluids" and "call if it doesn't get better" — before shooing her up to the receptionist to pay her bill. The first time she'd seen Dr. Vilk, he'd spent an entire hour with her, listening to her talk about her symptoms, checking her eyes, ears and reflexes, giving her almost a full physical. He'd even ordered a CT scan "just to be on the safe side."

This time, once again, Vilk's nurse called her back to an exam room after only a short wait. She smiled and remembered Alana's cat was named Caspar, which made Alana feel even more at ease. That was important. She didn't need any more reason for nightmares.

"How are you feeling?" asked the nurse, a thirtysomething, angular redhead with straight hair and bangs.

Alana pulled herself up onto the tan cushions of the examination table, leaving her legs to dangle over the side. "The same," she conceded. "If anything, it's gotten worse. I had this dream last night …"

The nurse put two fingers on Alana's wrist to take her pulse. It was racing. "Try to relax." She smiled reassuringly.

Alana's pulse didn't stop racing.

The blood pressure cuff was next. 147 over 95. Then the thermometer — at least they didn't stick them down your throat anymore; just touched it to your forehead for an instant, then pulled it away. Her temperature was normal, but she could feel herself perspiring.

The nurse took a step back and sat down on a chair facing Alana, looking her straight in the eye. "What did you dream?"

And Alana told her: "There was this crocodile … its teeth were dripping with blood," she said. "It wasn't normal, though. The blood was thick, like syrup, and there was stuff between its teeth. Stuck there. Like pieces of flesh and gristle." Alana felt herself shiver as she described it, but the nurse seemed unaffected, as if she'd heard it somewhere before. But that was impossible. She was probably just trained to keep her cool; not to upset the patients any more than they already were.

"Go on," she said.

But Alana couldn't. She shut her eyes tight, but that only made the image of the crocodile appear against the back of her closed lids. She even thought she could hear it breathing, a soft wheeze as it exhaled that pushed her back further inside herself. The creature's eyes were a sickly yellow, and its breath smelled rancid.

Her eyes flew open.

"It's okay," the nurse said, taking her hand and squeezing it. "Don't say anything more. The doctor knows all about this kind of thing. He's treated dozens of patients with dreams just like the one you've been having. It will be fine. Really." She smiled again and stood up, reaching into a transparent plastic magazine rack affixed to the wall and pulling out a copy of Better Homes & Gardens. "Look at this while you're waiting. It has some really cool articles. I've read it myself. The one on topiaries is really interesting. The doctor will see you shortly."

"Topiaries," Alana repeated, taking the magazine. She didn't give a damn about topiaries, but the woman's voice was at once persuasive and reassuring.

The woman turned and left the room, closing the door behind her. As the latch clicked, wordless background music began to play: *Killing Me Softly*, the insipid drone from the speaker punctuated by the tick-tock-tick-tock-tick of an old-style clock, with a white face, black hands and a red second hand that stuck momentarily at each minute notch before clicking forward. Alana thought she heard a faint whir in from the mechanism that kept it running; she didn't see a cord, so she assumed it to be a battery.

To the left of the clock were three certificates, one recognizing Dr. Vilk as a neurologist, the second announcing an advanced degree in psychiatry, and the third his diploma from NYU. She hadn't realized he was also a psychiatrist. Maybe that explained his easy manner with patients.

Alana's head snapped sideways as the door latch clicked and the brown faux wood swung inward. Dr. Vilk strode through the opening, his long, white gown swishing just above his ankles and a stethoscope dangling from around his neck. Alana thought for a moment it looked as if two tentacles were growing out of his skin there, and she looked away involuntarily.

"Good morning, Alana," he said easily, extending his hand. "I understand you aren't feeling any better than the last time we talked."

She shook her head, hoping he wouldn't ask her to repeat her dream about the alligator. She squinched her eyes together briefly at the thought of it, then opened them quickly, hoping he'd think she was just blinking.

"Can you tell me about your dreams?"

Alana hesitated. "I'd rather not, but if it will help …"

The doctor nodded his head once, deliberately. "I think it will. It will help you come to terms with them, bring them to the surface so you can deal with them — see them for what they are — until we can put an end to them."

Put an end to them. That sounded encouraging. She wondered how he planned to do that.

"Are you psychoanalyzing me?"

"No," he laughed easily. "I'm trying to make things easier for you. I am a psychiatrist, too, you know. What did you dream about this past week?"

She told him about the crocodile dream, wincing at the part where she described its teeth. She'd been afraid of sharp teeth since she was a child. A German shepherd from next door had gotten loose when she was five and had come bounding across the yard at her. It used to be a police dog, and it had been trained to help the neighbor lady, who was legally blind, find her way around. But there was something about Alana that had made it react differently. It had snapped at her, its white teeth sharp and glistening, as it barked and whined at the same time. Her mother had pulled her away in the nick of time, and her stepfather had shouted at her about getting too close to "animals that don't belong to you."

She had cried and screamed and wailed that the dog was going to kill her, but it hadn't mattered to her stepfather. It hadn't mattered to him that the dog had run onto *their* yard to attack *her*.

She remembered seeing saliva in the dog's mouth, flying off its teeth as it snapped at her, and she had a vague memory of the dog disappearing after that. She overheard someone saying it was rabid, and her stepfather cursing her for being stupid enough to get so close to it.

She'd had nightmares about that dog and its teeth — fangs — too, so she told Dr. Vilk about those. In the dreams, she was an adult, but the dog was still bigger than she was, the way it had been when she was a little girl. Its eyes were big and menacing, the markings over them making them appear that the animal was glowering at her, sizing her up and getting ready to *eat* her, drooling and frothing at the mouth all the while.

The doctor smiled softly and sadly as she told him. "I understand," he said. "What other dreams have you had?"

It occurred to Alana that it was strange for the doctor to be asking her this. But then again, he was a psychiatrist — he had training in this field — so maybe it wasn't so strange after all. She brushed aside her misgivings and continued.

"I was at a circus with my mother and stepfather," she said. She never said, "my parents." Her stepfather wasn't her parent. Not in her mind. "It was late at night — later than it should have been. All the other people at the circus had left, but the person in charge of the circus, the ringmaster, was putting on a show just for me. He brought out this beautiful tiger and made it jump through hoops, and I was so happy to see it all, like I was a little girl again. It stood up on its hind legs and pawed at the air, but then …"

"Yes?"

"Then it opened its mouth and the teeth inside — they were long like a saber-tooth tiger's, but narrow and pointy, like … I don't know … like railroad spikes, only white. They were whiter than they should be. Like a full moon on a dark night."

"What happened then?"

"The tiger jumped down from the platform and mauled the ringmaster, ripping at him with its claws. Then it opened its mouth and bit his head off, holding the head in its mouth and tossing its head back, like it had a trophy. There was blood coming from the head, like a fountain. There isn't that much blood in someone's head, is there?"

Dr. Vilk shook his head. "No, there isn't."

But Alana didn't wait for him to say anything more. She was talking over him now, as though she were back in the dream. The tiger had tossed the ringmaster's severed head aside, and it had landed in her mother's lap. She had screamed and stood up, wanting to run, but her legs wouldn't work. Her feet felt fastened to the floor, as if someone had taken a hammer and nailed them to the wooden stands beside the circus ring. The tiger was bounding toward her now, mouth open, those teeth seeming to grow even larger as it ran toward her. …

Alana's hands were balled up into fists; perspiration was dripping off her forehead. Her eyes watered and itched, as her head twitched nervously.

The doctor reached out and took her hands, jarring loose the images. "It's okay," he was saying. "You don't have to say anymore. Put it out of your mind. I had no idea the dreams were so vivid and … disturbing.

"I'm sorry, Alana," he said, his voice so full of sympathy it would have sounded forced if it hadn't been for the gentleness in his soft, brown eyes. Her breathing was ragged, and it came in fits and starts.

"Take a deep breath."

She heard him and focused on his voice. It was calming. She did as he told her.

"That's it. Now another."

Cool air filled her lungs as she pulled it into her. It felt good. The images at the back of her mind faded, gradually.

"Yes, good," the doctor said, then waited until she raised her head again to look at him.

"Have you had these panic attacks before?"

She nodded, and he smiled.

"I thought so. But here's the good news, Alana. I think I know the cause of it, and we can do something about it."

She swallowed. "You can?"

"Yes. I've diagnosed your problem," he said. His tone sounded hopeful, but behind it, there was a tinge of something else. He was holding something back.

"You're not telling me something," Alana said. "What is it?"

Vilk took what wasn't exactly a deep breath, but it was more deliberate than normal.

"It isn't the easiest thing to hear," he said finally. He paused for a couple of seconds to gather himself, then locked his eyes on hers, having apparently decided what it was he wanted to say. "Don't worry," he said, the syllables coming more quickly. "It's very treatable, and it's not terminal. No, not at all. It's just a little … graphic. I mean …" He stumbled over the words again. He had always seemed composed up until now, but he appeared nervous, like he wanted to tell her something unpleasant but was unsure of how do go about it.

"Are you uncomfortable with needles?" he asked.

She shook her head. "No. Why? Do I need a shot or something?"

He shook his head, then tossed it back, as if he were thinking. "No, no. Well, you might, but that's not why I asked."

Alana sat up straighter. "Doc, what's wrong with me," she said. "Nothing you can say would be worse than the nightmares I've been having."

The doctor nodded once firmly, as if pulling himself together. He took the stethoscope from around his neck and set it aside. "That's what I have to tell you. About your nightmares."

He stepped sideways to the wall at their left and flicked a switch; a fluorescent glow emanated out from behind translucent panels. Opening a folder, he pulled out a large negative and used a metal clip to fasten it in front of one of the panels. "Your CT scan," he said, using an open palm to beckon her closer.

She leaned in.

"Here," he said, his voice matter-of-fact, pointing to one section of the image. "See that area of the brain? That's your prefrontal cortex."

"Yeah. What's that dark spot? Is that supposed to be there?"

Vilk paused. "Uh … no. It's not."

"What is it?"

"There's not really a name for it," Vilk said. He still seemed to be tiptoeing around things.

"Doc, if it's cancer, just tell me. It runs in the family, and if I've got it, I'd rather know than …"

"It's not cancer," he said. "It's not a tumor or growth or anything like that. It's … a foreign body."

"In my *head?*"

"I'm afraid so. It's a kind of parasite."

Alana pulled back, away from the X-ray image. She'd heard about mad cow disease. Was this something like that? A parasite? Like a tapeworm? She remembered a story of about some guy in England who had felt something clogging up his sinuses and tried to blow his nose. He couldn't get any mucous out, but he could barely breathe, so he kept blowing. Harder and harder. Until blood started coming out, and then … a long tapeworm, seemingly never-ending, had begun to emerge from one of his nostrils. It had made the Englishman gag, causing him to wretch and vomit even as the parasite emerged, its segmented body torn to pieces by his violent fit.

Was *that* what was in her *brain?* Was it *eating* her gray matter?

Or was it something more like a leech? As punishment for some forgotten transgression, her stepfather had told her the story of how he'd fallen off a boat in the bayou one summer and wound up covered in leeches. She never knew whether the story was true or was just meant to scare her. He'd enjoyed scaring her, and he still scared her, even though she hadn't seen the man in more than twenty years. The images of those leeches clinging to his arms, his legs, his backside — he'd described it all, and the way they'd clung to his skin as he tried to pull them off. The blood that started dripping … was it from the man's body or from the leeches? The pink circles left behind as he pulled them away. … She saw it all in her mind's eye, and it was not something she'd ever wanted to see. But she dreamt about it even now. It was one of her nightmares.

All this raced through her thoughts in only a few seconds. She shivered involuntarily and felt suddenly light-headed. Was it the impact of what the doctor was telling her, or was she feeling that way because of the … the … parasite?

Vilk must have seen something in her expression, because he reached out with both hands and took her gently by the shoulders, steadying her.

"Please don't worry," he said in a tone half-apologetic, half-fervent. "We *can* treat this. We know what it is, so we know how to react to it. That's a lot more than we knew a week ago. It may not seem like it, but this is great progress."

Alana was still shivering, but managed to force a shaky nod. She couldn't bring herself to look the doctor in the eye, though, fearing she might see something there that his voice had been hiding.

He let go of her shoulders, but she still felt unsteady, as though she might teeter forward or off to one side. She stiffened both her arms and planted her fists on either side of her, making indentations in the exam table cushions.

She swallowed and came out with it: "Is this like mad cow disease?" she sputtered. "Will this thing *eat* my brain?"

In her nervousness, she almost laughed at her own question. What did she think this thing was? A zombie worm?

"No," Vilk said, but just as she started feeling reassured, he added, "not exactly."

Alana took a deep breath and held it, then exhaled slowly.

"It doesn't feed off the brain itself. It feeds off your dreams. It releases a hormone that stimulates a stress response, but only while you're sleeping. It's this hormone that produces the nightmares."

"Is there anything you can give me … to stop this hormone? Make that thing die? Can you make me stop dreaming?"

"That may not be possible. I don't know of anything, chemically speaking, that would suppress your dreams. We could deprive you of REM sleep, but that would likely increase your anxiety and, once the deprivation ends, you might be even worse off than before. I'll be honest with you: I've dealt with these parasites before, and the best way to treat them is to remove them."

"You mean surgically?"

"Yes."

"And you've performed this operation?"

"Yes."

Alana nodded firmly. "Then may I see one?"

Vilk's eyes widened slightly. He seemed surprised by the request. "See what?"

"One of these parasites. If you've removed them before, you must have a dead specimen lying around somewhere? Right."

"Well, yes ..."

"Then I want to see it, if that's all right. If I see, close up, what I'm dealing with, it will make me feel better — especially if the thing's dead."

Vilk hesitated. "That ... might not be a good idea."

Alana's eyes narrowed. She was still shivering inside, but she was trying to steel herself. How bad could it be?

"Why not?"

Vilk clasped his hands together and, for the first time, seemed to be avoiding her eyes, his pupils shifting to the left, away from her face. "It's not pleasant," he said, his voice lower than it had been. But then, looking back at her again, he said, "All right. Maybe it's for the best. I'll be right back."

The doctor returned a moment later carrying a Petri dish. In the center was a small, brownish-black *thing*, sitting motionless; not even a quarter-inch long, it looked like nothing so much as a slug that had crawled out onto the front porch during a rain. Or a miniature version of one of those leeches, the kind her stepfather had told her about. A tiny pool of slimy liquid surrounded it and, as she watched it, Alana thought she saw it twitch.

"Is that thing still *alive*?" she said, pursing her lips and pulling her head back as though from the stench of sour milk.

"Oh, no." Dr. Vilk's voice had shed its earlier, reticent tone; he had returned to its normal, reassuring manner.

She leaned in closer, but it didn't twitch again. She must have imagined it. It was disgusting to think a slug-thing like the one in the Petri dish might be inside her, but she told herself it wasn't as bad as it could have been. She remembered the video of the Englishman expelling the tapeworm from his nostril. It wasn't anything like that. Knowing it was in her *brain*, though, and was causing these nightmares. ... Well, Dr. Vilk was right. At least they knew the cause of it, so they could treat it. Even if it meant brain surgery, that was better than having something like *that* in her head.

"Here," Dr. Vilk said, handing her a magnifying class. "This will give you a better look at it."

Alana took the glass from him and put it over the thing in the Petri dish. Leaning in, she adjusted it up and down to remove the blur. It looked much larger; she could see what looked like red veins running across its brown-black flesh. Not flesh, really. More like a membrane. Those veins ... were they pulsating? It *was* alive. She was sure of it. She shuddered but forced herself to keep looking, up toward the larger end of it, what she thought must be its head. There, she saw ... screaming, she flung the magnifying glass away from her. It clattered to the floor and came to rest underneath a nearby cabinet.

Alana closed her eyes tight, hunched her shoulders and pulled her arms inward, protective.

She felt the doctor's hand soft against her back, between her shoulder blades, but despite its gentleness there was no comfort in his touch. She barely felt it, her mind fixed instead on the image that seared itself into her memory even as she sought to repulse it from her mind. Teeth. Dozens of long, sharp teeth extending from an open maw. Like needles ... the doctor had asked her if she was afraid of *needles*. Or like the crocodile from her nightmare. Was that *thing* feeding her subconscious mind images of itself, in a familiar form she could understand? She was shivering now almost to the point of convulsing. In her mind, she saw the red veins on the thing's slime-covered body throbbing, the mouth opening wider, the eyeless head curling back across the body to "look" at her.

"It's all right. It can't hurt you," Vick said, his soft tone caressing her ears.

Alana's head was shaking as she forced herself to open her eyes and look at him. "Get it *out of me*!" she all but screamed.

"Shhhh. It's all right. We will schedule a time …"

"Get it out of me *now*!"

Tears came, convulsive sobs, as she leaned into the doctor and put her wet eyes against his shoulder, dampening his lab coat. She felt him patting her shoulder. The next thing she knew, he'd be stroking her hair. What the hell? Was he doing all this to take advantage of her?

She pulled back.

He was just looking at her. Then he suddenly seemed to realize something and he stood up, taking a step backward. "Excuse me a moment," he said, and left the room abruptly.

Dr. Vilk closed the door hastily behind him, just as one of the nurses — a gangly twentysomething named Jason with a page-boy haircut — passed him in the hallway. Vilk caught the young man by the arm and pulled him in close, speaking just above a whisper.

"Nurse, I need you to prep the patient in Room 3 for the procedure."

The young man blinked. "Doctor, I didn't think we were equipped for invasive … " His voice was too loud for Vilk's liking, so the doctor pulled him farther down the hall.

"We're equipped for what *I say* we're equipped for," he said, his normally smooth tone gone; his cadence clipped and decisive.

Vilk had no intention of performing surgery, but he didn't need his patient — or the nurse — to know that. The woman was desperate, which was good. Desperation broke down resistance and moved the process along. But there was a fine line between desperation and panic, which could send a patient running for the door. Vilk had to guard against that. He had to strike while the iron was hot, but not make it so hot that the patient started to suspect she was getting burned.

So, he was careful to balance his own calculated, smooth demeanor against the disturbing image of the parasite. Precision was needed in order to alarm the patient without scaring her away. But he'd miscalculated by allowing her to cry on his shoulder. She'd thought he was trying to take advantage of her ... which he was, just not in *that* way. Jason was the perfect choice to smooth things over. With his boyish looks (he still struggled with a mild case of acne) and awkward bearing, he was as non-threatening as they came.

She would look at his face, reassured, and look at that X-ray he'd left behind in the room, the fluorescent light bleeding through behind it, and she'd know what she must do.

Jason would comfort her, get her to sign the needed forms, then leave her to change into the hospital gown.

"We'll take care of this right away," he'd say. "You'll walk out of here feeling one-hundred percent."

They weren't Jason's words; Vilk had told him to say that to every patient. It was all rehearsed.

He'd return to shave the side of her head — a pointless exercise in any practical sense, but a necessary ruse. The patient would have to believe she was about to have surgery, even if introducing the parasite to the patient's brain was far simpler. Just anesthetize her, turn her head sideways and moisten the ear canal with two or three drops of lubricant. Then use a pair of tweezers to — gently — pick up the creature and insert it into the aural canal. *It* would do the rest, wriggling and boring its way in over the course of the next few minutes. By the time the patient awoke, it would be firmly attached, feeding off her.

Yes, he would be inserting the parasite *into* her. It wasn't already there. The X-ray had been a fake, another ruse: It hadn't shown Alana's brain at all; it was, instead, the product of a CT scan performed on an earlier patient, *after* the parasite had been inserted. The nightmares Alana had experienced before she had come to her? They had been caused by nothing more than her own overactive imagination. The content of those dreams, with their toothy demons, was a fortunate coincidence.

Vilk had done this now more than a dozen times, and he was good at it. Attract suitable candidates, vet them properly with an extensive survey, then reassure them until they trusted him implicitly. The psych degree helped; it was real, not just a forged piece of paper. He didn't need one, because he really had done the work. What was so wrong with profiting from it?

And profit he did. He charged a pretty penny for his services, and even better, they were covered by most insurance. All he had to do was get the word out, and traditional advertising only went so far. The best recommendations came from satisfied customers … patients willing to tell anyone who would listen — preferably on camera — how much Vilk's "procedure" had helped them. People like Alana, or, rather, like she would be by the time she left his office today.

Alana had been the perfect candidate. On her survey, she had checked all the right boxes. Nightmares. Anxiety. Insomnia. Problems concentrating. Missed days at work. And her descriptions of those nightmares had seemed tailor-made for his procedure: so vivid, so debilitating, that she felt she had no other option but to trust him.

Alana got down off the table and paced back and forth for a few moments, putting her hand up to her temple, where her hair had been. She rubbed the newly bald spot, running her hand up and down across it. There was no mirror in here, but she imagined what she must look like. Her hair, long and silky brown, was one of her best features. Or had been. Now she would have to deal with it being gone until it could grow back.

After a few moments, she crossed the room to the plastic chair near the door and forced herself to sit down. Even so, her right toe started tapping uncontrollably at the floor. Something seemed off-kilter here, but her sleep-deprived brain couldn't pinpoint what it was. Whatever it might be, it wasn't as bad as the nightmares. It might even be a product of those nightmares, bleeding over into the waking world. She was having trouble telling the difference anymore.

Waiting made it worse. Sitting in a hospital gown that hadn't closed fully behind her, so the flesh of her buttocks was pressed up against the cold plastic of the chair. She'd taken off her underwear along with the rest of her clothes, putting them all in a pile on the floor; she thought about going to pick them up, but apart from her incessantly tapping foot, she felt paralyzed. Besides, the cold sensation on her backside was quickly fading as she warmed the seat.

When the doctor finally returned, he smiled and apologized for the delay. "We hadn't expected to perform the procedure today, but I was able to juggle some things and accommodate you," he said. "We're all ready, now. If you'll please follow me this way?"

She didn't follow, actually; he opened the door and ushered her out of the room and insisted that she walk ahead of him, keeping himself between her and the exit and they walked down the corridor, away from the building's exterior. Alana was vaguely aware of this and, on some level, found it mildly troubling. But everything troubled her now. The fluorescent lights assaulted her from overhead, making her eyes water; the sanitized smell of the doctor's office made her queasy; the tan walls seemed like a prison.

Suddenly self-conscious, she reached around behind her and

pulled the hospital gown shut. Why hadn't she put her underwear back on? Why had she taken them off in the first place? Vilk hadn't told her she needed to … or had he? There was that hug in the office … She'd heard about doctors taking advantage of their patients.

"Are you going to put me under?" she asked, looking at him over your shoulder.

"Just try to relax," he said. "Everything will be just fine."

"But …," she stopped in front of him, but he put a hand on the middle of her back and urged her forward.

She didn't have the energy to resist.

They moved forward.

Through a door and into another room, with a long surgical table covered in dark, square foam padding. There were restraints where the arms went, and her eyes immediately went to them.

"Just a precaution to keep you in place during the procedure."

She sat on the table and lay back.

"Are you going to put me under during the procedure?" she asked again.

He waited until he had secured the wrist straps before answering. "It's an invasive procedure, so yes, we have to," he said. "If we didn't, you'd be in severe pain. You don't want that, do you?"

The fluorescent lights overhead were making her eyes water even more, but she couldn't wipe them because her hands were tied down.

"Is something wrong?"

"My eyes."

The doctor pulled a tissue out of a cardboard box, and she saw it descend toward her eyes. She closed them and felt it dab against her face gently. Why wasn't the doctor wearing gloves? Or a mask?

"This will be a simple procedure," he said. "You won't be under for more than half an hour, and you'll feel like a new person once it's all over."

"The nightmares will be gone?"

"The nightmares will be gone."

She bit her lower lip and suddenly shook her head. "I don't want to be put under," she said firmly.

"That's the only way we can do this," the doctor said. "Even if we discount the pain, if you were awake for the procedure, you would move around too much. We're going to be operating on your brain. The slightest movement could cause something to go wrong."

"I don't think I want to do this." Alana's eyes were more than watering now; they were stinging. "Not today … I need to think."

The doctor put the X-ray in front of her face. She could see that *thing* inside her. Inside her brain.

She squeezed her eyes shut against the tears.

"That's what's inside you. We have to get it out. If we don't, it will grow as it feeds off your dreams, and it will begin crowding out your brain tissue. You will become a vegetable."

Alana shook her head. It didn't make sense. He hadn't planned to do the surgery today at all; now he was all but demanding to do it. With his *bare hands*. No one else was in the room. No nurse. No other doctor. Just him. This wasn't right. It wasn't …

She pushed up against the wrist restraints, but they held fast. She was weak from lack of sleep, but even at full strength, she wouldn't have been able to move them.

"Shhh. Relax now." The doctor's voice was melodic, almost sing-song. "It will all be over shortly. You have nothing to worry about. Really. Now I'm going to put this over your nose and mouth" — it was a piece of plastic connected to a tube; she could hear the gas moving through it — "and all you have to do is breathe normally."

Alana wanted to struggle, wanted to resist, but she had no energy left in her. Maybe she was imagining all this. Maybe the doctor really was wearing a mask. She was so tired, she couldn't think straight. Maybe this was part of another nightmare. She couldn't even tell the difference anymore. Whatever it was, it was still better than the things with all those gleaming white teeth that attacked her in the worst of her nightmares. The crocodile. That vicious dog from her childhood. All those *teeth*.

She was almost sobbing as the plastic nose-and-mouthpiece descended upon her. Then, before she knew it, the nightmare became real.

The parasite wriggled down into Alana's ear canal and burrowed its way into her brain. There was no blood. It was a simple procedure. All went as planned. It was seamless; no fuss, no muss. The doctor watched as Alana slept, her chest rising and falling in rhythm, with an occasional seizure every thirty seconds or so. This was part of the process; evidence that the worm was integrating itself into her being.

It wouldn't be long now.

The teeth. They were everywhere now. Snapping at her, saliva flying off them, their owners gnashing and snarling at her. Rabid dogs in a pack surrounding her. The crocodile climbing up through a layer of green slime out of black, fetid waters. A white tiger with red eyes. Hyenas laughing as they bared fangs that belonged to a rattlesnake.

"It's all just a dream," Alana told herself, but the more she told herself that, the more real it became.

How long had it been? She was vaguely aware she was supposed to wake up, but from what? She had forgotten.

Was she already awake?

Her memory was fragmenting along with her awareness, the way it does when you're driving a dark, abandoned highway in the middle of the night and you follow one curve after another until you're sure you're going in circles. Your eyelids get heavy, and it seems like you've been there before; you fight to stay on the right side of the broken white line that separates you from what you know must be disaster, but you forget which side of that line you're supposed to be on. Then the line itself fades from your consciousness and all that's left is the black strip in front of you, bleeding off into the darkness, becoming one with it. ...

Until you abandon your car and start running.

Toward something or away from it. Or both. And here, on this imaginary highway in the middle of Alana's nightmare, there were teeth. She felt herself spinning, as though she were drunk, but always she spun toward those teeth — never away from them. She turned away, and they were there. She ran, and they appeared out of a dark mist in front of her. She closed her eyes and they flashed open again involuntarily, staring into a gaping maw filled with row upon row of sparkling white daggers.

She felt the saliva fly out of that mouth and hit her in the face, run down her cheek, mingling perversely with her sweat, her tears. Becoming part of her. Surrounding her. Swallowing her. Becoming her.

She fell down, sobbing.

Time had passed. But how much? She didn't know.

It might have been hours or days or even weeks.

She realized vaguely, on the dim edge of her fading consciousness, that the restraints were gone. Her wrists were free.

But she was trapped. Inside.

At the brink of being severed from reality, she was dimly aware that she was filming a commercial for Dr. Abhijeet Vilk's dream therapy, smiling broadly as she told the world how Dr. Vilk's revolutionary methods had transformed her life — had cured her insomnia, had eased her anxiety, had saved her job. With her renewed focus, she had earned the praise of her supervisors and even received a promotion. She had met a man who treated her the way she'd always dreamed of being treated. ...

These words were not her own. She spoke them on the outside while she lay trapped and dying on the inside. They were whispered as suggestions in her inner ear by the parasite that Vilk had placed there, the sickening slug he knew how to manipulate to make her say whatever he wanted. That *thing* with its razor teeth and slimy, pulsating body. In the rare moments when her nightmares faded, it was the only image she saw. Soon it would be her only memory, her faithful companion in the darkness.

Abhijeet Vilk smiled at the success of his work. Alana's testimonial would bring in dozens of new patients, he was sure. All he would need was more of parasites to replicate the procedure, and for that he would need Alana one last time.

She made her final appointment with him six months after her own procedure and walked, docile, into the same room where she'd screamed and fought and cried so hard before. Now, however, she smiled sweetly as he put the plastic breathing mask over her nose and mouth, and inhaled deeply. This time, the doctor was wearing gloves and a surgical mask — not for Alana's benefit, but to be sure his true patients weren't harmed.

Cutting into the skin of her nostrils with an electrosurgical tool, he peeled the skin back up and over the cartilage all the way to the bone.

They would feel the cool air.

They would come.

Wriggling out, tiny and eager to start their new lives in his service.

One by one, the baby parasites emerged, slipping out of the cavity and down across her motionless lower lip, leaving a trail of slime as they tumbled down into the Petri dish where Dr. Vilk collected them. He wondered idly whether these small creatures remembered Alana's dreams and whether they might somehow transfer them to their next host. It was impossible to know, but it was of no consequence. What mattered was that they would serve his purpose — just as Alana had served hers.

Her body would heal from the operation, but her mind would

not. The shell of who she once was would seem happy and content, while the remnants of her true self wasted away inside a nightmare without end.

It was regrettable, but it was the cost of doing business.

Dr. Vilk took a deep breath and left the room with his prizes, for whom he would soon find suitable homes, planted deep and cozy in the recesses of another fertile mind. It was ironic, really, he thought to himself, that an endless string of nightmares should make his dreams come true.

The shell of the person who had once been Alana McCall sat down at her computer and let her fingers rest on the keys. They felt familiar, even though nothing inside her did. It was good to be back at work again.

Her fingers began moving, as if directed by something outside her. But the something was inside.

Deep inside.

The words flowed, as they always had when she was inspired. She had a new muse now, and all was right with the world.

"This is the story of my journey from terror to awakening," she wrote. "And it's all thanks to an amazing man named Dr. Abhijeet Vilk …"

A Never-Setting Sun

Panic stalks its prey in nighttime's depths
Where semblance swirls
Where terror twirls
Disguising future folly as regret

Anxiety is dreamtime's only heir
I like awake
I writhe and shake
A captive of this soul in disrepair

Stephen H. Provost

I lie here now; why should I rise?
What should I find with open eyes
Save cold reflections of my past
So ill-disguised by circumstance …

Which changes, yet is 'ere the same?
Complicit jailers, guilt and blame
Condemn me to this reverie
Of what has been yet cannot be

Each daybreak am I risen from the grave
I bathe in light
Until the night
Returns me to this prison I have made

Yet who am I to rail against the dark?
Which lives inside
Where night abides
Extinguishing the flame before the spark

Look not into the murky haze
Becoming captive to the gaze
Of your eyes staring back at you
From long ago, when hope was new

Reflections in the looking glass
Beyond which none save Alice pass
Invite us go where no one can
Without the ancient ferryman

My demons pitch their battles 'ere the morn
Consumed by need
To kill the seed
Of ev'ry hope or new desire born

Nightmare's Eve

My body heaves and shudders
    with each breath
I toss, I turn
As mem'ries burn
And comfort dies a thousand silent deaths

    If I should climb this endless stair
    And count the footfalls, each a prayer
    To absent gods, neglectful saints
    Who mock and scorn this mortal's plaint

    At least then should I stay the course
    Of endless reckoning's remorse
    Until my labored breathing fails
    Beneath the weight of these travails

Taunted by my own afflicted mind
Which ever spurned
What might be learned
From choices made and chances left behind

I linger wakeful, longing for new sleep
Yet fearing still
The sandman's will
I do forbear his company to keep

    Should I repeat the echoed cries
    Of fairytales and lullabies
    That happy endings did forsake,
    Of promises that parents break

Stephen H. Provost

To shield us from the barren truth
Assailing us beyond our youth
That ev'ry nightmare's sire is found
In waking sight and waking sound

Indulge me this, I pray thee, and forgive
That I should share
My own despair
And taint the joyous life you wish to live

For when I wish to wake, I slumber on
Then wakefulness
That cold caress
Ensnares me long when I would sleep anon

And if one day I lose my mind
Amid the rubble left behind
From fractured faith and shattered song
And fallen stars I've wished upon

Remember me with fondness still
This broken man of broken will
Who might have been and could have done
Beneath a never-setting sun

The Faithful Dog

Six shepherds took their flocks to pasture in the rolling hills many miles from the city. There they found a great expanse of grassland, and their sheep had more than their fill.

The shepherds were content until it came about that a pack of wolves came down from the forest and attacked the flocks. Five of the shepherds lost many sheep, but in the morning they noticed that not a single sheep from the sixth man's flock was missing.

They therefore went to the man and said, "What sorcery is this? How is it that the wolves have taken so many of our sheep, yet have not harmed a single one of yours?"

But the sixth shepherd said, "Friends, it is no sorcery. The wolves visited my flocks in the night as well, but my sheep were well guarded by my shepherd dog, Arturo."

Then the other men became jealous and said, "We do not believe you. We believe your good fortune is the work of a demon. If indeed your dog is such a fine protector, let him protect our flocks, as well!"

So the shepherd said, "As you wish."

The next night, however, the wolves returned. And though Arturo chased most of them away, he could not be in so many places at once. When he fought off one of the wolves from the north, another came in from the east. And when he guarded the eastern edge of the grassland, another attacked from the south.

One of the wolves came upon him from the west, and would not yield, sinking his teeth into the flank of a large, plump lamb. So Arturo growled and leapt upon him, fighting him fiercely until the wolf at last drew back.

But when the owner of the sheep heard the sound of the wolf howling, he rushed out to find the sheep lame and Arturo's coat strewn with blood.

He therefore cried aloud, saying, "See what this dog has done? Now we see who the real demon is!"

He went to the others and told them this, and together they made their way to the house of the sixth shepherd in order to accuse him.

"What treachery is this?" they demanded. "Your dog is the one who was attacking our flocks all along. This is why none of your sheep were killed!"

They beat the shepherd with their fists and stoned Arturo until he was so badly hurt he could no longer raise his head. Then they went back to their own fields, congratulating themselves for having preserved their flocks from such a demon.

But that night, the wolves came again, and neither Arturo nor his shepherd was there to oppose them. The wolves came in and devoured as many sheep as they could eat, for indeed it was a great feast. And when morning came, the shepherds were all dismayed.

They said, "What is this evil that has befallen us? Surely that devil of a shepherd and his hound from hell are behind this. They have struck out now at us in retribution, as is the way of demons. We should never have shown them kindness or mercy!"

They picked up sticks and stones, and they went straightaway to the shepherd's home, where they slew both the man and Arturo. Then they returned to their own fields, saying to themselves, "Now, we will know peace at last, and our flocks will prosper."

Yet again, the wolves returned, taking even more of their sheep, so that they became despondent and said, "Behold, the demons haunt us even from the grave!" But they knew not what more they could do. From that time forward, the wolves feasted every night, until not a single sheep remained in the fertile fields.

So it was that the five shepherds lived the rest of their lives as beggars and as paupers, never understanding that they had slain the ones who tried hardest to help them. For such is the way of men: They see what they want to see and believe what they wish to believe, regardless of what the truth might be.

Lamp Unto My Fate

England, 1896

Maximus insisted upon being called by his entire given name. No one referred to him as Max. Not his fellow barristers, not his business associates, not even the few members of his family with whom he remained, reluctantly, in touch.

At first blush, this has absolutely nothing to do with the matter at hand, but it's worth noting because Maximus Lynch was a fastidious sort. An attorney with the prestigious firm of Brimly and Brumly, he had developed a reputation for drawing contracts that were beyond reproach, a talent that had earned him the nickname Ironclad Lynch. Had he been born a hundred years later, he would likely have been diagnosed with OCD. But having come into this world during the Victorian Age, he was merely considered extremely obsessive and a tad compulsive (and never in the least disorderly).

He was always punctual, and one might have said there was never a hair out of place, save for the fact that top of his head was almost completely bald. For this reason, he always wore a hat — a

193

black derby to be specific — that was invariably tilted at a specific angle to shade his eyes from the sun at precisely five thirty-five in the afternoon on December twenty-seventh, the time at which he had purchased it from Harrington's Haberdashery.

Being fastidious and, therefore, abnormally encumbered by routine, Maximus Lynch would frequent the same few establishments whenever he went about his business. One of these was definitely *not* Abernathy's Secondhand Emporium on High Street, which was not only two blocks beyond his usual walking circuit, but was also (as the name was meant to indicate) a secondhand store.

He had never purchased anything secondhand in his thirty-nine years and seven months on this earth, and there was no reason to believe he would start now … were it not for a malfunction in the city's newly completed and much-ballyhooed sewer system, which chose this particular time and this particular place to display its shortcomings. Hundreds of gallons of water suffused with human urine, excrement and who knows what else spilled out onto the very avenue that Maximus traversed in his daily routine.

The sudden torrent of muck directly in his path sent him in the opposite direction at a pace uncomfortably more hurried than his normal gait. The river of filth seemed to chase him gleefully over the cobblestones, as though he were its quarry, until he turned abruptly up a side street — which turned out to be High Street. It was then that he found himself directly in front of, yes, Abernathy's Secondhand Emporium.

He would not have entered the business, even then, had he not glanced down at his shoes and found they had been sullied by the hated sewage. In the window, he saw a pair of shoes nearly identical to his own and, fortuitously, appearing to be the proper size.

Maximus Lynch hesitated only a moment. He weighed his consternation at the prospect of wearing a secondhand pair of shoes against his revulsion at remaining in his own soiled footwear a moment longer. The stench of it rising up to greet his sensitive nostrils decided the issue, and he strode forward, resolute, drawing back the door and entering a world the likes of which he had never seen before.

In the life of Maximus Lynch, everything had its place. But not so here. The hodgepodge of what passed for "merchandise" in Abernathy's began with a piled-up, fallen-down jumble of books in nooks and hats on hooks. Discarded purses lay strewn amongst threadbare coats and tattered, faded kerchiefs. Tables with missing legs had been stacked atop dressers without any drawers. And the bulk of this aggregated chaos stood between Maximus and the object of his interest: the shoes he'd seen displayed in the window.

"Hello," he called, failing badly to mask the distress in his voice. And then again, more loudly, "Hello!"

But no one was about. In fact, Maximus surmised that a burglar might easily abscond with whatever he wished from the shop — if, indeed, the shop contained anything worth wishing for. Which, in the view of Maximus Lynch, it did not. Except for the shoes, and even these were sought out of necessity rather than longing.

Maximus put his hands on his hips and scanned the corners of the emporium for any sign of Mrs. Abernathy, or whoever was supposed to be on duty at the establishment this day. Pulling out his pocket watch, he glanced furtively at the timepiece. He was due in court less than an hour thence, and tardiness was not to be contemplated, let alone tolerated. There was nothing for it: He would have to take matters into his own hands.

Reaching forward with one hand, he steadied himself against a grandfather clock whose jolly-faced silver-plated moon gazed down from its upper window. It appeared to be laughing at him.

He felt certain that it *was* laughing — in mockery — a moment later when the clock tilted precariously to one side as he pressed against it, then toppled to the floor, its chimes clashing and clanging as Maximus fell right along with it. Landing with his arms and legs akimbo, he found himself sprawled atop a dusty red military jacket, a torn petticoat and a pile of woolen scarves. From this position he glanced about, both embarrassed and, at the same time, hopeful that the racket might have alerted the proprietor to his presence.

Still, no one was in evidence.

As he stretched out one arm to pull himself up into a sitting position, his hand fell against something hard and cold. He might scarcely have noticed it, except that when his skin touched its surface, he swore he heard a grunt followed by a groan and a squeak. He nearly jumped, thinking he'd disturbed a family of rats that had made its home in the pile of discarded clothes and furnishings. But, no, when he looked down, he saw that his hand had brushed against what appeared to be a tarnished but serviceable oil lamp. The intricate engraving and fine metalwork seemed to indicate it was of some value and, likely, of antique vintage.

What was it doing here? he wondered. Pulling out his handkerchief, he rubbed it against the surface in an attempt to remove the tarnish. It was then that something quite unexpected happened: The lamp, though unlit, became to emit a deep, amber glow that somehow penetrated the surface, which nonetheless appeared for all the world to be quite solid. The glow seemed to permeate the designs etched into the metal, racing along the length of them like a spark from a matchstick up a fuse. It changed colors as it went, starting out bright yellow before descending the spectrum into shades of red, then burgundy, then purple.

As Maximus watched, the lamp began to shudder in his hand, like a child shivering in the winter's cold, and steam of the same bright colors that danced upon its surface began to rise from its long, fine spout. The cloud of gas, or vapor, or whatever it was seemed to hover for a moment over his head, then gradually began to coalesce into something solid.

He blinked and, after a brief interlude, found himself staring at … himself.

Maximus puckered his lips and blew on the apparition. A

moment ago, it had been mere smoke. Could he disperse it? No. The apparition flickered and glowed briefly, as if it were embers in a winter fireplace, but it appeared no less solid.

"A pleasure to make your acquaintance," it said, removing and then replacing its derby as it nodded politely.

"Likewise, I'm sure," Maximus replied, though his tone conveyed more trepidation than pleasure. Still down on his hands and knees, he scooted back a short distance, away from the thing. "Who are you, exactly? You look just like …"

"You. Yes, I know. It can't be helped, I fear. When you've been closeted away as long as I have, you forget what people look like, and it's easiest to take the form of the first person you encounter. You shouldn't find it too disconcerting. I daresay you're accustomed to gazing on your own likeness."

Maximus frowned, and the apparition laughed, sounding curiously like the clanging chimes from the grandfather clock. "No offense meant, my dear man," it said. "I could merely tell by looking at you that you are … very well put together. A few wrinkles in that coat of yours and a little dust from your recent tumble, but other than that, quite spiffy, I should say."

Maximus' frown deepened into a scowl, his trepidation giving way to annoyance. He was not in the habit of repeating himself. "Who *are* you?" he asked again, lapsing easily into one of his accustomed roles — that of courtroom litigator.

"Eugene E. Sercumspectillius IV," the apparition said. "Genie S. for short."

"Clever," Maximus observed tartly.

"Not clever," the genie rejoined. "Genius!" He laughed his clanging-chime laugh again.

Maximus was not amused. If anyone was going to play tricks with language, it would be him. And it would not be for fun. Maximus did not have "fun." In the courtroom or in life, he played for keeps.

"How long have you been in there?" he asked.

"Come, come now, man. Do you think a timepiece would fit in such a confined space?"

Maximus considered. "No, but I would not have thought *you* would, either."

"True enough," the genie chuckled. "But enough of these formalities. Let's get down to business, shall we?"

"Business?"

"But of course. You released me from the bottle, so it is both my duty and my pleasure to grant you a single wish."

Maximus stood up straight and tugged on his waistcoat. "I thought it was three."

The genie cocked his head to one side. "Actually, it depends."

"On what."

"On my mood. I don't have to give you *any* wishes, really. We have to agree to terms and enter into a contract first."

This genie clearly enjoyed this verbal sparring, and Maximus the litigator was quickly warming to it, as well. Contract law? He was in his element. "Very well then," he said. "One wish it is. What are the parameters of this proposed contract? What are you able to grant, should I request it?"

The genie stuck out his lower lip as if to pout; he looked wounded. "My good fellow, this is a *wish*, not a request," he demurred. Leaning in closer to Maximus, he frowned and fixed him with a razor-sharp stare. He then lowered his voice and proceeded, conspiratorially: "Do you doubt my ability to grant whatever it is you may command? If so, I am more than able and very much ready to allay those doubts. There are no limits to my power in this matter, my friend. Command me whatever you will, and it will be yours. You have my word on it."

A nervous smile crept across Maximus' thin lips, and he glanced around to make sure the shopkeeper was still absent. Relieved to find that neither the proprietor nor anyone else had entered the store, he turned his attention once more to the genie.

"Very well, then," he said, lowering his voice to match the

genie's. "I accept your terms. And having done so, you must recognize that we have, in consequence, entered into a binding verbal contract."

The genie nodded in mock solemnity. "Quite so," he said, his tone resolute. "But think carefully before you decide what to wish for. You only have one wish, and once I grant it, I will be absolved of any debt to you."

Maximus thought for a moment. "One wish," he said, more to himself than to the genie. Then, raising his eyebrows and staring directly back at the image of himself, he said, "I wish for an infinite number of wishes."

Maximus suspected that this was somehow against the rules, but the genie had assured him there were no parameters, and a contract was a contract. How, exactly, would he enforce it? He hadn't gotten that far yet. Should he alert the constabulary if the genie reneged on their agreement? They would no doubt laugh and ridicule him. His reputation would be ruined. But the genie had no way of knowing this. There was no telling how long he had been cooped up inside that lamp of his, without a clue of how the world operated on the cusp of the twentieth century.

He could worry about all that later. For now, he would simply let things play out. At worst, the genie would fail to deliver what he'd promised. At best, Maximus would have anything he wanted, whenever he wanted it, for the rest of his natural life. "Yes," he confirmed, speaking aloud. That is what I want: an infinite number of wishes."

"Are you certain that is your wish?" the genie asked him in a cautionary tone.

"Are you unwilling to grant it?" Maximus countered.

"Oh, no, no. Not at all, it's just that … are you not in the habit of understanding the implications of a contract before you enter into it? Of reading the fine print, as it were?"

"So, there are parameters, after all!" Maximus laughed ruefully. "Don't try to wriggle out of this by lecturing *me* on the law," he crowed. "I should apprise you that I have a reputation of being the finest barrister in London, and I know full well that there is no 'fine print' in a verbal contract. What we've stipulated is simple and direct: Unlimited wishes. Here and now!"

The genie shook its head, appearing to pout again. "There is one proviso," it said. "I must warn you that you may not, at any point, use a subsequent wish to invalidate one made previously. This would, in effect, break our contract."

"How?"

"Your wishes would no longer be infinite, as we specified, but would have been limited by your own devices."

Maximus considered this for a moment and, despite certain reservations, he couldn't argue that it seemed a fair interpretation. Infinite meant endless, and nullifying one of his wishes would make it less than so.

He would have to be careful, but he knew what he was doing.

The genie continued: "If you violate this contract, I'm afraid it would trigger certain ... penalties."

"What penalties?"

"I'm afraid you would be obliged to take my place inside the lamp."

Maximus scowled as he stared at the lamp, then brightened. Could the genie really make good on his threat? He doubted it. But even if such punishment were in the genie's power, he, Maximus Lynch, was the foremost litigator in all of London. Had he not just said so himself? He'd been in difficult spots before, and he'd always managed to find a way out of them. He nodded once firmly. "I accept."

"Very well," the genie said. "What is your first wish?"

"I wish for twenty million pounds in gold," Maximus declared, and immediately found himself sitting on a pile of gold coins that covered half the floor where the discarded clothing had been.

"Next," the genie said.

Maximus realized Sercumspectillius was calling for another wish.

"Wait a moment," he said, taking in the gold that now surrounded him. "I want to savor this. Maybe spend a little of it first."

"Is that your wish?"

"Well … all right. If I have an infinite number of them, I don't need to worry about wasting them."

The genie sighed. "I'm afraid that won't work."

Maximus frowned. A shadow crossed his eyes as his brow furrowed. "Are you going to violate the contract so soon?"

"I could ask the same of you," the genie replied smoothly. "Your initial wish specified that all contingent and subsequent wishes were to be granted 'here and now.' Hence, *you* would be the one violating the contract should I grant you any delay. I must therefore inform you that, if you do not make another wish within a reasonable amount of time, I will have no choice but to invoke the penalty."

The frown vanished, and Maximus' eyes widened instead. "A … reasonable amount of time?" he stammered. "You mean a week? A month? A year?"

The genie shook his head solemnly and produced (seemingly out of nowhere) a large, slender hourglass. This he inverted and placed on the grandfather clock, still lying on its side where it had fallen. The sand therein began to descend through the narrow bottleneck at what seemed to Maximus a frightening rate.

Realization dawned.

"But I asked for infinite wishes!" Maximus sputtered. "That means I will be wishing … forever … that I will never have time to enjoy *any* of my wishes!"

The genie shrugged. "That is not my business," he said nonchalantly. "I am obligated only to grant your wish, nothing more and nothing less. But try not to be alarmed, my friend. There is one fringe benefit to all this: In order to make an infinite number of wishes, you will need to live forever. Eternal life is a most excellent corollary of our agreement, I'm sure you will agree!"

Maximus stared unblinking at the sand, a quarter of which had already settled at the bottom of the hourglass. More granules were descending, forming an ever-increasing mound, as those that had already fallen ran skittering down the sides. He guessed the process would take two minutes at most, and his mind worked feverishly, in growing panic, to find some loophole — any loophole — to their agreement.

When nearly half the sand had accumulated at the bottom, he seized on an idea. Extending his right arm abruptly and pointing directly at the genie, he blurted out, "If I'm stuck here forever making wishes, you'll be stuck here with me granting them! Is that really what you want, Genie S? What do you say we agree, by mutual consent, to void our contract? I'll take my twenty million pounds, you can be free of your lamp, and we'll call it even."

The genie's laugh chimed louder than ever. "What makes you think I would agree to such a bargain?" he chortled. "Someone *must* occupy the lamp, and that someone will be either you or me. My money, for the moment, is on you. Eventually, you will run out of wishes. Or you will start to make wishes that are not, shall we say, in your own best interest. Out of desperation. But before that, you will probably fall asleep, at which point the sands will run out, you will be in breach of our agreement, and I will be free to go my way."

Maximus was shaking now. Only one-quarter of the sand remained. He balled up both fists, mind working frantically, then shouted: "I wish … I wish … I wish you were dead!"

The genie hung his head in what looked like sorrow, and for the briefest of moments, Maximus allowed himself the satisfaction of believing that he had bested his opponent. There was even the slightest hint of regret that escaping from his predicament required calling for the genie's death. But, then again, this had become a matter self-defense, a valid and universally recognized principle of common law.

"I am sorry," the genie said softly.

Maximus waited as the genie paused, then continued: "But my death would render me incapable of granting you any further wishes. This constitutes a clear breach of our agreement, for which you are entirely responsible. I do regret this, truly I do, but I fear I have no choice but to invoke the enforcement clause in our contract."

The sands ran out.

Maximus felt lightheaded, and for a moment he thought his panic was the cause of it. In the next instant, however, he felt himself being lifted off the floor as a strange numbness began to spread from his extremities over his entire body. He blacked out briefly, and when he regained consciousness, the interior of Abernathy's Secondhand Emporium had vanished. Instead, he found himself in a very tight, confined space with only a single window at the far end of a long passageway off to one side. The passageway was far too small for him to fit through, and there was no other entrance to the place.

He looked around, desperate.

The walls were smooth. Metallic. Unyielding.

Maximus realized to his horror that the genie had made good on his threat and had somehow deposited him inside the lamp, where he found himself entirely alone except for a single piece of furniture. It was the grandfather clock from the emporium, which now stood against one curved wall, miniaturized but still taking up nearly a quarter of the entire chamber. At the base of it was a piece of paper, which Maximus found bore a message, written with impeccable precision in what appeared to be his own hand.

"Please accept my apologies," it read. "As it turns out, a timepiece fits very nicely inside the lamp, after all. Leaving you this one small luxury was the least I could do. Consider it a token of our brief and fruitful acquaintance. I believe you will find it quite reliable, and you needn't ever bother to wind it. It will operate unfailingly for the remainder of your life, which is to say, forever. Best regards, Eugene E. Sercumspectillius IV, genie emeritus, attorney at law."

Attorney at law?

"HELP ME!!!!!" Maximus shouted in a voice that was no louder than the buzzing of a housefly. "HELP MEEEEEE!!!!!!!"

Maximus Lynch was a few minutes late for his appointment at the courthouse, a fact that surprised all those who were in attendance. It never happened again. Nor did Maximus ever lose another case during a long and illustrious career practicing law. Those who knew him remarked that, while he had always been a distinguished barrister, his skills as a litigator had grown even more formidable — so formidable, in fact, that they were without peer in his generation.

Especially when it came to argumentation.

Epilogue, 2018

Property records show that Annabelle J. Abernathy sold the emporium on High Street to a developer, who razed it along with the entire block of buildings to build a velodrome. Abernathy's had been in her family for centuries, but she no longer had any use for it in the spring of 1897. Indeed, she made a handsome profit on the sale, which was facilitated by none other than Britain's finest attorney "Ironclad" Maximus Lynch.

So great was Lynch's fame that the royal government called upon him to prosecute the case of Jack the Ripper, should a suspect ever be apprehended.

Of course, no one ever was.

Still, for the Widow Abernathy, it was helpful to have such a close family connection — even if only she was aware of Lynch's true identity, that he was, in fact, her maternal great-grandfather thirty times over: an Arabian merchant named Omar Khayyam al-Jafar who had settled in London shortly after the First Crusade.

Renowned for his ability to get the best of any trader in a deal, al-Jafar had built up quite a fortune, which he used to found a successful trading post in the city's marketplace. He adopted the anglicized name Eugene E. Sercumspectillius to avoid persecution as a "Mohammaden," as the devotees of Islam were derisively known, and flourished for many years. Meanwhile, he pursued his secret fascination with alchemy: a preoccupation that would prove to be his undoing. While seeking a means to transform base metals into gold, he had become imprisoned — through an ill-conceived experiment gone awry — within a lamp he had been using as a vessel to combine various substances in his research.

Upon his release from said lamp in 1896, the curse that bound his family to the emporium also was lifted. Once the business was sold, the contents were donated to an orphanage in London, with the lone exception being a priceless artifact that was retrieved from their out of their midst. The artifact, a lamp whose origins were traced to the Byzantine Empire in the early twelfth century, was delivered to the British Museum. There it remains to this day in a tightly sealed acrylic display case, protected by a network of sensors that ensure no one can get in.

Or out.

Nightmare's Eve
(Rotten Robbie's Christmas Comeuppance)

y any measure, Robbie had been a bad boy this year. He had stolen a handful of Tootsie Pops from Mrs. Addington's store on High Street, and had smiled when he'd gotten away with it.

He'd gotten away with other things, too, like cheating on his math test by looking over Annie Atherton's shoulder. Could he help it that the teacher had seated him behind the smartest girl in the class, just because his name was Bullwinkle and it came after "Atherton" in the alphabet? He was careful to miss one or two problems she got right, just so no one would wonder why the boy who never did his homework had done so well on his exam.

He'd threatened to poke out Brandon Seaver's eye with a needle after the boy cut in front of him in the lunch line. And he'd held

James Marx's head under water during a "bob for apples" game, nearly drowning him before Mr. Reynolds, the teacher, had pulled him off.

Then there was the time he'd captured Mr. Harrington's calico cat, Little Primrose, and trapped it in the Corrigers' mailbox down the street. He'd laughed in glee as it yowled and shrieked from inside the too-small metal box, shaking it on its wooden stand until it had finally given up going anywhere. When the mail had come the next day, Robbie had a front-row seat behind a hedgerow just across the street. He'd watched as the terrified animal spring out, eyes wide and claws flailing, at the startled postman when he opened the box, sending letters flying in all directions, into the bushes, the street and the muddy gutter.

The cat had run off and wasn't seen again until it turned up a couple of days later, dead, having been hit by a passing car on Mulberry Street.

Robbie had thought it was funny. Mr. Harrington, however, had not. Mr. Harrington's wife had passed away a couple of years back, and Little Primrose had showed up on his doorstep the next day, mewing and softly butting her head against the old man's leg. He'd taken her in, convinced his wife had sent her to keep him company. Or even, by some miracle, that his wife's spirit had taken up residence in Little Primrose. It was an old man's fancy, but it had made the grief almost bearable, and Little Primrose had been his constant companion until Robbie had taken her.

Robbie knew none of this, but he wouldn't have cared if he had. He knew nothing of Mr. Harrington's loneliness after his wife died or Little Primrose disappeared, because to him, loneliness was a good thing. He didn't like people at all, really. They were just nuisances to be toyed and trifled with for his amusement, if he felt like paying attention to them at all.

He didn't feel like paying attention now.

It was Christmas Eve, and he'd been shipped off to his Aunt Wilma and Uncle Giles' house, on the pretext that he would get to pass the holiday in a genuine manor house, but mainly because his parents didn't want him spoiling Christmas for his brother and two sisters. Because he always did. Spoil Christmas, that is. Throwing tantrums, opening the other children's presents "by mistake" (even though the tags were clearly marked in bright red ink), eating more than his share of the pumpkin pie and picking fights with his siblings over who got to sit where at the table.

He missed doing those things, and he didn't care about the manor house, even though he got to stay in a big room with a canopy bed, an antique writing table and its own fireplace.

Uncle Giles, unlike his parents, was not the kind of person to put up with Rotten Robbie's shenanigans. He was an old prizefighter who'd worked on the docks in his younger days and on the newspaper printing press when he'd gotten older. He'd inherited the estate from his father, and he and Wilma had kept the place up all by themselves. He might have been fifty, but his arms, still thickly muscled, and his booming voice made Robbie feel just a little afraid — even if he would never admit to it.

Despite all this, Uncle Giles was, underneath it all, a kindhearted soul. And because he was a kindhearted soul, he put Robbie to bed with a glass of milk and a cookie, and started reading *The Night Before Christmas* to him as he lay tucked snug under the blankets and Aunt Wilma's blue crocheted comforter.

"I don't believe in Santa Claus," Robbie said, defiantly. "It's Mom and Dad who put those things under the tree. I can read, y'know. The writing on the presents looks just like the writing Mom makes when she sends those notes with me to school."

"Notes?"

"You know, Uncle Giles. When I've been naughty and she has to say 'sorry' about it." He tried not to laugh.

"So, you've been naughty this year?" Uncle Giles didn't know about Robbie's mischief-making, because Robbie's parents hadn't told him. They'd been afraid he wouldn't take Robbie if he knew. That was the kind of fear Robbie had put into them, and it was the kind of fear he took advantage of every day. Something in Uncle Giles' voice, though, made Robbie realize he wouldn't be able to take advantage of the old prizefighter.

Robbie frowned. "No. I've been very nice. Mostly, anyway."

Uncle Giles frowned right back. "Tell the truth, Robbie. I can tell when you're fibbing, and Santa can, too."

"Santa's not real," Robbie protested.

"How do you know? Have you ever seen him?"

Robbie laughed. "Of course not. That's how I know he's not real!"

"Have you ever seen China?"

"Of course not!"

"Then to your way of looking at things, that must mean it's not real."

"But Uncle Giles, everyone knows …"

"That China is real? Yes, yes. And everyone knows Santa is real, too. But here's one thing you may not know: Santa is very different than he appears on Christmas cards and TV commercials."

"Or by the kettle in the mall?"

Uncle Giles laughed. "Yes! And you do know that isn't Santa, it's just some guy in a red suit dressed up to look like the Christmas cards and TV commercials. They have it all wrong, you know."

Robbie smiled. He liked Uncle Giles. He knew how to tease people, and Robbie could appreciate that, even if he was the one being teased.

"Tell me, Uncle Giles, what is Santa *really* like?"

Uncle Giles put his index finger to the tip of his nose, and his eyes sparkled knowingly. "Well, boy, maybe if you sleep tonight with one eye open, you'll see him when he comes down the chimney."

"He can't do that. Your chimney's too small!"

Some pine logs burning in the fireplace sparked and crackled, as if to protest Robbie's words, and Uncle Giles offered his own rejoinder as well: "Oh, you'd be surprised, boy. But since you don't like my stories, I think I'll just leave you to get some sleep. Christmas is in the morning, and I wouldn't want you to miss it, even if you've been so naughty Santa doesn't leave you anything this year."

Robbie caught his breath. He was naughty every year, and he always got lots of presents anyway. That's how he knew Santa wasn't real; his parents left those gifts. Some of the other kids said so, too. If there weren't any gifts for him in the morning, it would be because his parents weren't there with him this Christmas, not because he'd been naughty.

Uncle Giles closed the book, its colorful drawings of sugarplums, stockings hung by the chimney and the red-coated Saint Nicholas vanishing.

"Remember," he said, "Santa doesn't look anything like the pictures in that book. He's much *different*. If you see him tonight, you'll know." His voice was very serious — so serious that Robbie was a little nervous.

Uncle Giles turned the light off and said a brusque "good night" as he left the room. The hearth fire was burning down now, the embers glowing more faintly and smoke rising from what was left of the pine logs. Robbie focused on them, trying to stay awake … to sleep with one eye open, as his uncle had counseled. Part of him was curious, but a bigger part of him was scared. He couldn't quite figure out why, but he knew he had good reason to be.

Robbie didn't know how long ago he'd dozed off, but the next thing he knew, the glow had left the fire. Beams from a three-quarter-full moon drifted in through a large, multipaned window, illuminating the room and revealing the black smoke in the fireplace. Except the smoke wasn't rising.

It was descending.

Robbie rubbed his eyes and sat up straight.

A shriek echoed across the room, coming, he was sure, from the chimney, and a split-second later, a large bat flew into the room, black wings beating madly, buffeting the air all around it. Sickly stale air flew at Robbie's face, and he coughed violently, nearly choking on it, his eyes watering as he watched the scene unfolding before him.

The smoke that had flowed into the room from the chimney seemed to follow the bat, like a contrail, then envelope it, swirling about it in the moonlight. In the center of it, the bat seemed to be growing, changing shape. The frantic movement of its wings slowed, and the smoke around it grew denser, as though the bat and the sooty vapor that surrounded it were coalescing, becoming one.

Robbie gasped … and coughed again.

There before him stood a slender figure, dressed in a black robe that looked like something the Grim Reaper might wear. Indeed, the figure carried in one hand what appeared to be a scythe, its curved blade sharp and gleaming in the moonlight. Whether it was the work of that same moonlight or not, the figure's skin looked pale, almost ghostly, and the smile it wore raised goosebumps up and down Robbie's arms.

"Merry Christmas," the figure said, words almost oozing forth in extended syllables as they slipped from his mouth.

Robbie opened his mouth, but nothing came out, and the figure laughed a deep, otherworldly belly laugh. "Ho, ho, ho!"

Robbie shuddered. "Who … who … are you?"

"Why isn't it obvious, my dear boy?" the figured answered, its voice both thundering and hissing all at once. "I'm Father Christmas, also known as Father Time … or, if you prefer … Santa Claus."

"You mean …?" Robbie could barely speak. He'd never been this scared in his life. He wanted to run, but he felt frozen in place and was sure that, if he moved, the horrible thing standing at the foot of his canopied bed would lunge and take hold of him.

"I mean one's as good as another. Haven't you ever seen the pictures of Father Time with the Baby New Year? Ever notice how much he looks like Santa?" The figure smiled and turned his head in profile, raising his chin. He didn't have a beard, and his chest was flat, bearing not even the slightest resemblance to a bowl full of jelly.

"But … but … you don't look like Santa!"

The figure leaned in closer over the foot of the bed, and Robbie pushed his own back hard against the wall behind him. "I thought you didn't *believe* in Santa."

"I don't … I mean …" Robbie couldn't find any more words. He crossed his arms over his face and started sobbing uncontrollably, his body shuddering in waves and tears pouring down his cheeks.

"Now you know."

"What?" Robbie wailed.

"You know what Brandon Seaver felt like when you said you'd put out his eye. And you know what Mr. Harrington felt like when you took his Little Primrose, the only friend he had in all the world after his wife died. Now you know."

Robbie pulled his arms down, suddenly angry, his red eyes narrowing as he looked at the creature across his bed. "I didn't kill that filthy old cat. You did!" he wailed. "You did with that … that … *thing!*"

"It's called a scythe," the man said blandly. "And, no, I didn't kill them. They die at the appointed time, regardless of what I might prefer. The scythe is only an accoutrement."

"What's that?"

"Never mind."

Robbie's momentary flash of anger faded, replaced again by pure terror as he stared into the visitor's eyes.

This vile, distorted thing that called itself Santa was moving up from the foot of the bed, around to the side, a wraith gliding across the floor, its black robe flowing like storm-tossed waves on a foul and tainted sea. As it moved closer, Robbie could smell its breath, thick and raspy, an ill wind rising from unfathomable depths.

Robbie's stomach wretched, and he tried to hold his breath, failing miserably after a few seconds and gasping to avoid suffocation. Curling himself tight into a ball, he turned his back to the creature. Maybe it would go away. Maybe it wasn't even there.

Maybe this was a nightmare, and he could open his eyes, and it would be gone. But he didn't dare open his eyes and find it still *there*. He couldn't bear to look at it again.

He felt a bony hand on his shoulder that might have been intended as comforting … but no, the fingers were digging in.

Robbie spun around and stared into the eyes of Father Christmas, eyes narrow and sallow, shot through with veins.

He screamed as the creature opened its mouth, revealing a pair of long, pointed fangs, glistening white with saliva. Its mouth was watering. But before he could scream again, the jaws from which those fangs protruded had clamped down tight upon his neck, burying the twin canine daggers deep within his flesh. He winced in anticipation of pain but felt nothing. Only a rapidly spreading numbness, a timeless chill neither cold nor stinging. It felt like … *nothing*. Like nothingness was pervading his entire body. He tried to sit up, but he was paralyzed. Not a sound escaped his frozen lips. He was going to die, he felt sure. Or maybe he was already dead. Or maybe he was something else entirely.

Father Christmas pulled Robbie by his collar through the manor, dragging him across the floor. Robbie couldn't move. Couldn't speak. He hoped vainly that Uncle Giles might be roused from his slumber and come to his aid. Maybe the old boxer could deck this fiendish ghoul and free him from the clutches that held him. But somehow, he knew that wasn't going to happen. That it was too late. And worse than everything else, that Uncle Giles probably wouldn't come to his aid, even if he could. Uncle Giles hated him. Everybody hated him. And he deserved it.

"You're finally catching on," Father Christmas said with a chuckle.

Could this monster read his thoughts?

"Of course I can," came the answer.

But why …?

"Because you're on the naughty list, of course."

You're … you're … Dracula.

"No, no. He was on the naughty list, too, a long time ago, but he somehow managed to get away. Only time anyone ever did. I finally caught him and brought him home."

Where is home?

"The North Pole, of course."

But you're a … vampire?

"*The* vampire, more precisely. The original. How do you think Santa gets down chimneys so easily? The smoke trick works really well, especially since there's *supposed* to be smoke in a fireplace. No one ever notices. … not that it would matter if they did, but I prefer not to leave a mess."

If you're Santa, why don't you look like him?

"Actually, I do — to the children on the nice list. To the kids on the naughty list, well, what you see is what you get. If I can change into a bat, I can change into an old fat guy with a beard, too. It's kind of fun."

Father Christmas dropped Robbie on the front lawn, pulled out a burlap sack and deposited him inside, tying the opening around his neck so he could still see and throwing the whole thing over his shoulder. Striding quickly to the side of the house, he scampered nimbly up the outside walls like a daddy longlegs, reaching the roof, where a sleigh tethered to eight creatures was waiting. The creatures looked like Santa's reindeer … sort of. Their eyes were vacant and bloodshot, and large, black wings grew out of their backs.

Sensing Robbie's thoughts again, Father Christmas replied, "They have to fly somehow, don't they?"

Robbie wanted to cry, wanted to scream, wanted to do anything, be anywhere but here. He couldn't feel anything: not the crisp winter air, not even his own fingers or his toes.

It only took a moment for them to reach the North Pole. The zombie reindeer had to be fast to cover the entire earth on Christmas Eve.

To Robbie, it was more like Nightmare's Eve.

When he was younger and believed in such things, he'd envisioned Santa's workshop as a jolly place where elves sang merrily as they worked away on all the toys Santa would deliver to good little boys and girls around the world. But this place was nothing like that. It was more like a filthy factory, with smokestacks belching soot into the sky and the constant whining grind of cogs and gears and engines so loud he thought he might go deaf.

"Welcome to your new home," Father Christmas said proudly. "This is where you'll be working from now on."

Working? That's what adults do.

"It's what you'll do, too, now. All day and all night for the rest of eternity. You're a vampire now, too, which means you won't die. Of course, I can't let you loose among the general population. Too dangerous. But don't worry. We make synthetic blood up here. Kind of like nonalcoholic beer. It's a pity you naughty-listers never grow up to taste a drop of the spirits. You're really missing out. Of course, that's kind of the idea."

To Robbie, this place looked and sounded for all the world like the hell he'd heard about in Sunday school.

"Where do you think mortals got that idea?" He laughed. "Santa? Satan? Just transpose a couple of letters, and they're pretty much the same."

But Santa's not supposed to be mean!

Father Christmas looked genuinely wounded. "I'm not mean. Look at all the toys you'll be making for all the children on the nice list!"

Robbie knew he'd never been on the nice list. *So how come I got presents?*

"Well, you were right about that part: Your parents bought them for you. Parents are nice like that. They get gifts for kids on the naughty list to make up for what I don't bring. It's frustrating, because they're enabling the kids, and they just get worse until I have to come along and put an end to it." He shrugged. "But they're parents. They kind of have to love you."

He threw the bag containing Robbie off the sleigh and untied it. Robbie still couldn't feel anything, but he found he could speak once again.

"You said I'd be making presents? Does that mean, I'm an …?"

"Elf? That's right. Why do you think they're all so short? They're all kids from the naughty list who I … um … 'recruit' to help me out. Check out the ears."

Robbie reached up and felt, to his amazement, that the tops of his ears had grown pointy.

"One of the perks of the job," Father Christmas said. "Come to think of it, probably the only one." He laughed: "Ho, ho, ho!" Then his face grew long and Robbie thought he saw a tear forming in one of his pale, bloodshot eyes. Maybe, just maybe, he was sorry about having taken Robbie. Maybe he had made a mistake. Maybe he would let Robbie go back to his parents. He would change. He'd make it onto the nice list.

Father Christmas, who'd been reading his thoughts again, shook his head slowly. "Stop feeling sorry for yourself," he said. "I'm not sad for you. I'm sad for Little Primrose and for Mr. Harrington, who I'm due to escort out of this world tomorrow night. He wasn't supposed to go that soon, but without his friend, he has no more will to live. I'm not all-powerful, but if I were, I'd make it so the work you do here could bring Little Primrose back and she could purr for Mr. Harrington and bump her head against his leg and make him feel happy just a little longer. But you can't do that, and neither can I."

Robbie looked down at his feet, and for just a moment, he understood.

"See?" said Father Christmas. "I'm not mean at all. You're the mean one. That's why you're here: You wouldn't do good because you wanted to, so you'll be doing good because you have to."

For just a moment, the figure in front of Robbie changed into that of a jolly old man dressed in a red coat with white fur lining, a long white beard cascading downward from a plump face adorned with red cheeks and a jovial smile.

But the look of understanding faded from Robbie's face after a moment, replaced once more by one of fear mingled with deep resentment. "You're not real," he spat. And in that moment, the image of the jolly old elf vanished almost as quickly as it had appeared, replaced once again by the figure of a slender man dressed all in black, looking down at Robbie through sallow, bloodshot eyes and carrying a menacing scythe.

Robbie looked away again, and Father Christmas sighed.

Then he shouted: "Get to work!"

This Vale of Dreams

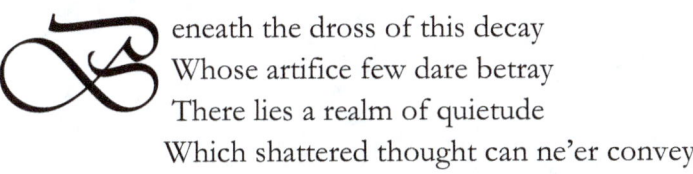

B eneath the dross of this decay
Whose artifice few dare betray
There lies a realm of quietude
Which shattered thought can ne'er convey

Betrothed to secrets (uttered not)
By phantoms of a day forgot
We hoard the baubles of the past
And cast away our treasures sought

So whence this futile reverie?
We sojourn long yet dare not see
We squander moments as they pass
To grasp illusions 'ere they flee

Stephen H. Provost

For darkness ever lies in wait
For those who act ... or hesitate
And light illumines ev'ry path
This frail heart doth navigate

Trust if ye will the hollow vow
Before the barren altar bow
And heed no more that lost refrain
Which conscious faith cannot allow

Or rend the fabric of what seems
Embrace the flow of timeless streams
Obeisant sanity unbound
To now abide this vale of dreams

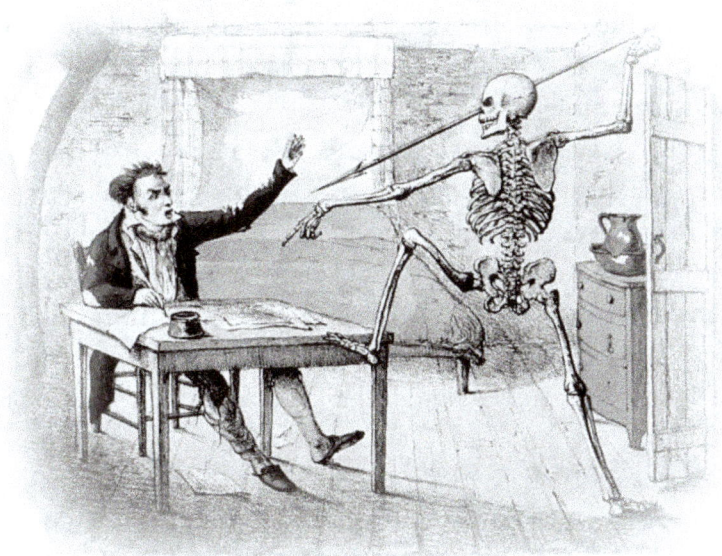

Stranger Than Fiction

Corey Fagin discovered his gift when he was in grammar school. Until that time, the adopted son of Charles and Pammy Lee Fagin felt and acted just like any other prepubescent child: climbing trees, playing video games and finding ways to stay up past his bedtime. That was before his fourth-grade teacher, Mrs. Billingham, assigned his class to write a short story about "what you see in your back yard."

Young Corey's back yard was, unfortunately, very boring — at least to his way of thinking. There was an uneven hedge against the back fence. There was a layer of Kentucky bluegrass littered with weeds and dandelions. And there was an old maple tree in the far corner that was fighting a valiant but losing battle with dry rot.

Nothing exciting at all.

The most interesting thing about the place was a bird bath that his parents had bought a few years back but had neglected to keep up. It had come in two pieces, which might have been why they got it on sale at Kmart. The winds from the first big winter storm that hit had knocked the bowl off its pedestal, cracking it down the middle as it fell upside-down. It wound up looking like the top of a dragon egg protruding from the lawn.

That had given Corey an idea: His story had been about the baby dragon that had hatched in his back yard. It had (according to Corey's imaginative account), pooped in the hedge, creating an odor like "the smell fireworks make," and spit fire from its nose at the old maple, making a mark that resembled "a drumstick from Champion's Chicken." The dragon, he wrote, had built a nest in the old maple and was living up there, having dislodged a family of robins from the same perch.

How does this relate to Corey's gift? Well, after he turned in the assignment, he returned home from school that day on the bus to find his parents frantically running around the back yard … chasing what looked like a very large winged(!) lizard as the family dog, a Dalmatian named Chipper, howled and barked. The little dragon puffed smoke and occasional sparks out of its nostrils as it ran, hopped and occasionally flew for short distances.

After the school bus brought him home that day, Corey stepped into the house and heard his parents shouting from the back yard. He dropped his backpack on the kitchen counter and ran out onto the porch behind the house, where he beheld everything he'd written about in his story: the baby dragon; the robin's nest lying on the ground underneath the maple; the trunk of which had been charred in the shape of a drumstick. A pungent smell of sulfur drifted across the yard from the vicinity of the hedge.

"Be careful, Charles!" Pammy Lee Fagin shouted as her husband closed the gap on the creature, then had to jump aside like a jackrabbit as it turned around and blew a stream of smoky fire toward his kneecaps.

"What *is* this thing?" Charles Fagin shouted as he paused in his pursuit, clearly concerned that it might not be in his best interests, health-wise.

"It's a dragon!" Corey shouted.

"Get him in the house!" his father shouted as his mother, at the same instant, began running toward him. "And call … I don't know, animal control or something!"

Animal control was, in fact, called, along with a fire crew that brought in a ladder to go after the beast when it scurried up the trunk of the maple. It was a huge kerfuffle in the town of Brimley Crossing, and the local WOLF Network affiliate even sent out a video crew to cover it. Cameras were rolling as two firefighters set up a ladder to climb the maple tree, but they soon learned that a dragon was far more difficult to corral than a treed cat. Just when they'd reached its nest, it spread its wings and leaped from the branch, catching an updraft with its leathery wings and soaring away far beyond their reach.

The TV cameras somehow failed to catch any footage of it, and pretty soon, people were saying it had all been a big publicity stunt for Charles Fagin's business, Super Snake Plumbing. The "dragon," they mumbled, had been nothing but a remote-controlled helicopter toy rigged up to look like a flying snake. Despite this, authorities issued an all-points bulletin urging the public to be on the lookout for a flying lizard that was "winged and dangerous."

No one ever saw the dragon again, however. The following day, when Corey returned to school, Mrs. Billingham returned his assignment, which was marked "incomplete." She took him aside after class and explained that the assignment had been to describe real events, not to write a made-up story, and said he would have to do it over again if he hoped to be graded. He did so, changing the dragon into a squirrel and removing the drumstick-shaped scar on the maple tree. When he returned home, the scar had vanished and there had arrived, in the maple's branches, a gray flying squirrel that had taken up residence where the dragon's nest had been.

His parents almost convinced him what the rest of the community was so quick to believe: that the squirrel had been there all along and that there never had been any dragon. Dragons didn't exist, did they? It was easier to believe that than to account for the fact that the creature had simply disappeared and never turned up again — even if it meant glossing over inconvenient details, such as why the fire department and a TV crew would have responded to a report of a dangerous squirrel on the loose.

Corey tried to gloss over those details himself, and he might have done so had he never resumed the activity that caused the problem in the first place: writing. In high school, Corey took a creative writing class, the purpose of which was to make up stories. So, he did. He made up a story about a mission to Mars, and the next day, news broke that a crew of four had touched down on the red planet. No one had heard, before this, that such a mission was even being planned, let along undertaken. The assumption was that it had all been a top-secret program, kept under wraps to prevent the Russians or the Chinese from getting there first.

Corey couldn't help but notice that the leader of the mission was named Roger Jones, the same name he had chosen for the main character in his story. Certainly, it wasn't the most uncommon name in the world, and such coincidences could happen, but the entire episode got him thinking back on the incident involving the dragon. It *had* been true, he told himself, and the mission to Mars could very well be proof of it.

He decided to put his theory to the test by writing another story, something he reasoned couldn't possibly be explained away as a squirrel or an undercover space program. This one involved a talking golden retriever that ran for mayor of Brimley Crossing — and was elected. The next day, it was announced that the mayor, Jessie Cumberland, had died suddenly and that the town council planned to convene an emergency session calling for a special election to be held in the spring. Mayor Cumberland's wife was quoted in the newspaper as saying she had no interest in running for her late husband's seat: "You'd be more likely to find our golden retriever, Lancelot, on the ballot," she quipped.

Nightmare's Eve

The quote, obviously meant as a joke, triggered an unlikely movement when no one else stepped forward as a candidate except for William "Bloody" Sunday, the owner of the local Dodge dealership. Almost everyone in the community despised him, and who could blame them? He'd sold some of them lemons, then reneged on the warranties, and he'd picked fights with his neighbors over everything from the property line to noise complaints. His campaign platform was simple: Raise fees on garbage collection and fire service, institute a curfew that would take effect two hours before most businesses in town currently closed, and declare City Hall an official sanctuary for "anyone who thinks they've been wrongly accused of anything."

To the vast majority of people in the 11,500-person town, Lancelot the golden retriever seemed like a far more rational choice. When the special election was held, they voted him in on a landslide, arranged for him to be neutered and built a doghouse for him out behind the police station.

Long before any of that happened, though, Corey was convinced his story was starting to come true. Just the quote from the mayor's wife was enough to confirm his hypothesis. All that remained was for him to decide how to use his newly discovered powers.

He soon realized he would have to be careful. A few days after he wrote the golden retriever story, news broke that the Mars mission was in trouble: The equipment wasn't adequate to sustain the astronauts for the entire trip back to Earth, and even if it had been, there wasn't enough fuel for them to get home. Corey had failed to provide any technical details in his story, so the astronauts found themselves on Mars in the kind of space capsule that would have made it to the moon just fine, but couldn't get them much farther — at least not without Corey's help.

Panicking at the thought he might be responsible for the astronauts' deaths, Corey ran to his room and quickly penned a new story that brought them safely home to Earth.

Nothing happened.

He tried to figure out what could have gone wrong. Had he just been imagining his role in these real-life stories, after all? That seemed unlikely. Everything he'd ever written had come to pass, in one way or another, and that *couldn't* be just a coincidence. What was different this time? He didn't know, unless … in every other case, he had turned his story in as an assignment. That could be it. The only difficulty lay in the fact that he didn't have another assignment due in that class for another three weeks. The news reports had said the astronauts only had enough supplies to last for ten more days, at most. Unless he could find a way to get them what they needed — the fuel, equipment and supplies for those ten days plus the six-month journey home — the astronauts would be dead.

For a moment, he tried to convince himself it wasn't his problem. If the mission wasn't the result of his writing, he wasn't responsible for it. But if it was, as he suspected, then weren't the astronauts themselves just fictional characters?

Maybe. Or maybe not. Maybe they had been real astronauts plucked out of their otherwise routine life and forced, against their will, to take part in a doomed mission at the behest of a seventeen-year-old kid from Brimley High School.

He couldn't chance it. Corey would have to find a way to turn in his new story, about the astronauts' safe return, at school before the ten days were up.

The next day, he waited after class to talk to his teacher, Mr. Madigan, about turning it in as extra credit.

"You know I don't accept extra-credit assignments," Mr. Madigan said.

"But can't you just read it and give me some feedback? I really want to learn to be a better writer."

The instructor, however, extended his hand, palm outward, when Corey tried to hand him the paper. "I'm sorry, Corey, but I don't have time right now. I have forty assignments to grade for my second-period class, and I have to proofread *The Bulletin* so it can go to press next Tuesday. *The Brimley Bulletin* was Brimley High's student-run newspaper, and Mr. Madigan acted as advisor for the journalism/yearbook club.

That gave Corey an idea. He had read about the astronauts' plight in the daily paper; what better way to put things right than to submit his own story to the school newspaper?

And so, he did.

A little more than six months later, the astronauts made it home safely, on the same day that Lancelot was certified as the official mayor of Brimley. By this time, Corey had graduated from high school and, like many high school graduates, he had big dreams for what he was going to do in life. The difference lay in how he planned to accomplish them.

Corey didn't stay in Brimley Crossing after high school. His grades were good enough for a partial scholarship to Worcester Poly, where he pursued and eventually obtained a bachelor's degree in journalism. Not only that, he was named the School of Communications' outstanding graduate, based in large measure on his work for the college paper, *The Clarion Call*. He spent all eight semesters there as the paper's ace reporter, declining an offer to serve as editor during his senior year because he wanted to continue doing what he did best: write.

He was a capable writer, but that wasn't what stood out to his journalism advisor, A.E. Kilpatrick. A reporter can always improve his writing skills, but the one thing Corey Fagin couldn't have possibly improved upon was his accuracy. Literally every story that the young Mr. Fagin submitted to the paper was one-hundred percent accurate, down to the smallest detail. It was Professor Kilpatrick's habit to fact-check students' papers for misspelled names, inconsistencies, mathematical errors and so forth. But about halfway through Corey's second semester, Kilpatrick hadn't found a single error in more than two dozen stories turned in by the young man from Brimley Crossing.

What he didn't know is that some of the stories Corey turned in were made up, but no one could tell because whatever he made up actually happened. This explained why *The Clarion Call* published so many more blockbuster stories after Corey joined the staff, and why nearly all of them carried his byline.

With Prof. Kilpatrick's recommendation, he applied for and received an internship with *The New York Star-Journal*, where he started off with the usual assignments for an intern: answering phones, monitoring the police scanner and writing obituaries. Not exactly glamorous work, but it was still *The Star-Journal*, the newspaper that had won more than a hundred Pulitzer Prizes in its illustrious history. Corey was convinced that, one day in the not-too-distant future, he would add to that total.

In the meantime, however, he had to put up with the drudgery of working the obit desk. Most of the time, he felt like nothing more than a glorified gofer, sometimes fetching coffee for the editor or running to the courthouse to check on the latest court filing for one of the "real" reporters. In his darker moods, it occurred to him that he might earn his ups by writing an obituary for some famous person who wasn't dead yet. Maybe a killer who had been acquitted on a technicality or the hardline dictator of some third-world country. But did he really want that on his conscience, even if it might mean a promotion sooner rather than later?

No, he'd bide his time, and he felt sure *The Star-Journal* would offer him a regular position when his internship ended.

Except it didn't.

Two weeks before his internship was scheduled to end, Corey was called into his editor's office along with the other summer interns. The editor was a sixtyish man named Carlton Franco, with a gruff demeanor that belied the gray beard and considerable paunch that would have made him an ideal candidate for mall Santa. The meeting was short, his message perfunctory: "Thank you for a great summer," he told the assembled interns. "We'd be pleased to have any of you on staff, but unfortunately, times are tough in our field, and we just aren't hiring right now. If there are any openings in the near future, rest assured, we have your résumé on file."

In other words, "Don't call us, we'll call you."

Corey knew he had to do something. He'd been so sure *The Star-Journal* would hire him, he hadn't sent his résumé or clips to any other newspapers. He stayed behind after the other interns left to plead his case. He had a story idea that would have everyone talking about *The Star-Journal* around the water cooler and on cable news the next morning.

"Look, kid," his editor told him, "unless you give me a scoop on the president being impeached, there's not much I can do. We just don't have the money to hire a full-time reporter right now."

Corey tried to tell him that he'd heard rumors the president *was* going to be impeached, and that he might be able to get a story written before his last day, but the editor just laughed at him and said, "You heard this rumor where? On the obituary desk?" He turned to walk away, then turned back to face Corey, "Listen kid, a word of advice: Never promise something you can't deliver. It'll ruin your credibility, and you won't be able to get a job anywhere in journalism." Chuckling again, he turned and walked back toward his office.

Corey balled up his fists and strode back to his work station, scowling.

"Something bothering you, Cor?" It was Lynne Farr-Jennings, who covered higher education — one of the few full-time staffers who actually gave him the time of day. He'd had a bit of a crush on her since he'd met her at the introductory luncheon the newspaper held for its new interns. Most full-timers didn't bother to show up for such things, but she had. And even though she was five years older, he'd been attracted to her immediately.

Despite that attraction, however, he didn't like being surprised, especially when he was distracted. Like he was now.

So, he blew her off. "Nothing. Just ... nothing."

She smiled.

Corey was vaguely aware that he was being rude, and was momentarily impressed that it hadn't fazed her. Then it occurred to him that maybe it didn't bother her because she didn't care. Maybe she was one of those people who was being nice just for the sake of being nice. She didn't care about *him*; she just cared about appearances.

"If you want to talk later, I'm off deadline," she said. "Hit me up for a cup of coffee in the break room when you're free."

"Thanks." Corey stormed off. Suddenly, he didn't have a crush on her anymore. Besides, he had more important things to worry about: like how to change Carlton Franco's mind about keeping him on staff. But how could he do that if Franco wouldn't even listen to his story ideas?

He knew how. The idea kept tugging at the back of his mind like a street urchin tugging on a pedestrian's shirtsleeve. He tried to ignore it, but it followed him down the sidewalk of his mind, demanding to be heard. It was this: Franco had told him that a story about the president's impeachment would get him a job, but he couldn't convince him to accept such a story ... and he couldn't get the president impeached without turning the story in. The only kind of story the metro desk would accept from him was an obituary. So ..., what if the president were assassinated?

Corey tried again to put the idea out of his head. The president certainly was unpopular. He'd raised taxes after promising not to, vetoed a bill that would have created a new infrastructure program that promised thousands of jobs, and was under investigation for a potential conflict of interest over stock he owned in a pharmaceutical company. There *was* a basis to impeach him, and a lot of people didn't like him, but that didn't mean he deserved to die.

Corey could always just accept the fact that *The Star-Journal* didn't want him and go back to square one. He was 21 years old and had his full life ahead of him … which just meant he didn't want to waste any more time than was necessary. The president, on the other hand, was 74 and in his second term. There were rumors he had prostate cancer and liver problems. How much longer did he have, anyway? If Corey didn't do something now, the old man would probably be dead before Corey got another chance to work for *The Star-Journal.*

His mind made up, he logged into his computer and opened up a new file, filling in the header as "Obituary: Notable," in accordance with the newspaper's style. This was meant to flag editors to the fact that what followed might be worthy of a full story.

"Might."

Corey laughed at the thought as his fingers played on the keyboard, typing out the words: "Garvey, Milton. 74. President of the United States. Survivors …" he checked the online archive and continued "… Dorothea Garvey, wife; Suzette Sullivan and Dana McPhee, daughters; Mitch Garvey, son; six grandchildren and one great-grandchild. Cause of death: gunshot wound to the chest. Arrangements by Ross and Petrie Funeral Home, Washington, D.C." That was it. *The Star-Journal* received so many obituaries that it only published the basics. The cost of newsprint being what it was, dead people weren't worth much ink unless they were famous or died in some extraordinary way. In a few minutes, President Milton Garvey would be the bearer of both distinctions — as soon as an editor on the metro desk opened the file and read the story.

He hit the "send" button and waited.

"What the hell is this?" Jill Bailey, the assistant metro editor, spun around to look at him from three cubicles away. "Some kind of practical joke?"

"No," Corey said, shaking his head, his face expressionless. Had he really just done this? He felt a momentary panic, a turn of the stomach. Could he undo it? No. It was too late. Jill had gotten up from her desk and was walking over to him, frowning one of those frowns that indicate in no uncertain terms that the recipient is in deep shit.

When she reached him, she stood straight, shoulders back, staring down her nose at him. "Go home, Corey," she said.

"Are you firing me?"

There was no response except, if it were possible, a deepening of the frown.

Then, from across the room, someone shouted, "The president's been shot!"

It took a split second for the words to register in Jill Bailey's mind, but when they did, she whirled around, and, in a virtual chorus with the rest of the newsroom, shouted, "What?!"

Carlton Franco came rushing out of his office. The news bulletin was appearing at the top over every work station computer now. "President Martin Garvey has been shot, the White House is reporting. More details soon."

Jill Bailey bent over beside Corey until her long, narrow face was next to his: "Where did you get this?" she said. "How could a funeral home have sent a notice like this across before the news even broke on the wires?" Her breath smelled of sour cream-and-onion potato chips.

He just stared at her.

"Fuck it," she said after a few seconds. "I don't care where you got it. Do you have any more information?"

Corey nodded.

"Then write the fucking story!"

She spun around and shouted across the room at Carlton Franco. "We've got an inside angle on this, Carlton! Working on the story now!"

"Who's writing it?"

"Corey Fagin."

"Who?" Franco didn't even remember Corey's name that day, but before long everyone would know it. Corey wrote a story about the death of President Milton Garvey that had details no other newspaper had. He wrote that Garvey had been shot by a blackmailer who had enough dirt on the president to force an impeachment vote. Dirt about payments wired directly from Draven Pharmaceuticals into a Swiss bank account that had been traced to the president — money that landed the day after he'd signed the Medical Research Protection Act, which had granted Draven the exclusive right to market drugs for more than two dozen serious conditions. Dirt about a child he had fathered out of wedlock during his time in the Peace Corps but had refused to acknowledge, even when the mother demanded a DNA test he refused to take. Dirt about an addiction to painkillers. About the fact that he had hidden a diagnosis of schizophrenia. Anything Corey could think of.

And it was all one hundred percent true.

Star-Journal editors confirmed the accuracy of official accounts referenced in the story before the officials had a chance to put out news releases or stage press conferences informing other news agencies. They verified the sourcing and quotes Corey had used. And they broke the full story before anyone else had a tenth of the information they did.

Carlton Franco called Corey into his office the next day and offered him a job as a general assignment reporter. It was typical starting pay, but it was a foot in the door, and Corey never looked back. Lynne Farr-Jennings forgave him his rudeness and actually asked *him* out on a date two years after he joined the staff. Soon, they were a regular item.

He produced one scoop after another, earning the nickname "Ace" and producing more bylines than any other reporter at the newspaper. Life was good.

The nightmares started five years later. Corey had managed to shove his role in Milton Garvey's death to the back of his mind until one of the television networks produced a five-year anniversary feature on the president's demise. His widow, Dorothea, sat for an interview in which she talked about losing the love of her life, and how the estate had been bankrupted over lawsuits stemming from the Draven Pharmaceuticals debacle. She still received angry emails and death threats from the families of people who had died because they couldn't afford Draven's prices for the medicine they needed.

Two of his three children shared similar stories in their own interviews. One of his daughters, Dana, had inherited his tendency toward schizophrenia and committed suicide after being fired from her job at a public relations firm that didn't want to be tied to Milton Garvey's "sordid presidency."

Corey told himself he shouldn't watch the TV special, but he couldn't help himself. Once he started watching, he couldn't stop. Then, when the program was finally over, it just kept playing over and over in his dreams. He drank warm milk to relax, but he couldn't. Insomnia became a means of avoiding the dreams, and trying to forget the guilt over what he had done. But the more he stayed awake, the more he thought about *why* he was staying awake, and things only got worse from there.

His relationship with Lynne ended when she told him she couldn't handle the angry outbursts that accompanied his severe fatigue. Soon, he was calling in sick to work more often, and when he did go into the newsroom, he found he couldn't think of anything to type. Editors had never needed to assign him stories, because he'd always come up with something better and juicier than anything they could have suggested.

Now, however, he was at a loss. It turned out that even the great Ace Fagin wasn't immune to writer's block.

His editors started pressing him, and the more they pressed, the worse it got.

He started thumbing through the paper's archives and reading novels at night in search of ideas. Then, while reading a historical novel on the case of the Boston Strangler, he hit on one: He would write a story about a serial killer. If there was one thing that got people to buy newspapers, it was blood — especially when the blood spilled belonged to innocent victims. Women and, especially, children.

The idea seemed like a revelation. He could keep the story going for months, revealing a new victim whenever he needed to turn in another story — and prolonging the time between stories by saying the effort required lot of research. If he could identify the killer before police did, he would tell his editors, it would win the newspaper another Pulitzer.

The adrenalin rush he felt at the moment of inspiration, however, was tempered by a wave of new anxiety. This time, he'd have to kill not one person, but maybe six, ten, a dozen or more.

But maybe there was an alternative.

He remembered back to the question he'd asked himself all those years ago, when he'd written his story about the mission to Mars: What if he wrote about people who didn't exist? What if he hadn't chosen to name his mission leader "Roger Jones," but had selected some other, unique name to be sure he wasn't actually killing someone living at this moment on Planet Earth?

There was still the matter of "creating" people in order to kill them, but if they were his creation, didn't he have that right?

He convinced himself that he did, and that they'd only be "alive" long enough to die, anyway. So, he set about being as sure as he possibly could that the names of the victims he wrote into existence were so unusual that they couldn't possibly be shared by a living human being. Names like Marcus Terwilliger Sandoval-Thyy and Cassiopeia Gingakurvetz. One of his favorites was a mashup of Celtic, Russian and Asian names: Pho Borzoi McIlheney. Another was Cyrus Andromeda Gilhooly.

When Corey returned to the office after a two-week vacation, he set to work on the project immediately. His coworkers noticed a marked change in him, a return to form and the re-emergence of the brash, energetic reporter who had joined the *Star-Journal* staff five years earlier. The dark circles under his eyes had vanished, and his shirts no longer hung from slumped shoulders as though they were draped across a hanger in his closet.

His first story concerned the death of someone named Zeddicus Rathbone Manticamezor, who was bludgeoned to death by a hockey stick once used by Gordie Howe that had been stolen from the Hockey Hall of Fame in Toronto. His next installment identified Pho Borzoi McIlhenny as the victim of a forced overdose of caffeine and whiskey; police had no trouble identifying it as foul play thanks to the inscription "I did it. Catch me." that was carved into McIlhenny's chest.

Each story got a little more intricate, as Corey got more and more creative. In between murders, he wrote about the investigation itself, and how the police would follow first one lead, then another, testing and discarding theories as they invariably hit another dead end. Each of the murders was committed using a different method, and there was no common motive for any of them.

Amidst it all, Corey was having more fun than he'd ever had, and copies of *The Star-Journal* were selling at a rate not seen in years. There was even talk that he might be nominated for his long-sought Pulitzer, and sure enough, after he'd covered the seventh murder, he learned his name had been placed in nomination.

On the eve of the Pulitzer announcements, Corey decided to celebrate by killing off another of his imaginary victims.

For his latest tour de force, he chose to kill off Cyrus Andromeda Gilhooly by decapitation. He sat down and typed the following sentence: "Cyrus Andromeda Gilhooly's head was found next to his desk at his workplace, having been severed by …"

Corey never typed another word. Lynne Farr-Jennings found his bloody, severed head on the ground beside his work station. No one ever caught the killer, who apparently was content on stopping with Corey Andrew Fagin.

Adopted son of Charles and Pammy Lee Fagin, natural son of Johnna Francesca Gilhooly.

Birth name: Cyrus Andromeda Gilhooly.

George & the Dragon: the Untold Story

anta Claus. The tooth fairy. The boogieman. During my childhood, the things I believed in seemed to slip away from me one by one. No matter how tightly I clung to them, there was always something that burst the bubble of what I discovered, a few years short of the precipice that is puberty, to be pure fantasy.

Such ideas, I came to realize, had been planted in my mind by grownups who had abandoned their own beliefs in such things, with equal reluctance, before I was born. They couldn't look each other in the eye and admit to accepting them, so they passed the beliefs on to me and other kids so they could believe in them vicariously through us.

This is how fairy tales survive for centuries while the historical deeds of real men and women who lived and died and made some sort of difference in the world get forgotten. It's how kids get disillusioned with their parents, and with the stories they hear in childhood.

Do I sound bitter?

Well, when you lose your mother at the age of seven and you find out years later that it had something to do with one of these fairytales, then you can talk to me about it. Try growing up without a mom — and with a father who hid the truth from you — and tell me you wouldn't be bitter about it, too.

As I grew older, like most kids, I left those fairytales behind. Over time, they faded into the forgotten corners of my childhood with the memories of family Christmases and kindergarten and Cub Scouts.

But one conversation always stuck with me. It was something my grandpa taught me; I'm not sure whether he'd heard somewhere or made up himself: "There's no better way to conceal a lie than behind a thousand truths, and there's no better way to conceal the truth than behind a thousand lies." Considering what's happened since, I don't think he shared this wisdom by accident. He was, after all, Mom's father, and I suspect he knew what was going on. He just didn't want to make things worse by telling me. I don't blame him. I'm not sure I wouldn't have made the same decision myself.

The saying has to do with Mom. And those fairytales. You see, I've come to believe that the lies we call children's stories, the ones that have been passed down to us for generations, have a very real purpose. They aren't just meant to entertain us until we outgrow them, and they're supposed to distract us from learning the truth.

Dragons are real.

And they're not at all what they appear to be, because the stories about dragons themselves are largely lies, meant to cover up humanity's shame at what we've done.

Oh, it's no secret — according to the stories, at least — that human beings drove dragons to the brink of extinction, just as we did with the passenger pigeon and the black rhino, and the Tasmanian tiger, which died out for the same reason: It was hunted and exterminated to protect livestock.

The same might be said for dragons, but, I learned, dragons were different. Humankind declared war on them hundreds of years ago, during the Dark Ages, long before we eradicated the passenger pigeon or hunted the black rhino into oblivion.

But there's something about the comparison that doesn't quite fit. The human population was much smaller back then, and we didn't have hunting rifles or elephant guns at our disposal. So how could this have happened? How could men, armed with nothing but swords and spears and longbows, have conquered flying beasts that breathed fire and rode the wind on wings that made condors seem like sparrows?

They couldn't have, obviously … which is why it's easy to dismiss the stories of the dragons' demise as just another children's fairytale. In fact, that's just what I did. Until I found the manuscript, that is.

It was one of the few things my grandpa left me, sealed in a leather folder inside a mahogany box. It has been almost twenty years since Mom disappeared, and my father never told me what happened. Mom had been special, and not just because she was *my* mom. She was the kindest person I knew, and fiercely protective of me. Dad had a violent temper, and he'd yell and scream and throw things when he got bent out of shape, but she never let him lay a finger on me. She always stood between him and me, even if it meant putting herself in harm's way. He never hit her — not that I saw — but I know he resented something about her, though I never figured out just what.

There were a couple of other things about Mom that made her unique. She had slightly webbed fingers, which she used to joke about, saying my grandpa was the creature from the black lagoon. (I knew this wasn't true, because he hated the water and couldn't even swim.) Then there was this weird birthmark she had on her neck that looked like three or four tiny leaves, one overlaying the other. She always seemed self-conscious about it and wore high-necked shirts or scarves to hide it.

Mom was the perfect mother. She read me bedtime stories, made me hot cocoa at Christmas and told my teachers at school to stop being so tough on me when I had a harder time learning to read than some of the other kids.

She was always there for me — until, one day, she wasn't.

Dad said she left and didn't tell him where she was going. I remember when the police came by the house to ask him about it, and I hid just around the corner in the bedroom to hear what he'd tell them. But he didn't tell them any more than he'd told me: She just left.

There was an investigation, and they kept the case open, but she never came back and they never found any body.

Just after she disappeared, though, I happened to see Dad burying something in the back yard. He saw me watching him, and he made me swear never to go nosing around there or he'd whup me. That scared me, but what scared me even more was what I might find there. Whuppin' or not, I didn't want to know.

My dad took charge of Mom's belongings — what she'd had before they got married — and I remember Grandpa shouting at him over it, saying some of those things were rightfully his. He didn't get anywhere with it, though. Dad was the surviving spouse, and she hadn't left a will, so the law said that stuff belonged to him.

But I don't think Dad realized that Grandpa had the manuscript — Dad probably never even knew it existed — and when he died at 46 of a heart attack, Grandpa let me move in with him for the next couple of years. Then Grandpa died, too, and left me a few things in his will: his old walking stick, which I'd loved to play with as a child; a few thousand dollars in savings bonds; and the key to the mahogany box where I found the manuscript.

It was a few pages long, laid on top of one another, all loose.

Nightmare's Eve

The paper was cracked in some places and torn in others. There was something that looked like a small coffee stain in the corner of one of the pages, and in another place, it looked like it had been singed by a candle. It looked very old, but I think it must have been translated from an even earlier script, because it was written in the first person.

Some lines (I don't know how many) had been lost — torn away from the top of the first page and then again at the end, but it seemed like the rest was intact. I could tell you what was in it, but it would be easier just to read it for yourself. Here's what it said:

… In those days, I sojourned for a time in the city of Silene, which is in Libya, and it is there that I came upon Lucinda, a maiden from that city who was in great distress, for she dwelt apart from her people in a cavern twenty leagues to the east. I happened upon the cavern quite by accident one day, as I was exploring the land at my leisure, and surprised her there while she was sleeping, a smooth stone as her pillow and a handful of straw as a blanket.

I startled her with my presence, and she rose quickly, taking two steps backward and making as if to flee into the cavern's darkness. But I besought her, assuring her that I would not harm her and that, should she wish it, I would depart straightaway.

Thereupon she hesitated, but shook her head slightly and bade me sit and rest a moment.

I did so, never once taking my eyes off the maiden. She was tall and fair and beautiful, with dark silken hair and ruddy cheeks, and eyes that glistened in the sunlight that danced off a pool of water there within the cavern. She spoke not a word for the space of several moments, like a young deer standing and watching at a distance, fearful that a lion might suddenly appear.

Then, ever so slowly, her shoulders relaxed and her brow unfurrowed, and I could see that she was becoming more at ease in my company. Truth be known, I was instantly taken with her, and she warmed to me quickly as I spoke to her of the lands I had seen in my travels and the wonders I had beheld as a knight in service of true wisdom.

She spoke little of herself, which I deemed strange, but when I rose to depart, she implored me not to forget her and, indeed, to visit her there often, as she was fated to tarry in this cavern until the next full moon.

I asked her why this must be, but she implored me: "Dear friend, speak to me of any other thing, but not of this, for I will breathe no word of it, even should you plead with me or threaten my life."

I wondered at these words of hers, but I did not press her, for it would not have been seemly to do so. Yet even so, they vexed me, for I wished more than almost anything to know how she had come upon this circumstance — more than anything, should I speak the truth, save that one day she might favor me with a kiss.

But she warned me: "Speak not of your visits to any man, lest you place yourself in danger, for this place is forbidden to my people. And when the moon next reaches its fullness, do not return here, but until then, be my succor."

So it was that I rode out each day to where she dwelt, taking with me palm dates and pomegranates and olives and wine to preserve her strength, for I had seen no source of sustenance in the cavern. These she gratefully accepted and, for many hours, we spoke of my travels, her childhood, my dreams and her regrets. And she lay with me, and I with her, for we loved each other. But though we spoke of all things dear to our hearts and to each other — our lips never dared touch upon the one thing I wished most earnestly to know: how she had come to be exiled there.

Although I had sworn by my honor that I should not ask her of this, I had not vouchsafed that I should refrain from asking another. Therefore, when I returned to the city one evening, I sought out an inn where men would congregate after sunset, my intention being to pose this question discreetly to some among them. One I came upon supplied the answer, which apparently was commonly known in the city:

The maiden was, he told me, the daughter of the king, and her exile to the cavern was the result of a cruel trick of fate. There dwelt in that cavern, the man said, a great dragon whose wings were wider — each one of them — than the building in which we were taking our leisure. The dragon's maw was filled with teeth sharper than a makhaira, and from the depths of its belly issued forth blue flame hotter than any from a blacksmith's forge.

The beast had departed the region for a time to raid the flocks of the shepherds beyond the city, but would return at the full moon. An oracle had revealed to the king that it could only be satiated by human blood and flesh, so he had called all the city together to cast lots as to who would sacrifice himself for the good of the people. The lot was drawn in secret by the king himself, and it had fallen to his own daughter, Lucinda.

With great sorrow had the king acceded to the will of the fates and banished his daughter to the dragon's cavern, where she went willingly and agreed to stay without even a guard being set there, with her honor as a guarantee that she would fulfill that for which she was destined. To the whole city, she had become an example of self-sacrifice and heroism, for she had given herself freely to save them all, and for this they were ever grateful.

"Yet would it not be better," I asked the man, "if one should venture forth to that place and slay the dragon?"

But the man only laughed at me. "What is your name, stranger?" he asked me.

"Jurj," I said, telling him my name in Arabic.

"Well … George, is it? … did you not hear the description I gave of the beast? What hope has any man among us of slaying such a winged demon, which calls forth fire from its belly and could fly away from us before we could even raise a blade against it?"

I said nothing, but thought to myself what a coward this man was, not to even to consider the attempt, when Lucinda had set forth unarmed to face the dragon on his behalf.

"Thank you, Friend," I said. "You have enlightened me far more than you know."

It was then that I determined it would be I who would slay this dragon, though it would require that I break my vow to Lucinda herself and appear in the cavern at the next full moon. I procured the services of a certain smith to forge a sword for me long enough, I judged, to reach the beast yet light enough still to wield. I also purchased a spear that could be thrust with the hand or hurled like a javelin, should I be unable to approach the beast too closely.

When the time came, I saddled my horse and set forth, weapons in hand, resolute of purpose and determined that I should not return 'ere the beast was slain.

I came to the cave and found there an eerie glow between gold and silver, the beams from the full moon cascading down off the desert sandstone and in through a small opening overhead. Lucinda was nowhere to be seen, at which I was greatly relieved, for I had no wish to endanger her by confronting the beast in her presence.

But my relief vanished when I saw the great dragon itself lying curled 'round its own body in the center of the chamber. Scales in shades of from yellow to gold to dark brown covered the creature as it slumbered, shimmering soft in the moonglow. Rising and falling with each breath, they seemed to ebb and flow in ripples up and down its back as it rested content upon the cool earth. Its eyes were shut in soft repose, its face marked with a diamond shape of darker scales across the forehead, and more clustered around its cheeks, with the rest of its countenance marked in gold and something close to crimson.

Two great wings rested in folds across its back, the flesh there devoid of scales, yet leathery and thick. I had never seen anything so wondrous, and for a moment I doubted my intent: How could I slay such a breathtaking creature? Was this beast not also God's creation? And perhaps, in truth, the pinnacle of his work! I nearly lost myself in a reverie admiring it, but then it stirred, rolling slightly onto its side and bringing me back again to my senses. I caught my breath, then released it after a moment when I had assured myself its eyes were still closed, and that the great belly, covered with lighter orange and yellow scales, was now exposed, along with ...

Was it possible?

Yes! When the dragon turned, it revealed something held close to its breast, something not visible before, when its body was curled 'round about it: A large egg, azure in color like the evening sky, and sparkling with what seemed like tiny stars winking out from its surface. A reflection of the heavens, or so it seemed, far larger even than an ostrich egg and cradled in a nest of straw like a bird might make.

The beast had come here to make its nest. But if it were here, resting, and Lucinda was gone ... was it possible she had fled? No, this I doubted. She had vowed to offer her own life up to the beast for the good of the city, and I had no doubt of either her virtue or bravery in carrying out this task.

Was I too late?

Had the great dragon already taken her? Did it now rest there, its meal finished, in sated slumber?

This was the only conclusion my mind could reach, and in despair's stark certitude, I felt a rage boil up from inside me. Righteous and unholy at once, it flooded through my body, a thirst for vengeance — the Lord's prerogative, and yet, I must have it. Lucinda had been too precious to me not to seize it, and as I gazed upon the creature before me, its beauty seemed to vanish 'neath the hideous mask of my own great wrath.

I let forth a cry as I rushed forward, and it stirred, opening its eyes. For a moment, I thought I recognized something behind those eyes, something familiar that, were it not for my fury, might have caused me to hesitate. But I was too consumed by my hatred at the beast for taking Lucinda from me to give my actions any pause. The slightest delay, and the beast would turn upon me. I had to strike.

Racing forward astride my steed with all the force that I could muster, I aimed my lance at its exposed breast, unprotected by the scales that covered the rest of it. My hand was steady and my aim was true, and I watched with satisfaction as my weapon plunged deep into the creature's body, calling forth a font of crimson from beneath the surface.

The dragon sent forth an anguished cry that shook the cavern from floor to ceiling, sending small stones cascading down the walls and rousing a handful of sleeping fruit bats that took to wing.

There was something in that cry that gave me pause — something almost human, as though the beast were crying, "No!"

Surely, I was imagining it.

I leaped down from my mount, blade drawn, and ran toward the creature's head, determined that I should show no mercy to the beast that had slain my Lucinda.

As its eyes looked up at me, dark and glistening, they seemed to be pleading with me silently to look deeper, to see something I was missing. But in my rage, I had no use for such pleas. I drew my sword and plunged it deep into the dragon's throat, drawing forth from it a hideous gasp of agonizing pain and ... it almost seemed like, disbelief.

I drew back as the creature thrashed wildly about, not wishing to be caught in the fury of its death throes, and watched as its will to fight and then its very life drained out of the massive body. The shimmering scales grew dull, despite the moonlight, and the wings fell limp. At length, it curled up tight around the egg that it had been guarding, and drew its final breath.

I stood there for some moments, watching it, after that, sword still in hand but no longer raised, held in place by something — I knew not what. I was about to turn and take my leave when I noticed the dragon's body begin to stir again.

Was it alive still? How could this be?

But no — no breath issued forth from its nostrils, and no other sign of life could I see. Its body was ... shrinking. Changing into something else.

I stood, transfixed, as I witnessed this transformation, horror mixed with dawning recognition that welled up inside my breast as the dragon's body slowly became something else entirely. Some*one* else. Until, at last, there lay before me the bloodied and broken body of a naked woman.

My dearest Lucinda.

Her arms wrapped tight around the egg that remained, as before, clutched tightly to her breast, almost as large as her own body.

What madness was this? What sorcery? What enchantment?

I fell to my knees and crawled toward her, anguish replacing the rage that had driven me, all hope lost from my empty heart. I had done this. Unknowing, but it had been I, no demon-beast, who had killed my own true love. How was this possible? I lifted her head and cradled it in my arms, and I wept bitter tears for what I had lost that could never be regained.

The news would spread that I had slain the dragon, and I would be hailed as a hero far and wide for my presumed bravery. And yet I knew the truth of it, that I had slain the only woman I had ever loved. This was my punishment for usurping the wrath of God and claiming vengeance, but what punishment had Lucinda deserved? Were it not for the child she left me, I would have taken my own life, but I owed my daughter a life of her own, and I vowed that I should bring her up to know her mother, whose eyes and visage were reflected in her own. I swore that …

That's where it ended, this story of Saint George and the Dragon that few others had ever read.

I wondered at the meaning of those last few lines. The writer hadn't mentioned anything about a child before then, and there didn't seem to have been enough time for Lucinda to have given birth. Perhaps George had adopted the child, but he spoke of it as if it were his own — his and Lucinda's together.

What did that mean?

I had no idea.

For a while, I thought about taking the manuscript to an expert, maybe a professor at the university or someone who knew something about the ancient Near East. But I decided, in the end, to keep the story to myself. It had been among Mom's belongings, and if she'd wanted to share it with the world, she would have. It wasn't my place to second guess her.

Besides, there were plenty of people who wouldn't want this story to come out — people who knew what they thought was the "true" story of Saint George and wouldn't want others reading this new version of the tale (especially the part where he had lain with the princess out of wedlock).

So, I kept the story to myself. I read and reread it every night for a month, and when that month was over, I put it away and never looked at it again. I didn't need to, because I could have recited it from memory. For some reason I couldn't quite understand, it felt real to me. It wasn't like Santa Claus or the tooth fairy; it seemed like a real-life adventure that real people had lived. It didn't matter that its supposed author was a Roman soldier from the Middle East who became the patron saint of England more than a thousand years after his death. The words he'd written, no matter how unlikely, rang true.

I put the manuscript back in the mahogany box where I had found it, used the key to lock it and put it in a safe place. I took the key to the bank and put it in a safe deposit box, and I never had any desire to open the box again.

But something else kept gnawing at me. If that box had contained such an unexpected treasure, what might be hidden in the back yard, where I had seen my father burying something as a child? I hadn't seen what it was — he'd been almost done by the time I saw what he was doing — and I'd always been curious what he might have been hiding. My father was gone now, and I had no need to fear getting whupped if he caught me digging around out there. Still, just the idea of it gave me a knot in my stomach. It was as though I'd be breaking some important taboo … or, more alarming, that I might find something I didn't want to see.

If the manuscript had taught me anything, though, it was that things weren't always what they seemed. If the story it contained was real — and I was convinced it was — it meant that all the superstitious bullshit about Saint George saving the princess from a dragon had been all wrong. He hadn't saved her at all. He wasn't a hero or a noble champion, but a broken man who had tried and failed to save the woman he loved from a fearsome beast.

I'd continued to live in my childhood home after my father's death; I was alone there now, unmarried and without any real attachments. My girlfriend and I had broken up a month earlier, and we'd never reached the point of living together anyway. I'd had a roommate for a while — a friend of mine from college who smoked too much pot and paid too little rent (you never really know someone until you live with him, right?), so we'd parted ways around the first of the year. The house was quiet most of the time, except for the creaky moans it uttered when settling or the echoes of Merle Haggard or Def Leppard when I listened to some music.

On this particular day, I was playing Billy Joel — not so much to drown out the house's creaking as to muffle the voices in my head. My doubts. My fears.

I had gotten out of bed this morning determined that I was going to do this thing.

I walked down the stairs and out the sliding glass door into the back yard, where fog sat dangling from the sky in tendrils that reached the ground and seeped into the soil. The gray mist hung among the branches of some fig, orange and tangelo trees my father had planted out by the wooden fence. Once upon a time, he'd thought to harvest them, but he'd never gotten around to it; the fruit had fallen from their branches and lay rotting on the ground.

I unlocked the small metal shed at the side of the house, its door rusted at the hinges. Stepping into the cold, musty air, I pulled the chain at the entrance, but the light must have burned out. Fumbling around in the half-darkness, I stubbed my toe on an old push-mower and knocked over a rake that had been propped up against the wall before I found what I was looking for: a long spade shovel with a splintery wooden handle. Fortunately, I found some gloves lying on a sawhorse beside me; slipping them on, I took the shovel and went back outside.

The sun, peering out through the veil of morning mist, looked more like a blurred full moon as I crossed the moist grass and patches of soft, damp earth to where I'd seen my father digging so many years earlier. I knew the exact spot where he'd been kneeling that day, looking over his shoulder at me as I stood on the back porch and fixing me with a look that said, "You shouldn't be here. Forget you ever saw this." He told me much the same thing in words later on, but it was that look that stayed with me, and I knew exactly where he'd been when he had seen his young son standing there looking at him.

He'd been about three feet this side of the fig tree, which had lost all its leaves as autumn crept toward winter and stretched out with barren branches to embrace the fog like a long-absent consort.

The ground where I planted the point of my shovel was bare; no grass grew in a circle about six feet around — and hadn't for as long as I could remember. It might have been that way before my father buried whatever he'd hidden down below, but something told me it hadn't been — that the grass had refused to grow there in the years since, its silent protest against any involvement in my father's deed.

The soil was compacted, and I had to push hard to get any purchase with the shovelhead, stepping on it with one foot and lifting my whole body off the ground as I thrust the point of it into the earth. It resisted, but I was able to dislodge a small half-shovelful of dirt and toss it aside.

I repeated the process.

And again.

The earth, disrupted, began to yield more readily, and my pace accelerated. I was half a foot down, then a foot, then two feet when I hit something. The scraping sound told me it was made of wood — maybe like the box that had contained the manuscript. But as I started removing more dirt, it was clear this box was a lot bigger. I kept digging and scraping the dirt aside and removing it as I went. It seemed the pine surface would never end. How on earth had my father managed to bury it by himself?

I remembered back to that day: He had dropped me off at my friend Jackie's house in the morning, but he'd forgotten to come get me, so I'd asked Jackie's parents to take me home. I'd walked through the living room, the kitchen and out onto the back porch — which is when I saw him. From the look of the box, he must have been at it the whole time I was gone.

I could tell by the position of the sun in the sky that it was nearly noon now, but the mist showed no sign of burning off. It would be one of those early winter days when the fog stayed put, an uninvited but stubborn guest.

By the time I was done clearing away the dirt, I had exposed a box that must have been twelve feet long and six feet wide.

A twist in my gut whispered what I feared might be inside, but I had to look.

It was nailed shut tight.

I went back to the toolshed and grabbed a crowbar, which I set in the narrow space where the lid was nailed to the side nearest me and pried upward. The wood started to give way, then cracked and splintered.

I tried another space, repeating the process and, at last, was able to pry the lid loose enough that I could get down on my knees and raise it up. Fetid air wafted up from inside, along with a thin plume of dust. And there, in the darkness, lay a human skeleton, not a shred of flesh remaining on the bones, but wearing a dress I recognized from childhood. I hadn't seen it in years, let alone thought about it. But I'd tugged at the white lace hem of that now-dusty blue dress many times when I was a toddler, trying to get the attention of the woman who wore it.

Mom.

I bent over and started to sob, all the grief that I'd had when she disappeared careening back into me. I'd known she was dead — I mean really known it, not just given up hope: We'd had a connection, the way mothers and their children often do, and I couldn't feel that anymore after the day she disappeared. Still, there was some part of me that thought she wasn't really in the ground somewhere; that she was alive, in some sense, even if it was only in my memories. The sight of her corpse lying there in a wooden box shattered that part of me, and I knew I'd never be able to piece it back together.

Dad had killed her. There wasn't any sign that her neck had been broken or that she'd been shot; it was as if she had just gone to sleep. But I knew my father had killed her; poisoned her, maybe, or put a pillow over her head while she was asleep. Still there on my knees, I balled up both fists and slammed them into the ground beside me until the knuckles started to bleed. I closed my eyes tight against the image of Mom lying there, but I could still see it against the back of my eyes, exactly the way she looked when I opened them up again.

What I had barely noticed, in my grief and shock, was that the box contained something other than her remains: There was a second box, set at my mother's feet, taking up most of the width of the larger box and measuring about four feet across. As I listened, I heard a sound coming from inside it, like an animal had become trapped there and was scratching or thumping at the wood, trying to get out.

I pulled the box out and set it aside on the ground, then closed my mother's burial box and shoveled the dirt back over it. I was grateful for the fog and the fact that we lived on a three-acre lot so no one would notice what was happening — just as no one had noticed when my father had buried her all those years ago.

I felt nauseated.

By the time I was done, I was dripping with sweat, despite the cool, wet day, the moisture of the fog and my perspiration mingling and running down across my forehead.

I picked up the box and carried it into the house, setting it on the table. Not only had the scraping sound intensified, I could feel it move a little in my hands, jostling back and forth.

What could be inside?

Using the crowbar once again, I pried open the lid and took a step backward as my mind struggled to make sense of what I saw in front of me. There in that box was a gigantic cracked egg, its contents struggling to break free. This was impossible. It has been almost twenty years since Mom had disappeared — had died. Whatever was inside that egg must have survived for *nearly two decades*. No animal I'd ever heard of had a gestation period like that. How could it have survived?

The question was moot, though, because it *had*.

Whatever "it" was.

I knew I was about to find out.

Reaching into the box, I inserted two fingers into the gap where the shimmering azure shell had cracked, curled them under and pulled back. The shell peeled away easily, revealing a gap underneath. I tried to peer in, but I still couldn't see anything; the shell jostled around some more, and I heard a noise that sounded like an infant's cry.

Hurriedly, I peeled back some more of the shell, and flaking it off piece by piece, until the cavity revealed its contents.

A little girl's blue eyes stared up at me, tufts and wisps of golden hair on her forehead and straggling down on either side of a round, cherubic face. Her little lips smiled, and she said something that sounded like "goo" as I picked her up and cradled her in my arms.

"Who are you?" I asked, knowing she couldn't answer. "Where did you come from? How did you survive all that time in there, little girl?"

She lolled her head back, her eyes blinking against the sudden brightness as she tried to look around. She appeared for all the world like any other baby, except she lacked a belly button and had a strange odor that seemed a little like rotten eggs. Well, she had come from inside an egg, so that made sense, but still, this smell wasn't *exactly* like that, it was more like something else — it reminded me of the mineral hot springs resort at the edge of town that had closed down a couple of years back.

"What's your name, little girl?" I asked, knowing she wouldn't answer.

But then, as I watched, the strangest thing happened: She laughed, and what seemed to be a puff of smoke came wafting up out of her open mouth. I looked closer, and saw a glow inside, a flash of something that was more than a spark but less than a flame … coming from inside her nostrils.

I looked again at the fragments of eggshell. They were blue, the same color that the writer described in …

Was it possible?

Had that little girl emerged from a *dragon's egg*? If so, where was the dragon? Unless …

I looked down at the little face again, entirely human and smiling up at me, but there was something else about her — something I hadn't noticed the first time I looked at her. Between the fingers of each of her tiny hands was a flap of skin that made her look like she was related to the creature from the Black Lagoon. And there, on her neck, was my mother's same birthmark of little leaves.

I looked closer. Maybe not leaves. Maybe scales.

I cradled the little girl in my arms, realizing I wouldn't be in the house alone anymore. I'd be sharing it with my sister, born a dragon like all the women in my mother's family, all the way back to George's beloved princess. And even if she was the dragon, it was my turn to do the protecting.

George may have gotten it wrong, but I'm going to get it right.

I know my family secret, and now that I do, I'm gonna make Mom proud of me.

Stephen H. Provost

The author writes about American highways, mutant superheroes, mythic archetypes and pretty much anything he wants. A historian, philosopher, novelist and veteran journalist, he lives on the Central Coast of California. And he loves cats. Read his blogs and keep up with his latest activities at stephenhprovost.com.

www.ingramcontent.com/pod-product-compliance
Lightning Source LLC
Chambersburg PA
CBHW070859250626
47159CB00003B/1124